Praise for Cindy Nord's
No Greater Glory

"Beautifully written, *No Greater Glory* shines a light into long-neglected corners of two human hearts as Reece and Emaline struggle against the currents of America's divisive Civil War. You'll savor every ounce of passion, adventure, and transformation in Cindy Nord's exquisite debut novel. I didn't want it to end!"

~ *Cynthia Wright, Romantic Times and Affaire de Coeur multiple award winner*

"*No Greater Glory* is a powerful, well-crafted Civil War era novel of complex emotions and beautifully drawn characters that explores the inherent risks of falling in love with one's enemy."

~ *Laura Taylor, multiple Romantic Times Award winner*

"The plot is very well done, with strong character development in a short amount of time... The love scenes are steamy yet tender. Recommended for anyone who enjoys historical romance, as well as those who would find appeal in a steamier Gone with the Wind."

~ *Library Journal*

Look for these other titles by Cindy Nord

Now Available:

The Cutteridge Series
An Unlikely Hero
With Open Arms

Coming Spring, 2018

By Any Means

No Greater Glory

Cindy Nord

I love to receive emails from readers who share their 'book thoughts' with me...let's connect! cindy@cindynord.com

No Greater Glory
Copyright © 2012 by DCT Associates
Cover by Lyn Taylor
Formatted by Jacob Hammer
Published by DCT Associates

Digital Edition ISBN: 978-0-9976573-3-3
Print Edition ISBN: 978-0-9976573-6-4

First Digital Publication: July 2012
Second Digital Publication: March 2017
First Print Publication: June 2013
Second Print Publication: March 2017

Dedication

I dedicate this work of fiction to my husband, Tom, the love of my life and in every way, shape and form my hero. To my sons, Christopher and Jeremy, who are my greatest blessings. And to Tex, who has made this thing called writing so amazingly fun.

Chapter One

October 1862

Seven miles west of Falmouth, Virginia

A bitter wind slammed through the tattered countryside, sucking warmth from the morning. Emaline McDaniels rocked back in the saddle when she heard the shout. She glanced over her shoulder and her eyes widened. Across the fields of ragged tobacco, her farrier rode toward her at breakneck speed. Lines of alarm carved their way across the old man's ebony face.

Emaline spurred her horse around to meet him. "What's wrong?"

Tacker pointed a gnarled finger eastward. "Yankees, Miz Emaline! Coming up da road from Falmouth!"

"Yankees?" Her heart lurched against her ribs. She'd heard of their thievery, the fires and destruction left in their wake. Teeth-gritting determination to save her home flashed through her. She leaned sideways, gripping his work-worn sleeve. "Are you sure they're not the home guard?"

"No, ma'am. I seen 'em, dey's blue riders, for sure. Hundreds of 'em."

Two workers moved closer to listen to the exchange, and the farrier gave them a quick nod.

"Everyone back to the cabins," Emaline snapped, sinking into the saddle. "And use the wagon road along the river. It'll be safer."

"Ain't you comin' with us?"

"No. Now move along quickly, all of you. And keep out of sight." She flicked the reins and her horse headed straight across the fields toward the red-brick mansion that hugged the far edge of the horizon.

The spongy ground beneath the animal's hooves churned into clods of flying mud. Aside from a few skirmishes nearby, the war had remained east along the Old Plank Road around Fredericksburg. Her mare crested the small hillock near the main house, and Emaline jerked back on the leather reins. Off to her far right, a column of cavalrymen numbering into the hundreds approached. The dust cloud stirred up by their horses draped in a heavy haze across the late-morning air. In numbed fascination, she stared at the pulsing line of blue-coated soldiers, a slithering serpent of destruction a quarter of a mile long.

Waves of nausea welled up from her belly.

"Oh my God…" she whispered. She dug her boot heels into the mare's sides and the nimble sorrel sprang into another strong gallop. Praying she'd go unnoticed, Emaline leaned low, her thoughts racing faster than the horse. *What do they want? Why are they here?*

Her fingers curled into the coarse mane as seconds flew past. At last, she reached the back entrance of the mansion. Quickly dismounting, she smacked the beast's sweaty flank to send it toward the stable then spun to meet the grim expression fixed upon the face of the old woman who waited for her at the bottom of the steps. "I need Benjamin's rifle!"

"Everythin's right there, Miz Emaline. Right where you'd want it." She shifted sideways and pointed to the .54 caliber Hawkins, leather cartridge box and powder flask lying across the riser like sentinels ready for battle. "Tacker told me 'bout the Yankees afore he rode out to find you."

"Bless you, Euley." Emaline swept up the expensive, custom-made hunting rifle her late husband treasured. The flask followed and she tumbled black crystals down the rifle's long muzzle. A moment later, the metal rod clanked down inside the barrel to force a lead ball home.

She'd heard so many stories of the bluecoats' cruelty. *What if they came to kill us?* The ramrod fell to the ground. With a display of courage she did not feel, Emaline heaved the weapon into her arms, swept past the old servant, and took the wooden steps two at a time.

There was no time left for *what ifs*.

"You stay out of sight now, Euley. I mean it." The door banged shut behind Emaline as she disappeared into the house.

Each determined footfall through the mansion brought her closer and closer to the possibility of yet another change in her life. She eased open the front door and peered out across Shapinsay's sweeping lawns. Dust clogged the air and sent another shiver skittering up her spine. Her heart hammered in her chest as she moved out onto the wide veranda. Five strides later, Emaline stopped at the main steps and centered herself between two massive Corinthian columns.

She squared her shoulders. She lifted her chin. She'd fought against heartbreak every day for three years since her husband's death. She'd fought the constant fear of losing her beloved brother in battle. She fought against the effects of this foolhardy war that sent all but two of her field hands fleeing. If she could endure all that plus operate this plantation all alone to keep Benjamin's dreams alive, then surely, this too, she could fight.

And the loaded weapon? Well, it was for her fortitude only.

She knew she couldn't shoot them all.

"Please, don't turn in," she mumbled, but the supplication withered on her lips when the front of the long column halted near the fieldstone gateposts at the far end of the lane. Three cavalrymen turned toward her then approached in a steadfast, orderly fashion.

Her gaze skimmed over the first soldier holding a wooden staff, a swallow-tailed scrap of flag near its top whipping in the breeze. The diminutive silk bore an embroidered gold star surrounded by a laurel wreath, the words, US Cavalry-6th Ohio, stitched beneath. Emaline disregarded the second cavalryman and centered her attention directly upon the officer.

The man sat his horse as if he'd been born in the saddle, his weight distributed evenly across the leather. A dark slouch hat covered sable hair that fell well beyond the collar of his coat. Epaulets graced both broad shoulders, emphasizing his commanding look. A lifetime spent in the sun and saddle added a rugged cast to his sharp, even features.

An overwhelming ache throbbed behind her eyes. What if she had to shoot him?

Or worse—what if she couldn't?

The man reined his horse to a stop beside the front steps. His eyes, long-lashed and as brown as a bay stallion's, caught and held hers. Though he appeared relaxed, Emaline sensed a latent fury roiling just beneath the surface of his calm.

Her hands weakened on the rifle and she leaned forward, a hair's breadth, unwillingly sucked into his masculinity as night sucked into day. Inhaling deeply, she hoisted the Hawkins to her shoulder, aiming it at his chest. Obviously, in command, he would receive her lone bullet should he not heed her words. "Get off my land!"

Colonel Reece Cutteridge spotted the woman the instant he turned onto the lane. He informed his comrades he'd handle the situation. But just how, he didn't quite know yet. The blazing animosity reflected in her evergreen eyes indicated she wasn't open to hospitality. The rifle in her hands underscored that fact. Of the many plantations he'd commandeered since the beginning of the war, most were deserted or housed civilians cowering within.

But not this one. This wasn't an outlandish act of defiance by some deranged old farmer. No, this woman was brash. Bold. Reece gritted his teeth, the sensation radiating against the firm set of his jaw. A quick glance around the front of the mansion assured him her weapon was the only immediate threat.

His gaze dropped in time to catch the slight tremble of her hands, the lone indication of her fear. He scanned the firearm and a faint smile touched his lips. In her haste to defend her home, the brazen little madcap had failed to place a necessary percussion cap in front of the firing hammer. An unprimed rifle posed no danger.

His shoulders relaxed. His thrumming pulse relaxed. Even the muscles in his thighs relaxed. Reece scanned her again, moving slowly from the top of her head to the tips of her muddy boots. Perhaps in her mid-thirties, she stood a breath above five feet. A thin line of defiance tightened her mouth; otherwise, her lips would be full. Lush. Coffee-colored hair lay in a long braid across her right shoulder. Errant wisps clung to the perspiration that glistened on the sun-stained curve of her cheek. A timeworn work dress extended barely to the top of her boots, the faded green and black plaid doing little to disguise the noteworthy curves that lay hidden from view. Without a doubt, he could encircle her waist with one arm.

That is, if he wanted to.

And that simple reflection, flickering back to life beneath the layers of emptiness and grief, startled him. He'd not had such a thought about a woman in years. But he had a job to do and took pride in doing it well.

Reece hardened the tone of his voice. "Is this the Shapinsay Plantation?"

"I said, get off my land."

"You don't need to do this, ma'am. We're not going to harm you or your people."

She raised the weapon a fraction further and widened her stance. "Turn your horse around and keep on riding. There's nothing for you here."

"Unfortunately, I can't do that. In the name of the United States government, I've been ordered to commandeer your home and grounds for my regiment's winter encampment."

"Your orders mean nothing to me."

The corner of his mouth quirked upward and he topped one hand with the other on the front of his saddle. "I can clearly see that. However, my men are exhausted after the long ride from Manassas Junction, I've got a camp to establish before nightfall, and the horses need tending." The smile vanished. "Now, I'm asking nicely. Lower your weapon."

She tromped down four of the five steps, the heavy rifle wavering in her grip. Edging into the shadow cast by his horse, she brought the Hawkins closer. "If you don't turn around right now, mister, you won't be alive to worry about anything else."

Before the woman could respond, Reece leaned from the saddle and wrapped a gloved hand around the rifle's barrel.

The unexpected motion startled her. She gasped and squeezed the trigger.

The hammer struck metal without firing. Her mouth dropped open as Reece raked the rifle from her grasp and tossed it to the soldier behind him.

He then leaned toward her, a surge of anger roughing his words. "The next time you aim a damn weapon at anyone, woman, I'd suggest you make sure it's properly loaded." He exhaled sharply. "Now you can make this easy or difficult. The choice is entirely yours. But make no mistake in understanding this: We're here to stay."

Her mouth clamped shut so hard Reece heard her teeth clack.

A gust of wind tossed an errant curl across her face and she reached up to rake it back. Ever so slowly, Reece straightened, the worn leather of the McClellan saddle creaking beneath his shifting weight.

Since riding east into the bowels of this war, he'd yet to meet such an uncompromising woman. And if he weren't so damned tired, he might have commented on her boldness and bracing spirit. Good God, thinking she could hold back his entire regiment with an unprimed hunting rifle.

He'd not seen such refreshing courage since Jenny.

The muscle under his eye twitched as he shoved the memory back into the darkened corner of his heart, crushing it up against his other misfortunes.

"Stay out of our way and you won't get hurt." He touched his hat brim in a curt acknowledgment before pulling Saguaro's reins to the right and galloping back down the lane.

Daylight surrendered to darkness as the sun sizzled from sight behind the farthest ridge of rolling hills. Apricot streaks painted a glorious sunset across the sky, but Emaline dismissed the masterpiece to stare instead at the macabre scene that now stained Shapinsay's canvas.

A ten-acre walnut grove stood to the right of the lane and the stately trees arched over a sea of white tents. In the six-acre clearing nearby, where corn had thrived each summer, scores of cavalry horses now grazed.

More than eight hundred soldiers swarmed across Shapinsay's secluded haven, hacking miles of whitewashed fencing into fuel for the cooking fires of a dozen canvas kitchens. The tangy aroma of cut pines infused the late-afternoon air, the trees stripped bare of limbs and honed into poles or flooring for the enemy tents.

All activity emanated from commander's row, where dozens of junior officers directed their troops. And Emaline knew exactly which tent housed their colonel. The blue-coated beast reigned supreme at the pulsing core of this living, breathing and all-too-organized hell.

She looked over her shoulder to the pile of military vouchers stacked on the nearby side table. The same brute who'd ordered the pillage beyond had signed every single one. As she stared at the signature scrawled across the documents, her thoughts tumbled backward an hour to when an envoy of his soldiers stood at her front door, one man shoving the official issues into her hand.

She glared at the officer. "How dare that man assuage his guilt with these scraps of papers? How can I care for my people if he leaves me nothing to feed them?" Her voice spiraled into a harsh whisper. "I demand to speak with him this instant."

"I'm sorry, ma'am, but Colonel Cutteridge is busy. I'll be certain to forward your request."

"You do that." She slammed the door in their faces.

Instead of the colonel appearing, however, Yankee activity increased and a dozen more vouchers followed. The brute ordered men to establish picket lines on the roads leading into Shapinsay, and gave them permission to plunder the hen houses, the milking shed and even the gristmill. He'd even had the gall to have them slaughter several of her pigs for their evening meal.

Emaline glared out the window at the broad-shouldered figure in the distance. He leaned over a camp table, a white map unfurling before him like a full-blown sail across the weathered wood. Her lips pulled tight. She had watched him issue orders to officers, enjoy a bite to eat, and even tend to his own horse. In fact, he took time for everyone and everything. Yet hours later, he still hadn't found the courage to face her again.

The mantel clock in the upstairs library chimed nine.

Emaline tossed the pencil to the desk and stared at the tidy numbers tallied in the ledger. Ciphering a dozen times still produced the same agonizing numbers, the same agonizing annihilation of her resources.

She flipped to the front of the leather tome and to yet another bundle of the colonel's military vouchers. In the past five hours, her house overflowed with his worthless documents.

She slammed the volume shut to block out the blasted man's signature. The clock's persistent ticking, however, could not block out the emptiness. Her eyelids slipped shut. Benjamin's death still left an aching hole in her heart, and she sorely missed her husband's wise counsel and friendship. He would've told her to inhale deeply and count to ten. Emaline's despair rose. Though lacking a passion only whispered about behind fluttering fans, their marriage had nonetheless been satisfying. The few times he'd taken his privilege with her, the joining failed to produce a necessary heir—an obvious defect in her delicate frame, he'd whispered, for Benjamin had been a stout and hearty man. After several attempts proved futile, he draped the banner of barrenness over her, took himself a mistress in Fredericksburg, and never entered her body again.

Emaline had not missed his absence from her bedchamber, and she'd accepted his infidelity with an expected dignity, however, she deeply mourned the loss of motherhood. Upon his death, management of Shapinsay consumed her and became *the child* she never had. Like the air she breathed, she needed the scheduled routines. Routines sustained her. Routines kept her sane. Now this horde of bluecoats had severed her from her very purpose.

The ache of disruption bled through her.

Emaline shoved the chair backward and stood, breathing deeply to push away the memories. The six-tiered crinoline beneath her dinner gown settled into place. She rarely wore the ensemble, yet tonight she needed familiarity. The caged hoops brought back a much-needed sense of control. She draped a white silk shawl around her shoulders and strode to the window.

The multitude of Yankee campfires beyond the panes of glass reflected her life's transformation. The flames within the fieldstone rings slowly consumed her home. Her gaze skimmed past soldiers playing cards or musical instruments to search for the man who had become her target of blame. The beast was nowhere in sight.

Emaline leaned forward, spreading her hands across the cool glass. "I cannot change things now, Colonel. That is true." Her whispered words veiled the panes. "But I'm finished with waiting for you to face me." The angry swish of brocade accompanied her when she turned abruptly, and left her upstairs sanctuary. Each resolute footfall down the carpeted hallway and main staircase only deepened Emaline's wrath.

She jerked open the front door in a full-blown and frenzied stride.

Reece lifted his hand to knock upon the mansion's wooden door.

Now that he'd established camp, he knew he needed to deal with the hellion. Ever watchful, she haunted him. And that fact alone irritated the hell out of him. But he was finished with intriguing women. By delivering this next order in person, he would also be finished with her. The massive door opened so quickly Reece didn't see who crashed into him. Instinctively, his arm wrapped around the warm body.

A startled gasp filled the space between them and he looked down into the woman's face. She blinked in confusion, then her features shifted into blinding contempt.

"Release me this instant, you...you..."

Reece stared down at her. Amid the dullness of winter, this woman's sparking wrath vivified his mood and the essence of lavender wafted over him to scatter all logic. Unexpected heat tripped up his spine, along with the disquieting thought that he should not be feeling such intense emotions simply from holding her. He dropped his embrace and stepped back.

Loosened by their impact, a pale blue ribbon drifted over her eyes and the crocheted netting that confined her hair slipped sideways. In one fluid movement, she pulled the piece off her head and sent a tangle of dark curls tumbling across her left shoulder and down over her breast.

As potent as the sting of whiskey poured over an open wound, the sight burned into memory. His stomach muscles clenched, and for one mind-numbing moment, Reece simply stared at the cascading cloud. Only God's intervention, and his own self-control, kept him from burying his hands in the glorious curls.

He fought for calmness.

And won.

Tight and controlled, his breath eased out in a low rush. "I understand you wish to speak with me?"

"Yes, Colonel Cutteridge. Six hours ago to be exact."

"I've been busy." He motioned to the glass panes that graced both sides of the massive front door. "I'm sure you've noticed from your many windows."

"How dare you stand here and state your duties take precedence over my concerns for my people?" Her hand rose and she fanned her fingers across a row of mother-of-pearl buttons. "It's my property you're destroying, and you're stealing the very food that would have fed us the entire winter! Have you no heart, you…blackguard?" A gust of wind wafted the crisp bite of burning pine around them to underscore her words.

Reece sharply exhaled. "I'm not uncaring about your situation, ma'am. Unfortunately, military orders take precedence over civilian concerns."

"Military orders such as securing Shapinsay as your spoils of war?"

"As I've already mentioned, we're bivouacking here to wait out winter and the arrival of the main army."

"The main army? So I can soon expect the whole Yankee nation to descend upon my home like a plague of locusts?" Her finger pointed eastward, the hair net a beribboned silk web dangling from her hand.

"My regiment will be the only one here. And you don't need to know the whereabouts of the rest." Though she was a woman, this one had already proven dangerous.

She tossed the netting and white shawl to the mirrored hall tree and then turned; it seemed she expected him to follow. She led the way down the wide passage toward a parlor and slipped inside. He waited at the doorway of the well-appointed room. Grabbing a pile of military vouchers from the side table, she whirled to face him, furiously wiggling the scripts in midair.

"Explain to me how these scraps of paper your errand boys keep delivering can ever hope to correct your thieving ways?"

Reece leaned against the doorframe. "They're payment vouchers for the things I've confiscated."

Her hand froze in midair. "Payment?"

"That's right. They're authorized payment vouchers. And you may redeem them for monetary compensation at the Quartermaster General's office in Washington D.C."

She stared at him. With each breath, her chest rose and fell. Then, she drew the vouchers to her stomach and her sharp laugh filled the room.

"Well, of course they are. How foolish of me. If you'll please excuse me, Colonel, I'll just go saddle my horse for the journey to your Yankee capitol to claim my…what was it you said? My monetary compensation? Yes, I'm certain to have no trouble at all crossing your main army lines to recoup my staggering loss." She tossed the vouchers to the side table and they spread out like playing cards.

Her voice swirled downward into a wicked whisper. "Do not mistake me for a fool. These are absolutely useless to me now and you know it."

Reece stepped through the doorway. In four strong strides, he loomed over her. Her attack on the war was one thing, but mocking him and his damned integrity, entirely another.

"Look," he snapped, his ire rising. "This war doesn't sort out or spare those who are innocent, and I have no control over its course."

"This war is nothing short of idiocy!" Her index finger jabbed him in the chest near the row of eagle-faced buttons. "I repeatedly told my brother this fact before he rode off with Stuart's cavalry. And I'm telling you now!"

His heart thumped against the spot where her finger stabbed. Reece pressed closer, crumpling the slender digit back into her palm.

"A well-championed point which matters little." The evenness of his voice surprised him. Her hand dropped away, and Reece caught the haunting glimmer of anguish in her eyes. From somewhere deep inside, unexpected and unwanted, a spark flared. He struggled to deny the empathy that swelled upward. Instead, he affixed her with a trenchant glare. "My regimental surgeon has requested the use of your house for his wounded. I agreed with him, and requisition the lower quarters effective tomorrow morning. A detail of soldiers will move your belongings at first light, however, your privacy upstairs will be honored."

She stiffened, sucking in an audible gasp. They stood so close his breath stirred the wisps of dark silk that framed her face. Soft lines creased the corners of both eyes. Her head moved in denial as a groan caught deep in her throat.

Trembling lips parted, and she whispered, "No…"

"I wouldn't do this if I didn't think it absolutely necessary." Reece reined hard on his irritation and turned away. When he reached the doorway, he paused only long enough to add, "And by the way, Mrs. McDaniels, the government no longer requires us to issue payment vouchers. And most officers don't bother."

He barely cleared the front door before she slammed it behind him.

Chapter Two

"The house is ready, sir."

Reece stood outside the command post under a large canvas tent fly, scanning the half-dozen soldiers clustered behind the junior officer. A myriad of weary expressions creased their faces.

"Did you encounter any problems?" he asked.

"Well, aside from her blocking us each time we entered a room and then following us up and down the stairs while we stacked her possessions in the attic, all the while demanding we remove our filthy Yankee hands from her cherished belongings, no problems to speak of, sir."

A sharp laugh filled the enclosure behind Reece and seconds later, the scent of burning tobacco melded with the aroma of frying bacon wafting across the encampment. Reece shot a glance over his shoulder before returning his attention to the courier.

"And, sir," the young man continued.

"Yes, Lieutenant?"

"We're all wondering if in the future we might be assigned some other detail that doesn't involve her."

Another deep chuckle spilled from the ten-by-twelve-foot enclosure behind him. Reece shifted his weight, his jaw tightening. He offered the soldiers a quick nod. "I'll keep your request in mind, gentlemen. I've had my own run-in with the hellion, so I completely understand. Thank you for your hard work this morning. Please notify Doctor Evans his hospital is ready."

"Yes, sir. We will, sir." The men saluted and Reece returned the gesture. He watched them head toward a row of Sibleys in the distance. The white canvas, teepee-shaped tents soared upward to resemble mountain peaks covered with snow.

Reece drew a steadying breath and exhaled before turning to face his second-in-command sitting inside the headquarters tent. Jackson Neale teetered on a camp chair's two back legs, his white teeth gleaming between lips pulled back in a broad, mischievous grin.

"Why do you always have to laugh at the most asinine times?" The scowl Reece aimed at his friend never quite reached his voice.

Jackson exhaled a thin stream of smoke into the air. A cigar propped between the two fingers he pointed at Reece waggled. "You know, if the Johnnies just recruited her, these bastards could win this war in no time."

Reece reentered the tent, then settled into a chair beside the table, pushing aside his coffee cup. The tepid brew sloshed over the side to pool beneath the battered tin. He stared at the widening puddle. "She's reckless, foolishly so. And headstrong besides." He swept aside the mess, and looked out the canvas opening toward the mansion, wiping his hand down his pants leg. A sliver of something real and raw curled inside his heart and sent an unexpected smile to his lips to disperse the contempt. "She *is* one hell of a woman, though…isn't she?"

His gaze cleared the front lawn and wide veranda, then skipped around the side yard to settle on the edge of the rough-hewn stable visible from where he sat. The audacious upstart was nowhere in sight. Reece swallowed his rising disappointment just as a warning flag unfurled inside his mind.

For someone who'd spent the past year ignoring the many fine northern ladies available at his beck and call, that he now should be searching for some rebellious southerner who surely despised him was rather discomforting. A wave of unrest spurted through him as he re-anchored his common sense. Engaging in an ongoing battle of wills with the widow McDaniels was nowhere on his list of responsibilities. Riding in and riding back out…detached and in control, *that* was his sole focus.

His gaze returned to Jackson. Still leaning backward, the major tested both the strength of the wood and Reece's uncoiling patience. An annoying, quizzical look furrowed his friend's brow. "She's quite the beauty, though, don't you think?"

Reece lifted the copy of D.H. Mahan's *Treatise on Field Fortifications* resting near his elbow. His left hand splayed beneath the worn cover as he nestled the book against his open palm, and his right searched for the chapter he'd been reading before the envoy of soldiers had reported in from their morning assignment.

"She's beautiful, yes. More noteworthy, however, is her tenacity, her determination; an anomaly seldom seen in women." He paged through the tactical, the words and drawings slipping by in a blur. That his heart raced at a ridiculous beat further frustrated Reece. And for some unfathomable reason, he couldn't keep his damn mouth shut. "Not many women could handle the day-to-days of a plantation this size with a mere handful of workers." The pages fanned past as his lips twisted into a wry grin, his voice deepening. "And not just any woman would've pulled that trigger."

Jackson lowered his chair to the ground.

The thud drew Reece's attention and he closed the book with a loud whoosh. Calloused fingers dug into the dog-eared cover as he realized, in that moment, where he'd slipped up in this conversation. Jackson's inevitable rush of concern would most likely arrive with his next breath. In fact, all the man needed was a banner propped on the brim of his slouch hat that proclaimed, *You're making a mistake here, you damn fool.*

Just as Reece dropped the treatise to the weather-beaten wood marred by a dozen or more campaigns, Jackson placed both hands on the other side of the camp table and drew forward. The gold fob chain from a tobacco cutter snugged inside his vest pocket swayed, kicking a glint toward Reece.

"Yes, she's quite bewitching, I'll grant you that," he stated, caution painting his words a scarlet red. "A neat little package just ripe for the picking. But let's not forget why we're here, all right? And while we're at it, let's also not forget we'll be moving out in a few short months."

Jackson's apparent compulsion to counsel him only deepened the disquiet simmering inside Reece. Unfelt amusement pushed his lips sideways as his gaze bored into his best friend's. "I'm well aware of my regiment's purpose and I do believe I'll know when it's time to move, since I'm the one who issues the damn orders."

The air inside the tent grew thick with things unsaid as the cigar returned with a flourish to Jackson's mouth. He settled back in the chair, smiling around white teeth that clenched the cheroot. The tip glowed red, just before another aromatic cloud bloomed into the space between them.

"Well that's good to hear," he quipped, his words wobbling past the thin cigar. "Let's just hope you don't forget all that when her fancy little derrière starts twisting you around in circles."

"Oh I'm sure you'll remind me," Reece said, stifling a smile. He lifted the coffee cup and paused just before the tin met his lips. "Now get the hell out of my tent and call the troops into order for morning inspection before I decide to court-martial your sorry ass for insubordination."

Laughter trailed off behind Jackson as he left the tent.

White clouds tumbled across the early morning sky to taunt the sunbeams streaming through Emaline's parlor window. Sunlight splashed across her feet and pooled upon the poplar floor, the claret-colored carpet of wool now rolled up and carried away. Dust motes danced in the bright beam, their ghostly caper oblivious to the changes in her life.

Soldiers earlier had stacked everything in the attic...everything except her beautiful Steinway. A gift from Benjamin on her twenty-fifth birthday, the piano was too heavy to lift so the blue-coated brutes simply pushed it against the twelve-foot wall and draped canvas over the magnificent instrument. True to the colonel's words, the only rooms left undisturbed were the second floor bedrooms, the small upstairs library, and surprisingly, the winter kitchen at the back of the house.

Emaline crossed through the empty sitting room and stepped into the center passageway dividing the house in two. The walls were bare, stripped of all paintings and portraits. The chandelier that had illuminated the entry hall was gone, its individual crystals either stolen or dumped into a box and carted up to the attic. Everywhere she looked, the area was devoid of furniture.

Her footfalls echoed in the emptiness.

Fighting back tears, she walked through the sitting room and into Benjamin's downstairs library. All of his books and portraits, everything except the heavy desk was gone. With silent, serene dignity, her home now waited to embrace the dying.

Emaline completed the circuit and reentered the front parlor just as soldiers added a plank of wood across two tables between the front windows. Flickering flames in the nearby fireplace drew her scoff. *Not a single pot of water set to boil on the hearth.* That absence told Emaline all she needed to know about the inadequacies of the colonel's medical team.

Years earlier, when Euley had trained her in nursing skills, the old woman insisted she boil things first. When questioned why, she answered, "'Cause I said so, dat's why." Even though Emaline never understood the reasoning, she still followed the woman's sage advice. For without that step, wounds putrefied. These Yankee fools obviously knew nothing about Euley's curative secret. Good! The entire multitude could rot together, and if God had any sense, he'd start with the colonel.

A commotion outside drew her to the closest window. Three mule-drawn ambulance wagons lined up across the front lawns. Snippets of conversations about a cavalry raid near Kelly's Ford that morning filled her ears. Her cheeks flushed; many of Benjamin's business associates resided there. Soldiers lifted wounded patients from deep wagon beds, carried them inside, and in a matter of minutes, a sea of agony sprawled before her. Emaline found no victory in their suffering despite her search to find such feelings.

She turned to flee when a sharp tug on her skirt caused her to jump in alarm. A wounded soldier, mumbling incoherently, had tangled his hands in the mauve-colored, bombazine folds of her day dress. A low gasp tumbled from her mouth when his pleading brown eyes met hers. Emaline winced. These were not her people, and these wounds were not the simple scrapes received while working Shapinsay's fields. She stepped back, yet her skirt flowed outward. The soldier gave another frantic pull. Another garbled sentence followed. Emaline tamped down a surge of panic when his pitiful words finally registered.

"…water, ma'am. Please. Help me."

Her bitterness melted.

She scanned the area and spotted a water bucket sitting on the floor near the window. A battered tin ladle hung from its side. Impulsively, she reached for it and dipped the metal spoon into the liquid. Droplets splashed across her once-polished floor. The implement met his lips and he drank. Then his eyes slipped closed, yet his fingers still gripped her skirt. Emaline replaced the ladle and slowly stood, waiting for his clasp to loosen.

A portly man shuffled into the room and nearly bumped into her.

"There you are!" he proclaimed, his voice warm and gregarious. "You're the mistress of this fine home, are you not?"

She pulled free from the clutches of the now-unconscious soldier, and turned to face the new arrival. Shocks of silvery hair poked in every direction from the man's head and deep lines curved around his cornflower blue eyes, resembling an aged pair of parenthesis. She scanned lower. A cottony-white moustache spilled over his thin lips, and swept upward to join thick, mutton-chopped side-whiskers that hugged his flushed round cheeks. The man stood barely an inch above her height of five feet, and his military frockcoat gaped open to reveal a disheveled ivory-colored shirt. Splotches of dried blood encrusted the cotton. He clutched a weathered satchel under his arm.

Is this bizarre creature their doctor?

He smiled. And Emaline swallowed, so captured by his distinctiveness that she imagined his eyes illumined with some mesmeric inner force. "Are you deaf, woman? I asked if this is your home."

She restrained the impulse to salute. "Y-yes. I'm the owner."

He crossed to the surgical table and placed his bag upon the plank of wood with a resounding thump. "Name's Thaddeus Evans, ma'am," he brightly announced, "I'm the colonel's regimental surgeon. I'm pleased you've come to offer your nursing skills. I'll take all the extra help I can get." He arranged the medical implements across the makeshift table, so entangled in his task that he failed to see the negative shake of her head. "I prefer doctoring inside as opposed to a drafty tent, but these damn fools keep forgetting that fact." He glanced up. "Pardon my cursing, ma'am, but I've repeatedly told them I work best when out of the elements." He returned to his chore. "Now the colonel, here, well he completely understands. And he's a damn good man, the colonel." He smiled at her again and then winked. "Pardon again, but, I'm relieved to get assigned to his regiment. These rooms here are exactly what I've been wanting." He gestured around for emphasis, a wicked-looking saw clutched in his hand. The pecan casements and expensive wallpaper embossed with magnolias and twining vines, as well as the rococo texturing and plate railing that circled the top half of the walls now seemed grotesquely out of place. "But I'm glad you agreed with him, ma'am. Damn glad. So jump in and help wherever you can."

Without any additional words, he moved away to attend to his first patient.

Emaline backed into the farthest corner, avoiding any more interaction with him. She simply observed him. He spoke to the soldiers who carried in the wounded, and to his anxious patients, and sometimes he spoke to no one except himself. Eventually, his soothing words lulled her, drawn to his crooning and gentleness like the dying drawn to heaven. He swiftly treated each patient, surveyed every wound, and isolated the injuries by severity.

Despite his disheveled appearance and odd manner, the stout little man worked with a fierce and efficient devotion, and other than not boiling his instruments before each use, she saw no fault. And for an unsettling moment, Emaline wanted to approach him and simply whisper, "Well done".

Instead, she slipped from the room and climbed the main stairs. She isolated herself away from the makeshift infirmary until the next evening when she vacated her haven by way of the servant's stairway at the back of the house. She sat at the table in the center of the winter kitchen and ate her meal in silence.

Twenty minutes later, Euley ambled in by way of the same stairs.

The old woman held a bundle of clothes between her calloused hands. "Me 'n' Israel...well, he's done asked me to marry him, and I agreed."

Emaline lowered her fork to the dinner plate, a smile winging her lips. "Goodness gracious, it's about time, don't you think? After all, you share two children She looked at the belongings clutched in Euley's arms and her cheerfulness vanished. "But...surely, you aren't leaving me too?"

"No, we ain't leavin'. But if it's all right wif you, I's wantin' to move out to the quarter to be wif Israel at night."

"The quarter?" Was she daft? Why would she choose a servant's cabin over the comforting appointments of her upstairs room? "Good heavens, Euley, winter's coming. And you have your own place on the third floor. I insist that Israel move up here to live."

"Israel don't want to live in da main house, Miz Emaline."

"I wish he'd not drag you down there. If I go ask him myself, do you think it'll make a difference?" She stood and started toward the back door, but Euley's words stopped her.

"Please don't. I want to go live out dere wif him."

Their gazes met.

"But, what will I do without you here?"

"I'll only be dere at night, and den over here to help durin' da day. And da colonel, he won't let his soldiers hurt you none."

The dark-haired man's image flooded once more through her misery, making her next breath harder to intake. Instead, Emaline huffed—the riposte a hollow echo in the room. Her heart wrenched against this newest turn of events—one more loss, one more reason to hate him.

She slumped back into the chair and stared at Euley until the old woman lowered her head, her chin dropping to her chest. Seconds ticked by.

Finally, Emaline closed her eyes, her heartbeat rapid as she drew in a deep, strengthening breath. She knew selfishness when she saw it, and she saw it in herself right now. Euley was so much more than a servant; she was her closest female friend and a true confidante. She deserved happiness. Despite all the madness around them and more so now that her own life seemed so lost, Emaline understood that all people needed love.

She slipped down in the chair and looked at Euley's downcast head.

Her chest tightened around her breath. "Please look at me," she whispered. The turbaned head lifted. Ebony eyes met hers. "I'm so sorry for denying you. Please forgive me. I do understand. Truly. And it's fine. You go out to Israel and make a loving home for him." Euley nodded, offering her a hesitant smile. Emaline returned one. "But you tell him I said he must take good care of you."

The woman's face brightened. "Take care o' me?" Her comforting chuckle once more filled the room. "More like I'll be takin' care of him, and Moses and ol' Tacker too!"

"Well, we're all blessed to have you care for us," Emaline said, a rueful smile tugging at her lips. "I remember the many times you've helped me over the years with the house or the cooking. Even with my hair before I swept off to some silly soiree in Falmouth." She raised her hands, her palms held upward as a forlorn chuckle fell from her own mouth. "These used to be the softest in Virginia, or at least that's what Benjamin used to say. Remember?" A fire burned low in the hearth to offer warmth, yet she felt chilled to the bone.

"You don't need no fancy hands to be important to us, Miz Emaline."

Emaline looked up and smiled. "Thank you, dear. I've always treasured your friendship. Now go on out to Israel and have a good evening. I'll see you again in the morning."

Euley nodded. And then, without another word, Emaline watched her last domestic house servant, from her original staff of ten, slip outside. More than the winds of November swirled in upon Euley's departure. Emaline stared at the closed door. She sat all alone in a broken home that housed the enemy.

Loneliness engulfed her.

She lowered her head to the table, but the muffled moans from the infirmary nipped at her misery. Emaline rose. Leaden feet carried her to the swinging door that separated her from the hellish disorder of her world. She pushed open the divider and the doctor's comforting chatter somehow found its way across her pain to embrace her. Hour after endless hour, the dedicated surgeon maintained his vigil, aiding where he could, in a bloody world gone mad.

Despair tightened her throat and brought up the bitter bite of contrition.

Nightmares taunted Emaline. In her dreams, Benjamin scorned her from all directions, ridiculing her and her inability to keep together the only thing that mattered: *Shapinsay*. She cried out, begging him to stop, to remove the unwanted burdens he had placed upon her. But he granted no respite. Instead, he blamed her for her inadequacies as a woman, his torment unceasing. From the tangle of bedding, he lifted her, swirling her around and around, until she looked down upon the empty shell of a widow lying pitiful, old and all alone in bed. Emaline clawed her way through the blackness until the horror of her dreams withdrew with a new dawning.

At noon, she forced herself to dress, and with a heavy heart she once-again descended into hell. She preferred anything to the ordeal that had torn at her emotions all night. Her fingers gripped the newel post at the bottom of the stairs and she peered through the parlor doorway in search of the doctor. He was nowhere in sight. Emaline edged around the opening and stepped into the room. Icy fingers touched her hand and she jerked, staring down at a young soldier on a cot beside the wall.

He struggled to prop himself up on his elbow. "I'm sorry to startle you, ma'am, b-but would you give this to Doc. He'll make sure it gets to my wife." Shaking fingers held out a small mahogany-cased daguerreotype.

"I don't know where he is right now," she whispered, linking her hands together in a firm clasp.

"Please, ma'am." His hand shook as pale fingers gripped the piece. "If you'll just take it, then I know he'll get it."

Speaking to the wounded soldier brought everything back into perspective. Yet, the foolishness of standing here quivering in the parlor like a frightened doe sickened Emaline. She never thought herself a wretched person, yet here she stood, displaying weakness in all its disgusting forms to this poor, unfortunate soul. The pleading in his eyes weighed heavy across her heart, and she swallowed. She could do this. Compassion was never wrong.

Emaline reached down and took the small case from his hand, then flipped back the tiny hook latch on its side to open it. Maroon velvet covered the left side of the piece. A dainty gold border edged the left and on the right, framed under glass, the faded likeness of a young woman holding an infant stared back at her.

Emaline's tension dissolved. She looked up and scanned the sea of wounded men. How many other women and children in the Yankee kingdom awaited their beloved's return? Were they so different from her? Didn't she wait daily for news from her brother? With each passing moment, it became harder for her to indiscriminately hate.

She smiled and asked, "What's your name?"

"Private James Anders, ma'am, from Mariah Hill." Pride for his hometown filled his trembling voice. "In Spencer County, Ohio, ma'am. And that there's Rebecca. My wife. She's holding my baby girl, Mary Margaret." Despite the bandage covering half his head, the injured man still managed a weak, wobbly smile.

"They're lovely, Mr. Anders. But you should keep this. You'll want it when you're better."

"Doc says it don't look good for me. So in case I don't…well, you know. Will you—"

"Yes," she whispered, slipping the case inside her pocket. She patted the spot for good measure. The young soldier nodded and then lay back upon the cot in obvious relief.

Emaline resumed her search for Doctor Evans and found him in the downstairs library. The surgeon straightened as she approached, his usual broad smile flooding his face. "Well, the little lady returns! I'd wondered why you left, but nonetheless, I'm glad you're back. Come along now," he said, sweeping past her. "I need your assistance with a young corporal in the other room. His wound's been oozin' for days, and I'd like you to take a look." Emaline stood her ground and just stared at the man shuffling around a maze of cots. "The colonel says more wounded will be arriving soon…" He paused when he realized she wasn't following. Turning to face her, he raised his hands to his broad hips. "Well, why're you still standing over there, woman? Come along now and tell me what you think about this ooze?"

Emaline inhaled. Once. Twice. And then, with a resolute heart, she did the one thing she vowed she'd never do — she stepped forward to help.

"I've decided to talk to the doctor about utilizing your healing remedy," Emaline said to Euley three nights later. The whir of the maple spinning wheel slowed as she relaxed her foot on the treadle. Her fingers pinched the woolen fibers together in her hand and then married them onto the leader yarn already spun into a strand on the bobbin. Her gaze lifted, connecting with the old woman's. "I believe it will help ease some of their suffering."

"You sure you want to keep helpin' dese Yankees? I mean, dey's tearing apart yo' home." Euley wrapped a long strand of yarn around one polished end of a hickory stick.

"I'm not helping Yankees. I'm simply lending aid to help fathers return to their children, sons to their mothers, and husbands to wives." Rationalizing her thought of assisting the doctor somehow made her decision to share the woman's curative secret a bit easier to swallow.

Emaline resumed her peddling, keeping the tension firm on the clockwise spin of the bobbin. She concentrated on the cream-colored roving in her hands and guided the strands into a proper twist, her fingertips softening beneath the lanolin-infused wool. "I can't watch people die, not knowing what I know. I don't care who they are. You understand that, don't you? I mean, if we shared your remedy, perhaps something good could come out of this tragedy."

"I know, Miz Emaline," Euley said, plunging the yarn bundle into the bucket of hot water resting beside her on the hearth. "And I agree with you, but dis ain't no secret. We's been boilin' things down here for years." She swirled the stick several times in the water, allowing the liquid to absorb and strengthen the strands. "You think dere doctor will even let you?"

"I hope so. I'll mention it to him first thing tomorrow." The churring whisper of the spinning wheel blended with the muted resonance of a bugle blowing somewhere in the Yankee encampment. *Musical orders.* "The doctor calls this tune 'Taps'," Emaline said, changing the subject as she stretched the fibers in her hand to keep the skein thin. "Following a battle this past July over near Harrison's landing, some Yankee bugler rewrote an obscure military song to create this one." The brass leads guiding her yarn onto the bobbin in front of her glinted in the fire's glow and resembled a handful of twinkling fireflies. "The doctor said the colonel liked the tune so much he now has his bugler play it for his troops. It's supposed to tell them to stop drinking for the night, or some such nonsense." Doc had shared the lyrics with Emaline several days ago, and by now, she'd memorized every word.

Impulsively, she began to croon, the *wooka-wooka* of her treadle and the whirl of the wheel, embracing her soft voice:

"Day is done.
Gone the sun.
From the lakes, from the hills, from the sky.
All is well.
Safely rest.
God is nigh. "

Unbidden, the colonel's handsome image flooded Emaline's mind and she stopped singing. Leaning forward, she peddled faster in an attempt to push away the man's unwanted features. The warmth in the room seemed to impinge upon her, and she swept a dark-blue sleeve across her forehead to remove the perspiration without losing any treadle momentum.

From the corner of her eye, she watched Euley pull the yarn mass from the hot water and place it on the blanket to dry beside the countless other bundles they had created tonight. A groan slipped from her servant's mouth and drew

Emaline's concern. They would stop for the night.

Lessening the pressure of her foot, she slowed the wheel and leaned back.

After nearly two hours, the repetitious work of making yarn for winter blankets had also laid a sheen across Euley's brow. Decision made, Emaline broke the main strand from the pile of lock wool in her lap. She slowly treadled to allow the last of the soft, curly fibers to slip through her fingers, and then through the orifice on her spinner. Just as the bobbin stopped twirling, the colonel's bugler finished his mournful tune.

"It's getting late." Emaline dropped the mass of locks into the basketful of cleaned and carded wool. The fibers inside the wicker resembled more a puffy cloud than fleece. "We'll want to get an early start so we can talk to the doctor. Let's leave everything here and just finish up sometime tomorrow. Come on, I'll walk you out to your cabin."

"I'll be fine, Miz Emaline. I'm just a bit stiff, that's all." Euley stood and stretched her thin frame, working out the kinks in her back. "Dey ignore me anyways." She stepped over the bundles of new yarn and headed toward the back door, opening it. A gust of chilly November wind blustered in, forcing the fire into a lively dance and sending shadows up all four walls.

"Rest well, dear. And thank you for your hard work today. I'll see you again tomorrow, bright and early."

The servant nodded and slipped from sight, pulling the door shut behind her.

Emaline exhaled in a slow rush. Leaning back against the chair, she stared into the flickering fire. Today was her birthday, and she'd almost forgotten. "Well, I'm thirty-four now," she whispered to the gamboling flames. "Three years ago, I'd been swathed in widow's weeds."

Emaline pushed against her knees and stood, stretching out her cramped muscles. The corset pinched under her left breast. She ran her hands down her dress, ruffling her work crinoline into place. After banking the fire, she made her way around the room and blew out the candles, then slowly climbed the servants' stairs. The colonel's melancholy tune moved up each step with her.

The following morning, Emaline raked her hair into black netting and made sure the part in the center was straight before she affixed the ruffled, white silk day cap into place. Closing the bedroom door behind her, she hurried down the hall. Euley would be arriving soon so she mustn't dawdle. At the top landing, Emaline swept her fingers over her head one last time to check for loose hair.

Her chest tightened the moment her hand gripped the polished banister. Like a black hole, sorrow opened up to swallow her. Emaline struggled to catch her breath. *Another alarming episode.* Was there no end to her despair? She leaned forward, her fingers tightening around the smooth wood. Short, static gasps escaped between parted lips. Rapid and frantic, they filled the top landing. Some unknown fear squeezed tight and Emaline helplessly waited for the morass to lift. The smell of Euley's lemon oil met her nostrils. She forced herself to take deep, calming breaths.

Inhale.

Exhale.

She took one comforting inhalation after another until the blackness slowly withdrew. Emaline peered into the passageway below. Several soldiers moved across the hall, entering sickrooms on either side to begin another day. No one appeared to have noticed her at the top of the stairs.

Or if they did, they paid her no mind.

She straightened and raised her chin. Sweeping her hands down the front of her dress, she composed herself. First one step, then the other, she descended, focusing on each footfall upon the wide, wooden risers. Her palm slid along the solid oak, and by the time she reached the bottom landing, the railing had become tacky beneath her grip. Emaline lifted her hand away, and swept the front of her red-and-black plaid to straighten the folds of her day dress. A quick hop settled her hoops into place, before she shook her arms to fluff her undersleeves. The white linen draped into a graceful swell around her wrists.

Emaline affixed a smile, ready now to face the doctor.

She stared at the front door, and the longer she waited, the farther her heart inched into her throat. The large, forged-brass handle no longer gleamed. Her lips tightened. Like the bottom part of the banister, it too had dulled beneath the muck of a thousand Yankee hands.

Her gaze dropped to the once-elegant floor Euley had spent a lifetime on hands and knees polishing. Gouges scored the wood in a dozen places and mirrored the deep gashes that marred Emaline's soul.

Everywhere her eyes rested, she saw transformation. Mud and streaks of blood caked the majestic pilasters that soared up both side entrances into the sitting and dining rooms. A glaring rip across a section of swan motifs on the Walter Crane wallpaper broke her heart. For a split second, Emaline remembered the delightful week the gifted artisan had spent with them, applying pristine flecks of red wool to his exquisite masterpiece.

She turned her scrutiny to the windows that embraced the front door. The filthy glass dulled the morning light as if somehow sensing the gloom that had befallen her world. She swallowed against the anger percolating upward. Like Shapinsay's sprawling grounds, her home's downstairs reeked of *Yankee*. Emaline shoved aside her resentment and remembered her objective just as the front door swung open. The surgeon stepped inside and offered her a warm greeting as he unbuttoned his great coat.

"Good morning," she replied, impatience flooding through her as she fought against the urge to deny him Euley's secret. She pressed her lips together and waited while he draped his heavy outerwear across a sturdy nail pounded into the wall beside a pair of entwining swans. "If I may, Doctor Evans, I would like to discuss a matter of great importance with you."

He reached for her arm and guided her into the sitting room. "Certainly, dear. Let me make a few notes, though, before I begin working. We'll talk for a moment after that, if you'd like." He settled at his desk, reaching for a ledger, his pen and an inkwell.

While he attended to his bookkeeping, Emaline lowered to a chair beside him, her crinoline skirts collapsing into a whoosh of bright Chinese silk. Swathed from head to toe in the trappings of privilege, she became acutely conscious of the fact that she looked out of place amid the suffering around her. That she should feel such ignominy pounding through her while sitting in her own home only intensified Emaline's frustrations.

A soldier sidled up to them and placed a steaming cup of coffee before the surgeon. The man nodded his gratitude and continued with his notes.

The private turned her way. "May I bring you a cup, Mrs. McDaniels?"

"No, thank you," she said, offering a tight smile.

He nodded, took the reports from the doctor, then scurried off.

Orderlies moved about the room, sliding emptied chamber pots under the cots of rousing patients, refilling buckets with fresh water, and coaxing coals into flames inside the fireplace to abolish the bite of winter.

A small pile of rubble resting near the hearth caught Emaline's eye and she swept her vision upward. A gaping spot on the ceiling revealed where expensive rococo plaster used to cling. She clenched her jaw and scanned the built-in beaufats flanking the ornate chimneybreast. A jumbled collection of soldiers' personal items claimed every shelf.

A fresh wave of despair rolled over her.

"So tell me," the doctor said, drawing her attention. He laid aside his pen and clasped his hands over his wide girth. "What's so urgent that demands you greet me at the door this morning?" A gentle smile lifted his well-manicured mustache.

"Yes, well…" Emaline paused, clasping her hands tightly together in her lap. "I would like to suggest a process that might help lower your escalating infection rate."

Interest lifted his craggy features. "My dear, anything that could actually do that would be a Godsend." He scooted his chair back a few more inches to face her, and crossed his legs, the scuffed toe of his brown brogan pointing her way. He took a sip of coffee and returned the cup to his desk. "Go on, madam. I'm listening. What do you think might slow my pace of infection?"

Emaline hesitated, her fingers intertwining. A knuckle cracked.

He's not the colonel. Just tell him.

"Well…I believe you should boil your instruments."

The surgeon's forehead wrinkled as one bushy eyebrow shot upward. "Boil my instruments? You mean, like Doctor Goldsmith's theory." He paused for a moment and raised his right hand, propping his chin on his folded fingers. "Yes, come to think of it, I have read his papers. If I remember correctly, he states inflammatory mischief and febrile disturbances following an injury are due to the influx of poisoning, decomposing blood."

Emaline's own brow puckered. She had no idea what the good doctor had just spouted, but she nodded nonetheless. "Over the years, we've utilized the procedure at Shapinsay on our servant population. I have personally seen wounds treated with implements boiled beforehand remain purulent-free. I'm not sure why, but the boiling does seem to help."

His lips pursed. A moment later, his hand dropped to the desk. He toyed with the handle of his coffee cup. "Amputation wounds are not simple field scrapes, Mrs. McDaniels. They require long and continued suppuration. In this case, laudable pus is acceptable. The lesser of two evils, if you will. Otherwise, patients might be dying of sepsis inside, while we thought they had healed. Because of that, we must allow miasm on putrified flesh. Acknowledging ooze is one thing, my dear, but boiling our instruments?" He shook his head. "We simply don't have time, I'm afraid. Ordinarily, we're an army on the move, and doing so would be ludicrous even under the best of circumstances."

"I understand. But, if I may, Doctor—"

"Please, my dear, call me Doc." He clasped his hands across his belly again and chuckled. "Everyone else does."

Emaline nodded. "All right. Then Doc, would you object to me boiling things while you're at Shapinsay?"

He tugged at his whiskers for a moment before releasing another breath on a pondering sigh. "I have no objections to you including your procedure, if you so desire. And I'll note your suggestion and generous offer of time in my daily report to the colonel." He reached for his journal and pen just as Emaline's toes squeezed into a tight curl inside her leather morning shoes.

Her eyes widened. "W-why does he need to know? I'm sharing this with you, Doc. Not him."

"I report everything to Colonel Cutteridge, my dear. He is in charge, you know." Another laugh followed as he leaned forward to scribble a few lines in the journal before flipping the booklet closed. "But you know, this might prove valuable. At least while we're camped here. And as I mentioned before, I can certainly use all the help I can get."

Emaline stood, her silk dress rustling like willows in the wind. With a barely perceptible and much-practiced heel tap, she settled her hoops once more around her. She bit her lower lip, fighting the anger pulsing through her at the mere mention of the colonel's name. She didn't want him to think she'd offered the remedy because he'd been giving her the blasted vouchers. Mumbling a hasty thank you, she whisked from the room. Three medical stewards stood near the front door, and she ordered them outside to the laundry shed to haul back one of her large cauldrons. Thirty minutes later, with boiling pot in place over the fire, Emaline put the primitive medicinal secret into practice.

For nearly an hour, she and Euley gathered and cleaned all the medical instruments in the house before moving on to other tasks. Emaline did not think beyond the repetition of her chores. Day waned into night. Chores were ticked off her list, and the last thing she did was sit beside her patients and write letters home for them. They offered heartfelt thank you's, some wiping away tears. She slipped their missives into envelopes and sealed them. The gratitude that radiated from their eyes made hers well with moisture and validated the time she'd spent with them. They were mere boys, after all. Most of them scared and hurt and far from home.

And for a while, she almost forgot they were Yankees.

Five days later, the arrival of a dozen more patients cramped the workspace inside the makeshift hospital. One more injured soldier, and the medical staff would have to begin stacking cots on top of one another. Emaline decided to abandon the decorum of crinoline hoops in favor of simple work dresses with several underslips in order to move about without disturbing the wounded.

She stood before the fireplace in the dining room; a bucket propped on her hip. Upending the container, Emaline tumbled the bloodied instruments Doc had used for the morning's surgeries into the cauldron of bubbling water. Scalding droplets splashed across her wrist and she recoiled, dropping the wooden pail. She hissed through clenched teeth and buried her hand in her apron.

A convalescing soldier resting on a nearby cot reached down and stopped the bucket's awkward wobble. "You all right, Mrs. McDaniels?" he asked.

"Yes. I'm fine." She shook her hand and inspected the damage. "I was just startled, that's all." A red blotch suffused her skin near the knuckle on her thumb, forcing a sigh from her. She knew better than to plop items into boiling water. Fatigue caused her to be careless. Euley's salve would prevent a blister, but until she could find time to retrieve some, she'd just have to cope with the sting. A rush of tears swelled upward, and she swallowed to stifle them. The unrelenting compulsion to cry was certainly far more than a splotch on her hand required.

The soldier lifted the bucket, and Emaline folded her fingers around the sodden rope handle, anchoring her smile into place.

A blush skimmed the man's face. "I sure do thank you for your kindness, ma'am. We all do."

She nodded, mumbled a hasty thank you, and then retraced her steps across the room, shaking her hand to dissipate the pain. More comfortable following an established routine, she pushed past the canvas-covered Steinway to reach another patient.

The pail in her hand thumped to the top of the piano. It seemed an eternity ago since she'd last entertained guests with classical selections of Liszt or Beethoven. Emaline stifled a mocking laugh. Leaning over, she rested her hand across the forehead of an unconscious soldier. The boy's fever had broken. Her eyes slipped shut. *This one might actually live to return home.*

Muffled words reached her from the hallway and she straightened, peering around the heavy piano. Two officers had entered the house. The man the doctor called Major Neale stepped in first. When he shifted, the solid image of Colonel Cutteridge filled her vision. Emaline's breath caught. Her heart lurched. She'd not seen the colonel in several days, and his unexpected appearance sent a shiver through her. She squelched the preposterous reaction to the man and leaned forward to listen.

"...whole of Burnside's army should be in Falmouth next week," Cutteridge stated.

"Everyone?"

"Yep. Five corps, nineteen divisions. Not counting artillery and the remaining cavalry units."

The major's forehead crinkled. "What about the engineers?"

"They should arrive sometime next week and begin laying pontoons. Burnside says he wants to press hard on Fredericksburg before the Rebs have a chance to consolidate their strength."

"Press hard? Hell, we've been sitting here waiting for nearly two weeks."

"I know, but Burnside told General Halleck that moving down from Culpepper with a hundred and thirty thousand men takes time. Once the city falls, though, it'll be an easy walk to Richmond."

Emaline gasped. *They're planning to attack the city.* The colonel swung toward the parlor and spotted her. His lips pulled taut. Slowly, she straightened and smoothed her hand down the front of her dress. Her chin lifted as she purposefully walked toward him.

Dismissing the major with a curt nod, Emaline turned and faced the colonel. "If you'll kindly step aside, I'll go tend to your soldiers bleeding to death in my parlor. Thankfully, they'll be spared having to face the dangerous horde of civilians waiting for you all in Fredericksburg." The tense set of his mouth faded into a smirk. He took a full step backward and motioned for her to proceed.

Emaline pushed between the two men, shaking her right hand at her side to relieve the sting of the blister as she turned the corner.

Captain Brennen Benedict dropped the missive into the fire. His long sigh filled the clearing. A hundred and fifty Yanks protected the supply line near Freeman's Ford. Which meant his men couldn't steal the much-needed rifles and ammunition heaped inside the Federal railcars…at least not tonight.

Sonofabitch.

"We'll wait," he told the young courier. "Tell them to come back." The private issued a hasty salute, swept into the saddle, and headed into the darkness to deliver the message to his comrades concealed along the ridgeline above Warrenton Springs.

A biting wind cut through Brennen as he raked a hand through his hanks of dirty brown hair. He hadn't had a decent cut in more than a year. Hell's fire, he hadn't had anything decent in more than a year. He pulled the tattered slouch hat into place atop his head. His fingers looped around the lanyard that fell down the front of his jacket and he gave it a hard tug.

Bastards. No matter what he did, the bluebellies kept coming.

His lips compressed. He was moving ever closer to home and ever closer to the memories of those glorious years before the war when foolish indulgences and cognac flowed faster than his goddamned coins did at the gaming tables in Richmond. Since riding in from the valley a month before with the rest of Stonewall's cavalry, one powerful image superseded all others in his mind: *Emaline.* Surely to God, his sister had evacuated to the safety of Richmond as she'd promised. Less than a hundred miles lay between him and Shapinsay—and the damn Federals now crawled all over that side of the river. *But Em promised she'd go.* His worry eased back a peg.

Popping musket fire resounded through the eerie stillness and caught his thoughts. The Federals had trigger-happy fingers and they'd sooner shoot at their own damn shadows than think.

Cowards.

Frigid air permeated his faded gray overcoat. He stared down at the thin wisps of black smoke curling around an iron pot slung over the fire. Boiled rice with sugar sauce for supper again—the tangy sweetness clung in nauseating layers and aggravated the empty ache in his gut. Brennen swallowed back the bile and reached over to check his Sharps, making certain the carbine's scabbard still held secure to the side of the Grimsley saddle. He dropped his hand, slipped cold fingers over the even colder metal of his saber, and allowed a lopsided smirk to lift his lips. He'd appropriated the sword earlier this year from some dead Yank over near Ball's Bluff. The threaded leather grip was always at the ready now along with the dead officer's holstered Adams resting on Brennen's right hip.

Dangerous work, this scouting business. When the Falmouth Guard first joined ranks with the Army of Northern Virginia, Brennen never dreamed they'd all be assigned as scouts. He knew the area better than most so command fell to him. He enforced discipline in the ranks and led his men with cool determination. Each mission—striking fast, withdrawing quietly. His methods became a calling card abhorred by the Federals, and within months the home guard earned the moniker *Gray Ghosts*. A smile cracked his features. He liked their signature nickname. He also liked risk-taking and the secrecy and raiding Yankee outposts and wagon trains, tearing up rail tracks, and ripping out Federal telegraph lines. Such exploits gave him the spark he needed in his otherwise gone-to-hell life. Besides, scouting for General Jackson kept him and his boys from mundane camp tasks and picket duty. Pride zipped through Brennen and shoved aside his usual reserve. In fact, Yank secrets uncovered by his men had made the difference in more than a few battles.

He leaned sideways and checked the girth strap on his saddle to make sure it was still tight. His smirk widened as he recalled the personal satisfaction of capturing a Union general over near Ox Hill last week. The fact that the bastard had been buried between some whore's legs at the time only enhanced the account. Better yet, the saddlebag recovered alongside the buffoon held a treasure trove of information about Union troop movements. Of course, the wench who'd shared details of her upcoming tryst had been well-compensated— and, at her eager insistence, Brennen even managed to find the time needed to finish what that bluebellied buffoon had begun.

The recollection stirred up a chuckle as the aroma of freshly brewed coffee swirled in the breeze around him. Brennen wrapped his fingers around a cup his sergeant had thrust into his hand. Nodding thanks, he raised the tin to his lips. The caustic brew burned all the way down his throat but managed to silence the gnawing hunger.

"Think we can stop 'em, Cap'n?" his lanky right-hand man asked, sloshing coffee into his own cup. A hiss filled the night as the brew splattered on the gloveless fingers. He swiped his grubby hand down an even grubbier pant leg.

Brennen nodded. "Hope so. We'll need to cut their ammunition supply to slow them down. That'll give General Jackson the time he needs to get to Gordonsville first. If the Confederacy loses Shenandoah Valley, we lose our food supply."

He scanned his men across the clearing. Fatigue etched deep lines in each face. Loyalty aside, his Ghosts were hungry now and dog-tired from being on the move. Their horses hadn't been unsaddled in three days. But they couldn't rest—not just yet. When the others returned, they'd grab a quick bite of the boiled rice, then follow the train southward, hoping for another opportunity to strike.

And they'd find one—it was only a matter of time. Brennen's smirk dissolved, and his lips compressed into a tight line. Once he'd been considered the best-dressed gambler in Richmond, but those times were gone. His commitment to the Gray Ghosts now filled the void.

And nobody would rein them in—not as long as he drew breath.

Nobody.

Dead tired from being on her feet all day, Emaline rested her forehead against the doorframe. A moment later, she reached for her heavy cape and draped it across her shoulders. Corded loops easily slipped over metal toggles to secure the garment. When the doctor suggested she take some fresh air, she welcomed the opportunity for a break from the pain and suffering of the soldiers.

A brittle wind scoured her face as Emaline eased open the front door. Snuggling into the folds of the woolen cape, she trudged onto the veranda. A pungent whiff of fried mutton wafted over her as flickering lights poked like pinpricks through the ebony canvas.

Now they're enjoying my sheep.

Each new day she scrambled to keep up with her losses, recording what she could in the ledgers. And each new day, her stack of Yankee vouchers grew. She stared at the campfires. Amber reflections, a myriad dancing forms of shadows and lights, flickered over an endless sea of white canvas.

She leaned against the closest column and sighed. Restless anxiety washed over her. With the disturbing news she'd overheard today, she knew something had to be done to alert the city. Her concern lay only for the citizens of Fredericksburg, not with army matters. If the men of this country wanted to kill each other, she wouldn't stand in their way. But innocent people always got caught in the middle. She smirked. Well this time...oh yes, this time she had information to prevent such a catastrophe. She would make sure news of the impending Federal attack got to the city officials.

From the shadows, a deep voice interrupted her scheming. "It's a bit chilly to be outside," he said.

Emaline recognized the man the instant he stepped into the moonlight. The colonel's very presence wrought havoc with her emotions as well as her plans. A tremor skimmed through her when he leaned forward, resting a black boot on the bottom step. His arm draped his upraised knee. "But this gives me a chance to thank you for helping the doctor."

He paused when revealing shuffles indicated several soldiers ambling past. He turned his head toward them.

Emaline scanned the colonel's profile, the handsome contours strong and well defined. Her belly muscles tensed, the tightness spiraling downward when he turned back to her.

"As I was saying," he continued. "He's a colorful fellow, don't you think?"

She glanced away. A queasy regret engulfed her, knowing she would betray him tonight.

"Colorful doesn't quite fit," she quipped.

He chuckled. "Did you happen to see the sunset this evening? It reminded me of home."

His relaxed mood and absurd question startled her, and her gaze raked back to his. A strong urge to flee zipped down her spine. Just as quickly, she dismissed the sensation.

He continued—his eyes luminous. "This god-awful cold makes me wish I'd never come east. I miss Tucson and the dry heat of the desert."

"What's Tucson?"

"My home. Out west."

"Well, why don't you resign your post and hurry back there. In fact, if you left tonight, you'd be enjoying the heat of your Tucson desert and those beckoning sunsets that much sooner."

One dark brow peaked. "If I were to leave, they'd simply send a replacement. And I assure you, he'd not be nearly as accommodating as I have been."

"Let me be the judge of that."

"Contrary to what you think, Mrs. McDaniels, I've been extremely patient with you. Remember, you did try to shoot me." Without warning, his smile transformed into a hard shove against her heart. "And I can promise you another officer would've dealt with your…spirit much differently."

The smile she offered barely moved her lips. "I was merely defending my home and people. If the tables were turned, I'm sure you'd do the same."

He replied without hesitation, his words direct. "When you say your people, you mean your slaves. And no, the tables could not be turned because I would never enslave Negroes. Among other things, we're fighting for their freedom."

Issuing her most direct glare, Emaline leaned forward. "I too abhor slaveholding cruelty, among other things…" She paused and scanned him from head to toe. "And upon the death of my husband, I changed many things at Shapinsay. My servants had the option to leave if they wanted to long before your President issued his proclamation…and most did." Her chin lifted and a rush of heat burned her cheeks. "But these 'enslaved Negroes', as you call Euley and the others, are here of their own free will. I love them as if they're my own family, and have even taught them how to read and write." Her heart slugged hard against her ribcage, forcing her words out in a clipped rush. "I shall always be grateful to them for their loyalty." She straightened, leveling her chin. Why did she feel such an oppressive need to explain her views to this man? She owed him nothing.

In fact, he should be apologizing to her.

His foot scuffed the step as he replanted his boot. The abrasive noise bounced up each nerve in her spine. "Well, I certainly commend you for your bold decision, Mrs. McDaniels, but among Southerners, you are in the minority."

"Minority or not, Colonel, is totally irrelevant to me. This is how I feel."

Firelight played across his face, and Emaline eased back against the uncomfortable wooden column. Having a conversation with this man about servitude, the weather and sunsets, or any other absurd topic, unsettled her. She forced her thoughts back into control, stifling the unease that fluttered inside. With an important mission to accomplish tonight, she must make certain he did not become suspicious. Indeed, the blue-coated beast would not best her this time. She tamped down her puzzling frustrations, and presented a dazzling smile.

"Isn't it ever cold in Tucson?"

She actually saw his jaw clench.

"Nothing like this," he said, "except in the mountains, of course. There's snow in the passes, but not in the lower elevations." He abruptly changed the subject. "Doc said your name's Emaline. May I call you that?" She nodded, ignoring the thrumming rush of blood that surged through her. "Mine's Reece. Please use that, if you'd like. It'll make things easier."

Easier?

This man apparently thought personalizing their names would force her back inside. "Reece," she softly said just to prove him wrong. "Colonel Reece Cutteridge. Yes, the name fits you. All the hard, rough edges match up with the even harder, rougher-edged man."

A mixture of humor and intrigue danced in his dark eyes. "I've been called many things, but rough-edged is one I shall remember."

His laugh, rich and solid, oozed around Emaline's animosity. Heat wrapped the back of her neck, slipped over her scalp, then settled into two hot spots on her cheeks.

She scrambled for control of the conversation and her reaction to this man. "This area here—this weather, is all I've ever known."

"You mean you've never been up north?"

The honeycombed light beyond the veranda held her spellbound, and she silently begged for a miracle to stop the ludicrous flutter inside her. "Nothing farther north ever interested me."

"I don't have much use for it either," he said, spilling another warm chuckle over her. "All my interests lie out west."

"And what might those interests be?" Someone as stalwart as this raw-boned brute probably had a wife and a dozen children awaiting his return.

"Dos Caballos." Two fingers rose as he finished his sentence. "It's Spanish for two horses. *Dos Caballos* is my ranch." His hand dropped back to his knee.

"And is there a wife out west with those two horses?" *Dear God! I actually asked him?* Why should she care if he had a dozen wives with horses?

His smile vanished. "There's no wife. Most women aren't able to endure that type of living."

Emaline stiffened. What could a ranch out west possibly require from a woman that plantation life these past years did not demand? Instead of challenging him, however, she baffled herself with another intrusion into his private life. "Don't you have any family?"

He nodded. "My sister, Colleen. I call her Callie. The ranch is well established, and she's managing things in my absence." Smoothness returned to his lips. "Callie's one of those rare women who can handle the wildness of the West."

Mystified, Emaline simply nodded. Somehow, this silly, civil conversation portrayed him as flesh and blood, a living, breathing mortal—not some judgmental, dark-eyed heathen who tied up all her spiraling emotions.

"I run horses," he continued. "The ranch has over ten thousand head. We sell them to the army. That's how I ended up back East."

"I couldn't help but notice your buckskin when you rode in. He's obviously not an army-issued Morgan. Is he one of yours?"

"Saguaro? Yes. I broke him myself. We've been together for a while. Since I'm an officer, I can choose my own mount, so I prefer to ride him." He shifted his legs and leaned forward again. "But what about you? Any family members other than a brother?"

The words came too easy. "My husband died of cholera in the spring of fifty-nine, and we had no children. I've only Brennen left." Her voice coiled into a soft whisper. "That is, if he returns from the war." Emaline's mood shifted abruptly. She should not be serving up such private slices of her life to this man.

"If he's anything like you, I'm certain he'll return."

"Like me?" She stared at him.

"You're a survivor. When your brother returns, things will be better for you."

Better? First, you confiscate my food and destroy my home, then counsel me on the cruelties of slavery. And now you have the gall to dollop out hope? How dare you!

She pushed away from the column and gestured toward the clearing behind him, clinging to her bitterness like a lifeline. "Take a look around, Colonel." She refused to use his name. "Do you see the damage made by your scores of horses and wagons? Or the empty smokehouse, henhouse and storage sheds? You've left me little to feed my people, enslaved as they are in their miserable life of bondage and chains." Sweat beaded her forehead even as the icy wind nipped at her face. "In fact, what tattered remnants of prosperity I had left has been effectively vouchered by you! Will things be better? I think not. In fact, it's because of you that nothing will ever be the same again."

Her thumping heart rattled her deeper than even her mocking words could reach. She turned, but the heel of her slipper caught in the hem of her cloak. Even though she managed to balance herself, he instantly responded, mounting the steps in two strong strides.

His hands slipped around her arms to steady her.

Emaline stared up at him. Under the rim of his slouch hat, his eyes narrowed and he studied her from beneath half-closed lids.

The camps beyond the front lawns evaporated.

Her harsh words of moments before faded. A maddening, nameless pain returned. Her husband's nearness had never created such an unguarded, unexplainable disturbance inside her—and only from the mere pressure of the colonel's hand. The craving for a man's touch, cloaked for years inside her widow's body, roused from its lengthy slumber and stirred fully back to life. Try as she might, Emaline could not ignore its beckoning. Regardless of the war, despite the differences in their worlds, he captivated her. He had at first glance. The aroma of leather and wood smoke embraced her, along with the warm musky notes of coffee and horses; subtle fragrances that only underscored the masculinity that oozed so easily from this man.

Emaline couldn't swallow past the knot in her throat. For an instant, merely a fraction of a second, she envisioned herself resting against him, his comforting, commanding presence made even more enticing by its very wickedness.

"Go back inside," he said, his breath ruffling the wisps of hair that had escaped her braid. 'Twas a miracle that gave her the strength to wrench free from his hold. Another miracle propelled her across the veranda.

A ragged curse spilled from Reece when the front door slammed. He leaned against the pillar, his fingers straining flat against the white column. Flakes of paint drifted to the weathered wood beside his boot. A stab of desire lanced straight through him, and he squeezed his eyes tight against the heady sensation.

Oh yes, he'd managed to force her back inside, but at a staggering cost.

Goddamnit. Don't touch her. Not ever again.

He shoved away from the column and descended the steps, heading straight for his tent and the unopened bottle of whiskey. The bracing liquid would help quash the fires of wanting a woman he would never take. But could it burn away the craving he'd just glimpsed in those incredible evergreen eyes?

Chapter Three

Shapinsay shimmered beneath the glow of a brittle moon. Silver light spilled across the barn and stables, the summer kitchen, washhouse and chicken coup. Emaline eased out into the clearing. The stench of mold welled up around her in musty waves when she crept past the water wells. She flitted in and out of the shadows. And fifty feet later, she flattened up against the weathered wall of the stable.

From inside the soft whickering of horses greeted her. With an ancestry dating back nearly a century, each sleek Andalusian was worth hundreds and all were Benjamin's pride and joy. He'd spent years developing the herd, placing a few choice stallions into stud when the highly sought service met Benjamin's equally high price.

Several seconds passed while Emaline caught her breath. Satisfied no one could see her, she moved across the open yard. When she reached the blacksmith shed, she winged a prayer heavenward in hopes Tacker had reached the boat dock on the Rappahannock per her instructions earlier this evening. Just before supper, she'd visited the quarters and informed her servants of her plan. They begged her to send Tacker with the news, but Emaline ignored their pleas. Fredericksburg officials would be wary of information of such magnitude delivered by him, fearing it to be a trick. No, she would have to be the one to go. And with bigger plans than fishing tonight, the little dinghy would carry her ten miles downriver to the city.

A tangled boxwood ran fifty feet behind the stables.

Emaline dropped to her knees and crawled the distance. The sound of shuffling feet halted her as a sentry on patrol passed by just on the other side of the hedge. Her breath caught, but several anxious moments later, the man moved on, continuing his circuit. Several moments after that, Emaline resumed her quest and reached the rough post of the broken fence line.

She rested her head against the splintered wood, and calmed her pounding heart. The drum of galloping horses echoed in the distance. She peered in the direction of the sound, but the darkness and bracing breeze cloaked the riders. With time, the hoof beats faded. Despite the malevolence of November's wind, perspiration beaded her forehead. Making certain the sentry had moved from sight, Emaline scrambled to her feet and then broke into a run across the icy ground.

Lifeless tobacco stalks emerged before her like ragged corpses. Clods of earth caught on the heels of her riding boots, nearly tripping her. She pressed onward and thirty minutes later, the brackish smell and the rushing splash of the Rappahannock greeted her.

She chanced a quick glance back over the fields.

In the far distance, washed in amber by the enemy camp, her columned mansion glowed. The sight refueled her purpose and Emaline dragged in a sustaining breath. She worked her way down the embankment, rocks and bushes hampering her progress. Reaching the pathway, she skirted past a dense copse of trees that lined the water's edge. In summer, the willows provided much needed relief from a glaring sun, but tonight the tangled branches grabbed her hair and cape and whispered of unseen dangers.

I've come too far to give up now. She pushed onward.

Her foot slipped and both hands flew out to brace her fall. Her elbow crashed down upon the rocks provoking a sudden, sharp pain. She stifled a cry, climbed back to her feet and kept going. A sudden gathering of clouds covered the moon and stole the pale light. With outstretched hands, Emaline shuffled another twenty paces until she heard the faint thud of wood against wood.

"Bless you, Tacker," she whispered. Following the slapping din to the tiny boat, she grasped the rope and slicked her hands along the corded length to the knot. It loosened, and sent her emotions soaring.

Suddenly, the light from a lucifer split the darkness and wafted the sulfuric stench over her. Emaline gasped and whirled to find the source. Several dark forms stood on the crest of the riverbank. From the cluster of soldiers, a tall figure descended the hill to loom before her.

"I knew you'd try something like this." The voice identified her captor seconds before the clouds parted and moonlight flooded over the colonel's face. A raging storm cloud gathered in his dark eyes, anger raining down on her. Her gaze darted left and right, weighing the possibility of escape. Reading her intent, Reece signaled his men to secure the boat. "Did she speak to or dispatch anyone else?" He directed the question into the darkness behind her. And seconds later, a shadowy figure emerged from the river path she'd just traversed.

"No, sir. She met no one." The soldier clothed in dark wool brushed past her to join his comrades.

Her throat tightened and she fought back a sob.

He had me followed?

Would the current be strong enough to whisk her toward Fredericksburg? If she could remain afloat, surely someone downstream would rescue her. She shifted her foot toward the water's edge, but hesitated a second too long.

Reece clamped his hand around her upper arm, his fingers biting into her skin through the cape.

"Don't even think about it," he grated. A faint trace of whiskey reached out to tease her. "It's too damn cold for a swim, and I'm not getting wet trying to save your idiotic ass. Good God, woman, you never cease to amaze me. Sergeant Conners!" he bellowed.

A soldier stepped forward. "Yes, sir."

"Walk her back to the upstairs library. And if she gives you any trouble, you have my permission to bind and gag her."

"Yes, sir. I will, sir."

Reece turned and climbed the embankment, the chink of spurs echoing from the river rock. The remaining soldiers turned and followed him, carrying away the light. Moments later, the sound of galloping horses faded back into the night.

Emaline's vision shifted from the empty space where Reece had stood to the lone soldier. He motioned for her to move up the incline, but she shuffled sideways.

The grizzled man blocked her way. "Don't make me bind you, ma'am." He pulled her away from the river and onto the main wagon road. An icy gust of wind whipped at her sodden cloak. "You should be glad he stopped you," the soldier continued as they began their trek toward the house. "You might've gotten hurt."

"It was worth taking the chance."

"You never had a chance, ma'am," the sergeant quipped. "He's had you watched from the moment you overheard his conversation with the major this morning. He assigned details and posted guards right afterwards."

Emaline seethed. So his foolish chatter about southwestern ranches and blazing sunsets was just a ruse. The beast was only watching.

And waiting.

She sniffed, longing for the comforting numbness of her life prior to Colonel Reece Cutteridge. The blast of wind across the open fields burned her cheeks, yet she stumbled alongside the now silent soldier, embracing the heat of her wrath to keep her warm. Their steady pace gobbled up the distance and thirty minutes later, the soldier marched her through the house and up the stairs to the library to complete his assignment.

A small fire bathed the room in flickering shadows. Silence encapsulated the tall figure standing near the hearth. Like a dark avenger, he crossed the room and slammed the door shut behind her. When he turned, dwarfing her, Emaline's chin rose. Her hand slipped out to brace against the desk when she met the spitting malice in his eyes.

His words raked over her. "Had I known you were so damned eager to die for the cause, I'd have arranged a far easier method." He stalked closer, a sable-haired heathen sheathed in shadows. "Have you no idea what might've happened had I not discovered your asinine plan?"

Her mouth tensed at his vulgarity, anxiety coiling into a tight knot in her throat. "Did you honestly think I would stand by and do nothing while you murder women and children?"

The tip of his boot bumped against hers and he leaned down, his nose scant inches from hers. "I'm not in the habit of murdering women and children."

"And you expect me to believe an attack on Fredericksburg would leave innocent people unharmed?"

"Unfortunately, war sometimes causes a few civilian casualties."

"A few?" Her scathing laugh filled the room. "How comforting—merely a few blameless souls to ease your brutal conscience." Her fingers worked the corded loops of her cloak to unfasten the garment. In a swirl of black wool, the cape landed across the chair back.

Reece drew a ragged breath and raked his gaze down her form. "You've obviously never heard of Bull Run. When the Rebs pushed north, dozens of women and children were injured while picnicking on a hillside." He placed space between them. "People get hurt, Emaline. It's the ungodly way of war. But since I have it in my power to protect you, I'll do exactly that…protect you even from your own self."

She infuriated him to a point past reasoning. He stalked to the side table and helped himself to another generous glass of her dead husband's whiskey. Turning toward her, he downed the contents in one long pull. The liquid set his throat ablaze, but did little to burn away his conflicting emotions. He wanted to wring her neck.

No…he wanted to pull her to him and bury himself inside her.

Her erratic heartbeat fluttered in the hollow of her throat. He stared at the small indentation. The perfect spot for… His gaze shifted, then scoured the curves of her body. Her slender waist. The generous swells hidden beneath the swath of cotton.

Sonofabitch. This was hell-bent agony, yet he could no longer squelch the returning rush of emotions too long suppressed. "I'll not argue the finer points of this war's morality with you," he ground out. "The riverbank opposite the city is crawling with sharpshooters. Had you even made it that far, Burnside's pickets would have made short work of you."

A sarcastic smirk broke her face. "At least that would put an end to my suffering."

Her words landed like a well-aimed blow in his gut and his voice spiraled downward into a harsh whisper. "Your suffering?" Four strides brought him before her again. "You've suffered little in your life, sweetheart." She attempted to snap back, but he cut her off with a surge forward. His gaze bored into hers. "Five years ago, I returned from a horse drive to find my father murdered, staked out and tortured to death. A slow and suffering demise, you can be sure." His voice dropped lower. "The Apache brutally beat my mother. Her suffering lasted days before she died in my arms. But Jenny? No, my Jenny wasn't nearly as fortunate." He paused only long enough to draw breath. "I spent two agonizing days tracking those bloody butchers and when I finally found my wife, the sonsofbitches had raped her, scalped her, and then staked her out for the coyotes and wild boars to enjoy. And you think you've suffered?" His guttural laugh ended in a painful growl. "You're whining over pigs and corn and flattened flower beds and calling it agony. I've no patience left for your drivel."

"I've...known suffering," she whispered. "It's you—"

He loomed closer. "I haven't made you suffer one damn bit. Good God, woman, I'm trying to protect you! There's nothing you can do to change the course of this war. Nothing. And trying to prevent the inevitable is not only dangerous, it's ludicrous. I don't want you hurt too." He dragged in a deep breath, realizing he'd said too much, revealed too much about himself and his unbalanced concern for her safety. He must leave the room.

Right now.

He shoved himself back three steps, then snapped, "Do not attempt the river again, Emaline. I won't be nearly as forgiving the next time."

He was gone before the heavy door hit the back wall.

Emaline stared at the empty threshold. A strange sense of desolation engulfed her. He enraged her, yet at the same time, his scorn pierced her heart. Did he truly believe her to be such a shallow creature? Was she? Suffering took many forms, didn't it? The raging beast had given her little opportunity to explain about the responsibilities she'd shouldered all alone or the anguish that consumed her at her obvious failure to maintain Benjamin's home. Emaline fought back tears. She might even have wanted to share sympathy for his lost family. But he denied her that too.

She sighed, weak with exhaustion.

Then a frail voice inside reminded her he was her enemy. She owed him no such revelations. Why should she explain away her lifestyle to him? She hadn't shaped the world she'd been born into. She hadn't asked him to invade her home or force his way into her life, either. And she certainly didn't want his opinion regarding her character. Inexplicably, however, the memory of his dark eyes searching hers earlier this evening on the veranda penetrated all her denials. She turned slowly and scanned the library, seeing the same desk, the same books, but everything now seemed different.

Emaline resolved many things that night.

In a hazy yellow wash, dawn filtered past the curtains in her bedroom. War made people behave differently than they would under other circumstances; the comparison between her brother and the colonel kept her tossing all night. Brennen would do exactly as ordered, regardless of the consequences, regardless of the situation.

A sigh rolled from her lungs. All along, she'd placed the blame for everything squarely on the colonel's broad shoulders. The realization he knew and accepted her censure, in fact, he even agreed to shoulder her animosity, forced her to see him in a new light. The day he rode onto her land, he promised no harm would come to her or her people. And so far, he'd kept his word.

A new day broke, providing her renewed strength. And with it came her solid vow to be more reasonable with the man.

Emaline returned her hairbrush to the glass-and-silver tray, taking comfort in the thought her personal items could be in order. She skimmed her hands over the sides of her head, smoothing down the errant wisps that refused the braid's confinement. Yes. She'd be more pleasant and continue to assist the doctor with the wounded. She could not help the people of Fredericksburg, but at least she could help someone here.

With her affirmation fixed into place, she finished her morning toilette and then donned a fresh camisole and corset. She pulled on a white flannel underslip, tied it securely at the waist, and slipped on a green work dress. After placing the china pitcher back inside its matching bowl on the side table, Emaline left the room, a frail smile fastened in place. Before she resumed her duties downstairs with the doctor, however, she needed to record more entries in her ledger. When she visited the quarters last night, Tacker informed her that the Yankees had vouchered more chickens.

Emaline crossed the hallway and pushed open the library door.

Her eyes widened in surprise.

Reece Cutteridge sat at her desk, boldly examining the entries in her ledger.

"What are you doing?" she demanded, closing the door behind her with a firm shove. He glanced up as she strode across the rug, then continued his study of the tome. She reached across the desk and flipped the volume closed, her heartfelt resolution to be pleasant toward the man squashed beneath the intricately tooled cover. "I'll ask you again, Colonel. What are you doing in here?"

He leaned back and steepled his fingers. "I'm impressed with the horses in your stable and wanted to look over their bloodlines. They come from excellent stock." A faint smile curved his lips. "The extent of your recordkeeping is remarkable."

His compliment disturbed her. In fact, everything about him this morning disturbed her.

She straightened and locked her arms across her chest. "I've always kept excellent household records. I would've told you what you wanted to know without you snooping. In fact, I can reel off the pedigree of each animal as easily as a child can the *ABCs.*"

The chair moved backward. He stood and rounded the desk, then came to a stop directly in front of her. Beneath his unbuttoned frockcoat, his white shirt lay open at his throat and a hint of dark hair teased her from the vee-shaped opening.

Emaline swallowed, squelching the preposterous urge to touch that sun-darkened spot.

Heat prickled down her spine. She averted her gaze and settled on the taut set of his shoulders. The rush of warmth spread across her belly and down her legs. She attributed the sensation to emotional and physical exhaustion.

She refused to attribute it to need.

"Men aren't the only casualties of war," he said, his silky smooth words drifting over her. "We lose good mounts in battle, too." She looked back and nearly shuddered at the coldness reflected in his eyes. "When we leave, we'll be taking your horses with us."

"W-what?" she stammered. "You can't take them. It took years for Benjamin to achieve that bloodline."

"I didn't ask for your permission."

White-hot fury poured through Emaline. All her good intentions, all her attempts to understand this man, died in the wake of his words. She didn't grieve the horses; they were another casualty of war.

What hurt most was how much he enjoyed this.

"No, Colonel, you never did ask, did you? You pilfered my supplies, mocked my character and lifestyle, filled my home with your dying, and had the audacity to lure me in with your heartbreaking loss. Then when you had me falling under your wretched spell, you boldly proclaim you're here to also steal my family's heritage." Her words tumbled out in a maddening rush. "Tell me, you...despicable heathen, do you plan on leaving me anything when you leave?"

He smiled flatly. "Vouchers."

Vouchers!

Emaline nearly buckled. "I live for the day you ride into battle and are blown straight back to hell, for that is surely where you've spawned."

"And that may well happen, Mrs. McDaniels, but when it does we'll be riding your horses."

With lightning speed, Emaline's palm connected with his jaw. The blow rocked his head to the side. The echo hardly faded before he reached out to band her waist. With a strong jerk, he brought her up against him. His belt buckle pressed into the softness of her belly. He leaned forward, dark eyes narrowing as he growled, "You will be paying me for that one."

His hold tightened and he bent her backward. His other hand slipped up to bury fingers in the base of her braid. The lower he bent, the closer he loomed. Until, in a fierce possession, he finally covered her mouth with his. Hard and demanding, he deepened the kiss. His hand freed her plait, moving down the arch in her back, then farther down over the curve of her buttocks.

With an easy sweep, he lifted her and nestled her against him.

Emaline pummeled his shoulders.

He only tightened his hold.

An incomprehensible pressure gathered deep inside her. The longer he branded her and the harder she fought, the more mesmerizing the sensations spiraled.

Unabated. Unrestrained.

Until finally her entire world tipped out of control.

Her flailing ceased. Her hands dropped back to his shoulders. She no longer could fight against his intoxicating onslaught or staunch the flow of emotions cresting over her. In fact, she could no longer remember why she needed to fight this man at all. An incredulous yearning ignited somewhere deep inside and she issued a husky, guttural groan, her lips softening beneath his just one small fraction.

An acquiescing moan followed. Abruptly, he straightened her and when his pressure lifted from her lips, Emaline's breath caught in her throat. Her eyelids shuttered open and through a shimmering veil, she watched his mouth shift sideways into a smirk. The sight slammed hard against her ragged nerves. The fragile flame of desire, so precious and new, sputtered and then flickered out. Unable to force words past her tingling lips, she simply stared up at him. Deep inside, however, she found her fury. Like a soothing balm, she smeared it across her heart, praying all the while for God's flaming hand to strike him dead on the very spot he stood. With their gazes still locked, he reached sideways and retrieved his hat from the desk, then settled it upon his head. A heartbeat later, both he and her leather-bound ledger were gone.

Chapter Four

The woman struggled to remain upright, but cloying emptiness beckoned. Mud seeped between bare fingers and toes. Her body ached. Still, she pushed onward, shuffling footsteps taking her to the summit.

At the top, caustic haze engulfed her. She fought back a wracking cough, her arms lifting. With frantic waves, she worked to disperse the smoke. By slow degrees, the miasma dissipated and the valley below shimmered into view.

Desolation spanned out before her. Acres of ripe tobacco and grain were gone, replaced with row after row of weathered canvas. Lush, summertime grass, usually clipped short by meandering goats and sheep, now smoldered in a morass of destruction and rotting carcasses. Death's mordant stench nipped at her nostrils while scores of horse-drawn artillery and ambulance wagons rumbled over once-exquisite gardens of roses, sculpted elderberry and boxwood.

She dropped to her knees, her arms thrusting skyward. A groan rose deep in her throat and escalated until a heart-wrenching wail poured out. The belching rumble of cannon-fire rocked the valley, masking her lamentations. Explosions ripped apart the night as uncontrolled fires raged across the battlefield. Caught by the treacherous wind, flames swept up the hill toward her, carried faster and faster upon the consuming tongues of hell.

Too weary to move, she resigned herself to her inevitable death.

Then something alerted her senses. A horse! Indeed, the miraculous, unmistakable consonance drew nearer, approaching fast. A strong arm, honed to muscled perfection, swept out, then banded her waist.

Higher and higher, she rose until she landed face down across the beast.

The impact stole her breath and the swell of saddle bored into her belly. In a frantic attempt to breathe, she jerked her face sideways, scraping her cheek across coarsely textured blue wool. Looking upward, she faced the handsome countenance of Colonel Reece Cutteridge.

Another barrage of artillery blasted across the sky and the spirited stallion beneath them reared upward, front legs slashing the air in powerful defiance. Terrified beyond reasoning, she slipped into the ebony realms of unconsciousness.

The loud crack of thunder awakened Emaline.

Another rumble brought her bolt upright in bed, an erratic heartbeat echoing in her ears. She leaned forward, gasping for breath. Lightning ripped a jagged scar across the sky and illuminated her bedroom in momentary brightness. Heavy raindrops pelted the windowpanes and the staccato tapping slammed against an unraveling panic. Her nightgown had twisted around her legs, trapping her, and she gripped the coverlet with such intensity her hands cramped in pain.

Glancing around the room, she recognized the heavy wardrobe, the matching dressing table and the chair near the inlaid-tile hearth where the red-hued shimmer of coals professed dying testimony to an earlier blaze. She lifted her head. Sheer curtains draped the top of her poster bed and continued down all four sides in a ghostly, gossamer sweep of cream and tan.

I'm home.

And safe.

Her hands rose in front of her face. No mud. Not even a trace. 'Twas another nightmare. And this time, enhanced by the thunderstorm that ravaged the night. She worked to calm her pulse. *Inhale. Exhale.* Finally, she slumped back against the pillows and with a determined jerk, pulled the eiderdown quilt up to her chin. Her fingers tapped out an exasperated beat. That blasted man dominated even her sleep now.

Unbidden, his powerful image nonetheless returned.

She struggled to breathe through the tightness in her chest, her body tingling from the remembered strength of his embrace. She slipped her tongue out to moisten dry lips, but only drew back the warm and wicked taste of him. In one fluid movement, Emaline kicked off the blanket and left her bed.

How dare he kiss me. How dare he!

With each agitated footfall, her nightgown swept the floor in a whisper of rage.

Is that music?

Emaline wiped her hands across the bibbed front of her apron and scrambled to her feet. The scrub brush dropped into the bucket with a loud plop, sending dirty water over the side of the pail.

Yes. It was definitely music.

The reedy notes of a harmonica filtered through the house.

Like a rat behind the Pied Piper, Emaline followed the tune through the sitting room and across the large entry hall. She came to a stop at the doorway leading into the dining room. Several convalescing soldiers had clustered near the wooden storage boxes, and two of them were engaged in an awkward, shuffling dance.

Her hand covered her smile.

As one man dipped, the other clumsily sashayed and she forgot her issues with the colonel in the face of such comical antics. A small giggle escaped and the harmonica's pleasing notes stopped. A dozen pairs of eyes turned her way. Emaline clasped her hands in a plea for forgiveness. "I'm sorry for intruding. Please don't stop." The soldiers sheepishly grinned at one another.

Two men approached her.

"Please don't leave, Mrs. McDaniels. Come join us," one soldier begged.

Another lad added, "Yes, come show these clumsy fools how to dance proper." A chorus of other pleas joined in and seconds later, Emaline found herself pulled into the room.

"Goodness no, I can't dance with...you men," she sputtered, attempting to disengage from their strong clasp. The men ignored her as another round of persuasive petitions flooded the room.

"Please, ma'am, one dance won't hurt you none. Will it? And we could all use a lesson, don't you think?" They shoved aside supply boxes to make additional space, their boyish enthusiasm more than contagious.

Emaline allowed them to lead her into the room. "For heaven sakes, you men should all be resting," she chastised, but the scolding never quite reached her voice.

"If'n you show us how to dance properly today, ma'am," proclaimed the young private from Cleveland she'd just met yesterday. "Then we'll promise to rest all day tomorrow."

A dozen affirmations joined his fervent pledge, and another soldier—this one from somewhere called Cincinnati—pushed forward, adding his declaration. "Absolutely, ma'am. I promise."

"And we promise too." Three more stepped up. "Please, ma'am. It's been so long since we've danced with a real lady."

Two more chimed in. "We won't take up too much of your time."

Emaline exhaled in a long sigh. "Well, I suppose I could maybe offer just a few moments of instruction."

"Me first," the closest one announced, jostling nearer and lifting his arms into position. She tentatively stepped into his embrace. The music resumed and they whisked off into a waltz. Around and around they turned, and with every spin, Emaline noticed more men filling the room. At what point a small guitar, a banjo and a makeshift drum joined the musical ensemble, she couldn't quite say. She only knew she was twirling while clapping hands offered a strong tempo. When one dance ended, another soldier stepped up to start the whole process again, and the dancing continued long past a few instructional moments.

Emaline changed partner after partner, and as the music moved from a lively jig, to a waltz, to a fast-paced reel, all the churning disorder inside her from the colonel's stolen kiss seeped right out of her body.

Flushed from exertion, her hair loosened from its stern chignon at the base of her neck, Emaline smiled up at the next partner to step in place. He politely bowed then slipped his arm around her waist. She laughed, and off again they went, twirling to the harmony of the musical notes. *I haven't moved this way in years!* Yet each step flooded back into recall. Breathless from the frolic, she knew she would dance with every one of these homesick men until they all either had their turn or she dropped to the floor from exhaustion. For more than an hour, the music and laughter encompassed her afternoon, and Emaline's smile widened when old Doctor Evans stepped forward to claim the next spin. Still spry in spite of his years, the surgeon waltzed her around and around the dance floor.

Music?

Reece pushed aside the map and climbed to his feet.

Yes. It was definitely music, and not just the simple tunes common throughout camp—this music was organized and accompanied by raucous laughter. And hand clapping. He swept open the tent flap and stepped out. Scanning across the encampment, he searched for the source.

The manor house? Reece crossed the rutted ground, climbed the front stairs in two steps and entered the house. Soldiers filled the entire foyer. He could barely get through the crush of men.

Within seconds, they recognized him and immediately stepped aside to allow him room to pass. He moved through the crowd, nodding to acknowledge their salutes. A wide space was created for him at the entrance of the dining room. Music pulsated around him and he spotted several members of his regimental band clustered near the fireplace. And then Reece saw Emaline twirling past in the embrace of one of his young privates. Her hair cascaded down her back in a tangle of riotous dark curls. She swept past, her laughter spilling over him like a much-needed breeze on a sultry summer day.

Reece swallowed. Spellbound, he could only stare in fascination.

From nearby a voice hollered out, "Step up there, Colonel, and catch her on the next spin!" Several amiable pats on the back followed. The dancers stopped directly in front of Reece, and Emaline's partner dropped his hold and melted back into the crowd. Crimson flags blazed high across Emaline's cheeks as she gasped for breath.

Her eyes lifted, then widened. The smile disappeared from her face.

The crowd urged him onward. "Reach on out there, Colonel, and take her in your arms." And another bellowed, "You remember how to hold a woman, don't you?"

His men roared with laughter.

Reece hadn't seen her in days and the memory of their kiss seared straight through him. His earlier guise of indifference vanished along with her smile. He took a hesitant step forward, his heart pounding like a repeated volley from the most accurate marksman.

"Step lively, sir, or you'll be losing your chance. Everyone has had a turn." The thundering pulse of the music overwhelmed the raucous roar of the crowd. "Take her in your arms."

More than anything, he wanted to draw this woman into his embrace again. He leaned forward, the muscles in his arms tightening as he started to raise them upward. Then, above the music and laughter, Reece heard her gasp, the timbre brittle and overwhelming.

Sanity pushed into place. What the hell was he doing? He stepped backward, bumping into several soldiers. A half-dozen hands clapped him on the shoulder to stop him. "Whoa there, you're going the wrong way, Colonel. She's the other direction!"

Everyone exploded in laughter.

Except Emaline.

And him.

Reece swallowed. Hard. Yet the lump inside his throat refused to budge. The music vibrated as her sweet, intoxicating fragrance drifted over him. Her dewy skin glowed. The silky curls a tousled frame outlining her face. He spun and shoved back through the crowd. It didn't matter that it was only a dance. Even that innocent gesture was more than he could allow.

He didn't dare touch her again.

Emaline stared at the back of the broad-shouldered man as he pushed his way through the crowd. He soared above the others. A leader who had no equal. The music vibrated around her, yet the joy inside her died.

The music lost its luster.

"I must go back to work now," she mumbled.

Turning, she worked her way through the crowd in the opposite direction, a wobbly smile propped into place.

"Yes. Thank you," she repeated—a dozen times or more to the soldiers who clapped and cheered her on her way. "An enjoyable afternoon, for sure." And, "You're more than welcome, indeed." She nodded to some, shook hands with dozens more, yet inside she could barely function, and the ache continued to grow. *Don't think about him. Keep moving.* Emaline placed one foot in front of the other, over and over again, until finally she stumbled into the winter kitchen and the door thumped closed behind her.

Her eyes squeezed tightly closed.

She willed her mind to forget the warmth of his mouth on hers. Still, the emptiness inside her blossomed. What did it matter that he'd cut her in front of everyone by refusing a dance?

Would she have even allowed one?

Yes, her heartstrings vibrated.

Absolutely not, her sanity proclaimed.

The burning behind her lashes dulled as the enormous lump in her throat lessened. Her eyes slowly opened and mercifully, the need to weep slipped away to join the myriad of other unshed tears locked deep inside her soul.

Emaline bent over the soldier and found him dead. She sighed, and bit her lower lip to stop its tremble. When had she become such a staunch advocate for peace over any kind of conflict? The fear of losing those she loved escalated inside her. Her brother's face filled her mind. *Brennen, please be careful.*

She settled the woolen blanket over the dead man's face. A little girl in Mariah Hill, Ohio, was now fatherless. Misery swelled inside Emaline. More deaths had occurred in the past three weeks than she'd known from a lifetime of living. The broken promises made to her husband upon his deathbed in regards to the plantation paled beneath such tragedy. Tears pooled in her eyes, years' worth of unspent emotions threatening.

Doc rested his hand on her shoulder. "I see the Anders boy finally died. God rest his soul."

She nodded. "I sent the picture case h-home to his wife last week." A tear slipped unchecked down her cheek. "But the mail service is s-so bad now, I don't even know if she'll get it."

"I'm sure she will. And he was blessed to have your caring friendship." Doc gestured toward the door. "Go on. I'll take care of this."

Emaline nodded as every ounce of her being fought to stay in control. She wouldn't cry in front of this brave and self-sacrificing man. Her chin rose. She inhaled and straightened her shoulders, then headed for the front door.

The winter wind nipped at her face when she stepped onto the veranda.

A courier pushed past her, clunking down the front steps. He headed across the rutted ground toward the command tent, the current list of casualties clutched in his hand. The overcast sky above him held the grim threat of snow.

Her thoughts turned to Reece. She'd not spoken to him in well over a week and he'd made no attempt to see her. Her chest tightened and she swallowed hard. Dear God, how much more could she endure? She was slowly losing her mind…bewildered by a man who wanted nothing to do with her.

Tears gathered. Emaline blinked faster and faster, yet they spilled down her cheeks anyway.

Clamping a hand over her quivering mouth, she stumbled down the front steps and headed for the stable.

Another soldier's name added to my growing bivouac of the dead.

Reece dismissed the courier and passed the medical report over to Jackson, who sat close by writing dispatches. He watched in silence while his friend scanned the report, then reached for the *Dead Ledger* to enter Anders's name beside the others. Eighty-nine men had died in the regiment this past year alone. *Eighty-nine.* Good God, how much longer could this war last? How many more good men would he lose?

He raked his hands through his hair. "I'm sick to death of waiting."

Jackson closed the ledger. "Things are bound to happen soon. Go get something to eat. And while you're at it, try to rustle up a bottle of whiskey on your way back."

Reece snorted. A hell of a lot more than whiskey would be required to remove the taste of Emaline from his lips. "We're officers, you idiot. We have to set good examples."

Jackson stretched his legs and stacked one booted foot atop the other. "I know. That's why I'm sending you. Hey, if nobody sees then nobody knows."

"You need help." Reece looked back to the house and saw Emaline disappear around the side of the mansion. Abruptly, he straightened from his leaning position against a tree.

"What the hell are you up to now?" he mumbled, before tossing the words, "I'll be back," over his shoulder toward Jackson.

Reece headed across the clearing after her.

A week… He'd purposefully avoided her for an entire week and not dancing with her only added fuel to an already stoked fire. He owed her an apology for his crude behavior in the library. Of course, he'd been upset at her attempt to cross the river and concerned for her safety. But that other part he'd thrown at her…the suffering part? His lips tightened. She wasn't selfish or shallow and he'd no right to say her misery was any less severe. And the kiss? Well, he charged that to his damnable temper, a quick reaction to her slap.

His stride widened. She deserved an apology and now was as good a time as any to give it. A grin wobbled near the corner of his mouth. *She'll probably tell me in so many words to go straight to hell again.*

At the stable door an unexpected sound reached his ears. Muffled. Sorrowful. Reece stopped and braced his hands on the wooden frame.

My God, she's crying.

Should he turn around? Should he go in?

She sobbed again and his chest tightened around a shielding resistance.

Seconds ticked by, her pain pummeling against his resolve. His anguish grew alongside hers. His hold tightened upon the doorframe, fingers digging into the weathered wood. Acceptance and denial warred within Reece. One more sob and his decision was made.

He stepped across the threshold and the smell of hay hit him full on. Tack eerily hung above the empty stalls. Empty because he'd taken her horses. Empty because of another *insufferable* loss in her life. He scanned the area, then stopped at the sight of her hugging a wooden post near the mare's stall, her horse, the only one left behind.

Fragile shoulders shook from the force of muffled tears. Misery twisted his heart. She needed comfort, deserved comfort, and although he was the reason for her torment, Reece longed to relieve her distress. He knew the hollowness of loss. He'd lived it…and had somehow survived.

Without hesitation, without arguing against the foolish impulsiveness of his actions, he crossed the distance and reached out for her. When he touched her shoulder, she instinctively whirled in surprise.

Her eyes widened with recognition.

He gazed into the rich green pools and his blood roared anew in his ears. Then her breath quickened beneath another swell of tears. Reece slid his hands down her arms. He couldn't stop the madness ripping apart her world, but at least he could shield her inside this stable. As long as he stood guard, she was safe. With a gentle pull, he embraced her. And with an unforeseen surrender, she accepted, gripping the front of his coat.

She laid her head against his chest. As she sobbed against him, Reece tightened his protection around her while inside his body hammered for more. Two minutes or two hundred years…time didn't matter. He held her until her tears dissipated, and still she remained against his chest. Little by little, the tension drifted from her body until she relaxed against him, her hands unclenching the fabric of his coat. A single eagle-emblazed button remained clasped between her finger and thumb.

He pulled her closer as his thoughts tumbled back to that night on the veranda. Had his desire for her begun there? Or in the library the next morning when he'd lost his sanity and kissed her. He knew he was her wicked oppressor, yet his heart told him something more.

Strong and steady, his heartbeat thumped where she rested. And then she shifted, her head lifting from his chest. She gazed up into his eyes.

Reece slipped one hand from around her, and cupped her face, the pad of his thumb wiping away the moisture glistening on her cheek. Her lips trembled as her evergreen eyes widened, but not in anger. Not this time. An unspoken petition as old as Eve reflected behind her tear-spiked lashes. Reece shoved aside all caution, all logical restraints. This time, he ignored the colors of blue and gray—the opposing realities of their worlds. And at this precise moment, he didn't give a damn about the war. She was all that mattered.

The wall he'd carefully constructed around his heart since Jenny's death crumbled. He wanted this woman. And he wanted her badly enough to forget the impossibility of keeping her forever. A familiar ache pushed against the hole in his heart, but he shoved it aside. Both hands slid up her back to the nape of her neck. With a soft tug, he pulled away the crocheted netting confining her tresses. Heavy curls tumbled across his hands and Reece furrowed his fingers through the silken waves.

Slowly, he tilted her face to his.

Without hesitation, without waiting one second longer, Reece answered her silent plea and covered her mouth with his.

Her lips parted beneath the pressure of his and he molded them into a flawless fit. When his tongue slipped inside, teasing and stroking and branding her his, she quivered in his embrace.

Her hands climbed over his shoulders, snagging briefly on his epaulets, before her fingers curled into the long hair at the nape of his neck. She clung to him, and just like she'd done in the library that morning, she again offered the sweet gift of her passion.

A voice flowed in through the stable door and twisted into a maddening tangle around Reece's bliss. "Miz Emaline, you in here? Da doctor sent me to fetch—Lord A'mighty...I...I's sorry."

Tacker's stuttering shattered the moment. Sanity returned. Reece tore apart the kiss just as Emaline pushed against his chest and broke free. She stumbled backward until she flattened against her mare's stall.

Reece spun to face the old man, his voice a hot rasp. "What is it?"

Tacker's tone spiraled down into a sporadic whisper. "Da doctor, sir...h-he needs Miz Emaline—back at da house."

"Tell him she'll be there in a minute," Reece growled. His chest rose and fell, frustration loading each breath. The servant nodded and fled.

Reece turned back to face Emaline. When his eyes met hers, his heart lurched. He never imagined anything could be as beautiful as this woman.

Her eyes slipped closed.

Behind her, the sleek mare pawed the ground. The pounding echoed the tumult surging through Reece.

"Look at me," he said. Her gaze slowly rose and he met a storm cloud of passion radiating from her extraordinary eyes. He could drown in the depths of them. She had matched his desire with hers, yet now she shook her head in denial.

Frustration catapulted through Reece. He swallowed, then straightened his shoulders. His lips compressed into a tight line. Without uttering another syllable, he stepped aside.

And Emaline bolted for the door.

Chapter Five

Reece stalked toward his tent.

What in God's name just happened?

One minute he was searching for Emaline to apologize, and the next he was wrapping her in his arms. And kissing her again.

He almost choked on his anger.

The ruts flew beneath his boots as he lengthened his stride. No matter how much ground he covered or what pace he set, the warmth of Emaline's kiss swirled up from inside him, intoxicating him all over again. Goddamnit, he was an officer in charge.

He knew better.

A group of soldiers passed nearby and saluted. He acknowledged them with a scowling nod and kept walking. The interlude had been nothing more than a mishap of the moment. He was tired—and fatigue made one careless, his saner side reasoned. Besides, she needed comfort. These were unsettling times. It was as simple as that.

Think again, you damn jackass. That one won't work.

Reece swept the white canvas aside and stepped inside his tent, then ground to a halt when he saw Jackson shove a waist-sash into his valise. White cotton dress gloves dropped on top of the yellow silk.

"You mind telling me what you're doing?" Reece snapped. Frustration banded his chest and his second-in-command received the full brunt of it. Too late, he realized the hard tone of his voice had hoisted another red flag.

Jackson closed the leather satchel and quipped, "What does it look like I'm doing?" He lowered to the nearest chair and fished inside his frockcoat's breast pocket for a cheroot.

"Don't play games with me, dammit. I'm in no mood."

"Then don't be an ass. I was gatherin' your dress gear. Don't want you embarrassing the regiment by looking disheveled in front of royalty." A trace of humor lightened his words.

Reece surged inside the enclosure, his temper the polar opposite of amused. "What the hell are you talking about?"

Jackson handed him a dispatch. "This arrived while you were...*out.* Of course, I took the liberty of reading it. To sum up the details, General Burnside wants his commanding officers assembled by noon tomorrow for a meeting with President Lincoln. For what reason, I have no idea, but our division commander wants you in attendance." His laugh punctuated the tension building inside Reece. "So you're riding to Belle Plain whether you want to or not."

"Sonofabitch." Reece dropped the missive to the table, his slouch hat slamming down beside it. "I can't go now." His jaw clenched and he tunneled his fingers through his hair.

"And why not?"

Turning on his boot heel, Reece strode back and forth in front of the opening. *Because I need to deal with these goddamned feelings for Emaline. That's why not.*

Jackson rose from the chair, impaling him with a sharp glare. "You want command of the brigade one day, right? This is how you get it." He issued a strident breath. "And this display right here is far more related to that widow up yonder than to any commander's call in Belle Plain."

"You've no idea what you're talking about," Reece growled.

"Like hell I don't. This is exactly what I knew would happen."

Reece turned a hot stare on Jackson. "What?"

A harsh laugh filled the tent. "All this. With her. Christ almighty, why are you allowing this to happen now?"

"Nothing's happened."

"Now that's a damn lie." The unlit cigar dangled between Jackson's fingers as he pointed at Reece. "You're forgetting I know you, pal. And your brain ain't doing the thinking here. We both know what's calling the shots right now." He paused for a full heartbeat before dropping back into the chair. "Look. I know this type of woman. I grew up surrounded by a passel of them just like her. My mother. My sister. Surely you realize she'll expect more than you're willing to give. She's all about babies and doilies and serving up little tea cakes. Letting you have your way with her and then watching you ride off into the sunset ain't part of her plan."

Reece turned and gripped the center post at the entrance to the tent, pushing aside the canvas to stare out across the encampment. The poignant truth of Jackson's words cascaded over him. "I know all this," he ground out, his ragged tone and bunched shoulders unfortunate consequences of his frustrations. "But what I don't need is your ass sitting there smugly reminding me."

"Well that's too bad, because there's a war going on out there that demands your full participation. Either bed the damn wench or move on."

Disgust undulated through Reece and his mouth tightened. "Shut the hell up, and go tell Lieutenant Glave he's riding over with me."

"He'll be delighted." He rose, knocking over the chair in his assent. Jackson muttered under his breath and brushed past.

"And you're also in charge while I'm gone," Reece reminded.

Jackson moved into the spill of sunlight, a sarcastic smile curving his lips. "Perfect. You know just how much I enjoy that too."

"Wait a minute." Reece grabbed his friend's arm to stop him. "I'll go find Lucas. I need you to do something else for me before I leave."

The unlit cheroot returned to the man's mouth and dangled near the corner.

"What?" He ground the word out around his cigar as he shrugged off Reece's hand.

"She's storing her vouchers in the top desk drawer in the upstairs library. Get them and bring them to me."

Jackson's eyebrows rose in surprise. "You taking them back now?"

"Something like that. Just tell her I gave you permission to go upstairs." He sighed. "Anything else?"

"Yes." Reece paused, searching for the right words. "I want you to… Will you just keep an eye on her while I'm gone?"

Silence lengthened between them. Somewhere beyond the encampment, bellowing sergeants issued drill commands. Discharging pistols echoed in response. Jackson tightened his mouth and then finally, he pushed a lopsided smile across his face. "You know I will, you damn jackass. But I'm telling you, you're messing with fire here."

He turned on his heel and headed toward the mansion.

Throughout the remainder of the day and well into night, Emaline remained dedicated to her patients. Keeping busy kept her mind away from Reece. When Doc finally headed for the front door that evening, Emaline panicked. For a ridiculous moment, she even considered asking for a sleeping powder to ease the torment she knew would arrive when she was finally alone with her thoughts.

Just as quickly, she dismissed the idea.

"I've heard the colonel's gone," Doc said, shrugging his arms into his greatcoat.

"Gone?" Emaline swept his fingers aside and secured the brass buttons across the front of the light-blue garment for him. "Gone where?"

"He received orders this afternoon to meet up with President Lincoln. Major Neale's in command during his absence."

Swift and strong, the ache of Reece's absence slammed at her heart's door. "H-how long will the colonel be gone?"

"Don't know. Could be a few days. Maybe longer. They don't tell me much about their military moves. Well, my dear, thank you again for helping. I'll see you in the morning."

Emaline bade him goodnight and leaned against the closed door. Tears gathered in her eyes, dampening her lashes. She rested her head against the doorframe and dragged in a sustaining breath. Blinking fast, she stifled the tears as well as the quiver quelling inside her heart.

No other options existed. Deny as she might, the truth held firm. Her late husband had been a staunch supporter of slavery. Her brother fought gallantly for General Stonewall Jackson.

And Colonel Reece Cutteridge wore blue.

Chapter Six

December 8, 1862
Belle Plain, Virginia
Two Weeks Later

"I'll be right back." Reece didn't wait for his aide-de-camp's response. Instead, he shifted the saddlebag across his shoulder, entered the quartermaster's office, and headed straight for the man seated near the back of the room. The soldier looked up when the heavy leather bag thumped onto the desk before him.

"What can I do for you, Colonel?" the clerk inquired.

Reece pulled out the bundle of vouchers and handed them to the bespectacled man. "I need these redeemed."

The quartermaster flipped through the coupons and a soft whistle followed. "This is quite a large sum, sir. I'm sorry, but I can't issue redemptions of this value without my superior's authorization."

Nodding, Reece pulled a letter from his breast pocket and tossed it to the desk. "This is all you'll need, Captain." At the bottom of the dispatch rode General Edwin V. Sumner's jagged signature.

The clerk scanned the document, a smirk lifting his lips. "Yep, I reckon that'll do just fine." He gathered the vouchers into a neat stack and shuffled them like playing cards before placing them on the desk again. "Who's getting the money?" He reached for a nearby ledger. "I'll need the information for my records."

"Just write Mrs. McDaniels—Shapinsay Plantation."

The clerk chuckled as he tapped the cover of the ledger with his pencil. "You know, for you to get ol' Bull Sumner's mark, your lady friend here must be quite extraordinary, eh, Colonel?" His eyebrows rose in a suggestive manner and he leaned back in his chair. "Yep, I've seen a lot of this going on with these local gals down here, but this woman must really be good at keeping your bed warm. I mean for her to earn such a high payout and all. Care to share the details?"

A wave of heat washed up Reece's spine. He dipped forward, placing his hands flat upon the desk. "Now I don't believe that's any of your damned business is it, boy?"

The clerk laughed, winking behind the metal rim of his spectacles. "Well, it's kind of a tradition around here, Colonel. You see, I get to hear all the juicy whore details since I'm the one dispensing the money to these lusty wenches."

Reece's jaws tightened and his teeth scraped together. A series of churns roiled deep in his gut as his mouth formed a thin, hard line. He'd tossed on his cot more nights than he cared to admit wrestling against the desire to bed Emaline, but the sheer thought that anyone would dare put her in the same category as a prostitute drove a spike of rage straight through him. He struggled to breathe, to remain calm and to tamp down the truth of his escalating emotions. "So, that's the way you like to run things here, is it?" He smiled, but the muscles knotted in his jaw.

"Yes, sir, that's the way."

"I see." Reece ground his teeth through a long moment, biting back charged words that crawled from their billet inside him.

The clerk's words continued to tangle around Reece's building rage. "… and if you ask me, it's a fine arrangement. I mean, your little whore gives us information about the Johnnies and the U.S. Government pays her for her services. Hell, it's a win for both of you."

In one heartbeat, Reece leaned across the desk, grabbed the front of the clerk's jacket, and hauled the wide-eyed quartermaster across the saddlebag. He glared down into the boy's face. "Just fill the goddamned order. Then I won't have to bore you with a lecture on good manners." Too stunned to protest, the clerk stared at him, his mouth agape. "And for your information, you moronic bastard, Mrs. McDaniels is far from being a whore. She's the strongest woman I've ever met, and I will not allow you or anyone else to besmirch her good name. You got that?" He shook the clerk, the force bobbing the young man's head back and forth. "She's earned every damn dollar without once spreading her legs, and if I hear another word about her from that grimy hole you call a mouth, I promise it'll be the last thing you say. Do we understand each other?"

Panic radiated from the clerk's eyes and he nodded frantically. His glasses shifted upward to rest upon his wrinkled forehead, and Reece reached over with his free hand and shoved the spectacles back into place. "Now redeem my vouchers quietly, and I'll think twice on whether to tell *my* commander how you like to run things over here."

Reece shoved the boy into the chair, the force nearly toppling the rickety spindle-back. Without another word, the captain leaned sideways and opened a black-lacquered Diebold-Bahmann safe.

With surprising efficiency, he counted out the cash, entered the dollar amount into the ledger beside Emaline's name, then pushed the stack of bills across the desk toward Reece along with a leather binder.

"I-If you'll just sign here, sir, that'll complete the transaction."

Reece knew he'd lost control, but by God no one would sully Emaline's good name. Especially, not some wet-behind-the-ears jackass who'd no idea of the courage the woman possessed. His heart thundered so hard in his chest, he expected a broken rib would follow. A hasty scrawl across the line where the clerk's shaky finger pointed completed the deal.

Reece jammed the pencil to the desk, then gathered up the greenbacks and shoved them into the saddlebag. His behavior more than validated the truth he knew now lived inside his heart. These weeks away from Emaline had only deepened his feelings for her.

Sonofabitch.

He tossed the leather pack over his shoulder and headed for the door. With knob in hand, Reece paused and glanced back. The clerk had yet to straighten the rumpled front of his sack coat. Had he been too rough on the boy? *Probably.* The glass in the weathered frame rattled as he slammed the door on his way out. He had far bigger things to worry about now.

Like falling in love again.

Flickering flames in the fireplace draped shadows on the oak-paneled wall of the upstairs library. The comforting smells of leather and slow-burning pine blended around a trace of lingering cinnamon. Emaline inhaled, calming the thrum of her heart as she waited for Major Neale to settle into a chair. Tall and lean, the man commanded attention even in his relaxed state.

Her pacing resumed.

She wrung her hands in front of her corseted waist. A knuckle softly cracked. She didn't want to feel anxious about Reece's whereabouts. In fact, she tried hard not to, but to no avail. When she'd exhausted all other avenues to uncover information about his location or time of return, Emaline surrendered to her heart's demand. By way of Doctor Evans, she sent an elegantly scripted invitation to the major, asking him to meet with her after dinner.

"Thank you for responding to my request," she said, stopping in front of him.

"Certainly, ma'am. What can I do for you?"

She swallowed, frustration over her upcoming actions pitting her stomach. In place of her usual work dress, she'd donned an expensive dinner gown. A Charles Worth. Her favorite designer. The reassuring perpetuation of proper attire, demure gentility even during such troublesome times lent Emaline strength and control tonight. She straightened her shoulders, knowing that the sweeping bertha neckline and cap sleeves solidified the clear message she hadn't always worked in the fields. A large caged crinoline beneath the folds of emerald silk allowed the garment to swell into an enormous bell. She hoped her presentation proved intimidating. She'd even swept her tresses into a chignon at the base of her neck. Oh yes, she would get the answers from Major Neale tonight even if she had to wring the man's neck to achieve her goal.

"Yes, Major," she replied, clasping and unclasping her hands. "Unfortunately, there is something I'm forced to discuss with you."

His forehead crinkled as his brow lifted. "What might that be?"

She nodded. "Though slight, it is nonetheless disheartening."

"Well, if it's in my power to amend things, I certainly shall."

"Thank you." She lifted her chin and plunged onward. "Well. I'm quite concerned about…my vouchers." She cleared her throat. "The colonel promised me I would get vouchers as payment, but then you took them away from me." A blush heated her cheeks and she compressed her lips to hide their slight tremble. At the moment she cared far more about Reece's whereabouts than her blasted voucher collection, but she couldn't broach the subject of one without questioning the other.

Major Neale inhaled then released the air in a long, nerve-grinding sigh. "As I explained at the time, Colonel Cutteridge sent me to retrieve your vouchers. I gave them to him per his request. I know nothing more than that. I'm sorry." He began to rise from the chair, but her next words eased him back into the leather.

"While I appreciate your candor, unfortunately that isn't good enough."

His eyebrow again rose. "What more do you require other than what I've already explained?"

"I need to know when Colonel Cutteridge will return to camp so I might discuss this in greater detail with him." *There, dear God. I've said it.* "Though you have temporary command, surely you know his return date."

The major sighed again, and Emaline's pulse kicked up a notch. He leaned back and folded his hands in his lap. "You're correct. I am in temporary command of the regiment."

Is the man dimwitted? She willed herself to relax, though her thoughts raced with a will of their own. Perhaps Reece had been injured or killed and no one thought to tell her? Panic swelled inside Emaline but she quickly squelched the tingling rush of fear. Doc seemed quite fond of her. Surely he would have shared news of such magnitude. Her pacing resumed and the rustle of silk overrode the crackle from the fire. She came to a stop in front of him once more. Each tick from the Bailey Banks Biddle mantel clock further frayed her patience.

"Allow me to rephrase my words then, Major," she said. "How long do you expect to retain temporary command?"

This time, he had the audacity to laugh. She stared at him, her tension escalating faster than the beat of her heart. A shaky breath escaped.

Laughter surely meant Reece hadn't perished after all.

"Well now, ma'am," he said between chuckles. "That's difficult to say."

"Try," she snapped. Her lips pursed and three steps took her to the closest chair. With an impatient rustle she lowered into the wingback. "Let's stop mincing words here, Major. You either know or you don't."

Another smile played near the corner of his mouth. He leaned forward and placed his elbows across splayed knees. A black slouch hat dangled from his hands in the space between. "So let me get all this straight. You want to discuss the length of time I shall retain temporary command of the regiment and know the return date of the colonel so you might further discuss the status of your vouchers?"

In that instant, Emaline realized he was toying with her. Her fingers fluttered to the blood-red ruby the size of a Liberty half-dime resting against her throat. Matching earrings brushed the sides of her neck. "Yes, Major. That's exactly what I want to know."

"I've already told you, I have no answer regarding your vouchers. And about Colonel Cutteridge? Well…" He paused, his smile disappearing. "Why don't you instead tell me the real reason for our meeting tonight?"

Emaline's indignation waned. Silence lengthened as weariness seeped from her body. Her words spiraled into a broken whisper. "Please. I must know if he's…returning."

Something flickered inside his eyes and a shiver passed through her.

"I see," he finally replied, working his hands around the hat's brim.

Her breath caught. "Wh—what do you see?"

"What I see has absolutely nothing to do with vouchers."

Raw awareness welled inside Emaline. Pent-up breath rushed out in a sharp gust. She'd been wrong. This man was no imbecile, and that only deepened her remorse. *Humiliation blistered her cheeks.* "I've asked everyone if they know his return date, but no one provides me an answer."

He rose to his feet.

She followed him up, her heart squeezing so tight she feared it would stop beating.

"And I would tell you if I knew, Mrs. McDaniels, but since this is the military, plans can change at a moment's notice." He stepped closer, his words direct. "Allow me the liberty of saying, however, regardless of what unfolds between you two, you must understand this: At all times, the responsibility of his command controls Reece. That will never change for him. I am his friend, and I tell you this to save you from heartbreak." Turning on his heel, he headed to the door, his boots leaving a trace of mud on the rug. When he glanced back, the metal scabbard of his sword caught the fire's glow—glinting a final reminder of her foolishness.

In numbed silence, she watched as his hand tunneled through long brown hair. Resettling his slouch hat, he offered her a faint smile. Although her spine was ramrod straight, Emaline desired nothing more than to sink to the floor.

As the door clicked shut, her eyes drifted closed. The yoke of irrational behavior draped heavy. *I've completely lost my mind.* An entire horde of Yankees wrought chaos across her property, destroying the very foundation of her world. Abject disorder ruled. Yet here she sat pining for the enemy. She released a ragged breath and opened her eyes. The smudges on her expensive Aubusson rug shimmered into view. When had her common sense perished.

Under the penetrating warmth of his mouth.

A chill seeped into Emaline's bones as a single tear spilled down her cheek. Far more than her carpet needed tending, yet she knew no way to bank the coals of desire that now burned inside her heart for Reece.

Chapter Seven

A week later, the Yankee encampment awakened to the resonance of thousands of galloping horses. Campfires sparked to life as soldiers stumbled from wedge tents to toss logs onto dying embers. Temporarily assigned the entire brigade, Reece led the incoming cavalrymen down the lane, the reinforcements swelling the number of soldiers under his command to two-thousand, nine-hundred strong.

He reined to a stop in front of officer's row and dismounted, tossing Saguaro's reins to the waiting soldier. "Water him good. It's been a long ride."

"I'll take excellent care of him for you, sir." The young wrangler faded off into the darkness with the buckskin just as Lieutenant Glave sauntered into view.

"Notify the junior officers and their adjutants, Lucas. Have them report to my command tent in one hour."

"Yes, sir." The aide-de-camp sprinted away.

Reece scanned the mansion. A single light flickered from an upstairs window. He knew Emaline watched. Three weeks had passed since he'd held her in his arms and kissed away her tears. And those twenty-one days, every damn one of them, had been the longest of his life.

A ragged curse fell from his lips and he turned, nearly bumping into Jackson.

"About time you showed up," Jackson said, pulling a blue sack coat over his rumpled shirt and pants. "I was gettin' tired of carrying your load."

"Is that right?" Reece chuckled. "Well, I brought you company this time."

"I can see that."

"I've been assigned command of the brigade while Colonel Thomas recuperates, the bumbling ol' fool."

"We heard. He sure picked a bad week to be thrown from his horse." The smell of sulfur radiated between them as Jackson lit a cheroot. "Got a dispatch from Headquarters this morning," he said, tossing aside the burnt lucifer. "Said we're to move out upon your return. So we're ready, then?"

Reece nodded. "We'll leave at dawn." They walked to the campfire and the pot of coffee suspended over the low flames. The brew would be thick and strong and just the way he liked it. Reece poured a generous cupful and brought the metal rim to his mouth. The long swig burned his throat and cut through the bitter cold swirling around him. "They finally laid the pontoon bridges across the river at Falmouth, yesterday," he said, raising the mug again. He swallowed, scanning the area. A multitude of junior officers organized the new arrivals into an impressive appearance of order. "You'll retain command of the regiment, Jackson. I'll need you on my left flank."

"Where're we crossing?"

"At the United States Ford."

"The U.S.? Why not Banks Ford? It's closer."

"All indications show Banks is too fortified. My orders are to keep the U.S. clear and curtail the Reb sharpshooters that'll surely surface once we begin our crossing. Burnside wants us to hit the river road hard."

"This should've been done weeks ago. I'm sure those Johnnies are dug in deeper than ticks by now. Their damn scouts are just itchin' to pick us off."

"You're preaching to the choir, my friend." Reece took another swig. Raucous laughter erupted across the encampment. Eager soldiers anticipated the eminent battle. He watched the moon slip behind a thick bank of clouds, then surrendered to his heart's demand. "How were things while I was gone?"

"Militarily or otherwise?" Jackson asked, a smile lifting his lips.

Reece released his breath with a vaporous sigh. "Otherwise, right now."

Jackson braced a boot upon one of the stones that ringed the campfire and leaned forward. "Well, she's been asking about you for days. First the doctor and his staff and then when no one had answers to your whereabouts, she scheduled an appointment with me. I was forced to tell her you're a damn slacker and we didn't know when your philandering ass would turn back up."

Reece chuckled and reached inside his greatcoat. A large leather pouch appeared in his glove-covered hand. "Here. Make sure she gets this, will you?" He passed the bundle over to Jackson, who weighed the package in his palm.

"Let me guess. The voucher money?" Reece nodded and his friend's voice lowered another degree. "I'll take care of this, but I don't mind telling you I'm damn glad we're moving out." His empty cup dropped to the ground and he turned, fading from sight.

Reece stared into the flames, listening to the crunch of Jackson's departing footsteps. He poured the remainder of his coffee into the fire. The flames sputtered and sent up a pungent coil of smoke.

Damn cowardly, sending his friend to do the dirty work. Reece flattened his lips into a hard line. The world had a wicked way of taunting him. He spun on his boot heel and with as much force as he could muster he threw the empty cup into the darkness. From the shadows, between him and the lighted window, a tin chink resounded against stone. Dammit, he didn't want to be this close to loving again.

Not ever again.

Not after the unbearable price he'd already paid.

Chapter Eight

December 13, 1862

Saturday, just after sunrise

Brennen lowered his field glasses and muttered a scathing oath. A field of advancing Federal cavalry emerged from behind the tree line. Two regiments, at least. Possibly a full brigade. The soldiers floated through the early-morning fog in wave after wave of blue, a steadfast enemy in a determined push to the river.

A biting wind lifted the shaggy hair off his neck and he tugged his slouch hat lower to ward off the chill. Artillery explosions resounded downriver near Fredericksburg; the Federal infantry assault in town had already begun.

A rider beside him whispered, "Looks like they're gettin' ready to cross, Cap'n. Just where you said they would."

Brennen lifted the field glasses again and sighted in on the four long columns. "The U.S. Ford is the logical crossing for this many." Bluecoats poured forth from the sheltering row of hickories and white pine, moving along the water's edge as the early morning mist swirled around them in miasmic layers. Beneath the stabbing hooves of thousands of horses, the embankment churned into a muddy quagmire, but he knew the rock-encrusted ground would support them all. "Ride back to headquarters and let them know the advance has started."

"Ain't ya comin', Cap'n?"

"No. I'm going closer for a better look."

"Don't get cut off from our lines, sir," a soldier on his left said above the faint report of gunfire.

Brennen nodded and spurred his mount deeper into the underbrush.

He reined to a stop just as another round of artillery shells exploded from the direction of Fredericksburg. Darting a look upriver, he tightened his jaw. Em's plantation sat less than two miles from this natural crossing.

He raised the field glasses once again, searching for any uncased flags to get an idea of the strength in numbers they were facing. A moment later, he spotted the U.S. colors fluttering in all its glory. Directly beside the Stars and Stripes danced a blue, swallow-tailed flag emblazoned with the number three. *A Brigade silk.* He focused upon a cluster of soldiers, a dozen or more, mounted on horseback beneath the standards. His lips twisted into a smirk. The command knot. He spied the highest-ranking officer—a colonel.

What the hell are you doing here?

The dark-haired, dark-bearded man shouted orders, prominently involved in the crossing. Rare to see such high brass in the middle of the fray. Ordinarily, they liked to stay well out of danger and let the rank and file minions do the dirty work. But not this one. No, this sonofabitch kept a tight rein on his men, controlling order as he brought each company into position. He allowed no chaotic crossing, nothing that resembled a lack of discipline.

Brennen lowered the field glasses and a niggle of fear mingled with an odd respect.

This big Yank knew exactly how to lead an army.

"Form the line away from the river on the opposite side, Captain," Reece shouted. "And, make certain scouts are posted well in front of the formation. I don't like surprises."

The young officer reined back hard. "Straightaway, Colonel." He galloped back into the melee. Snorting horses and clanking metal resounded through the clearing as sabers, canteens and bridle rings reverberated together. The air thickened with the cursing of cavalrymen struggling to keep their horses in line.

"Get that animal moving!" Reece bellowed, pointing to the Morgan bogged in the mud near the rock-strewn pathway. A frantic private atop the hulking beast fought for control of his horse. "Sergeant! Get over there and help him."

A burly soldier responded, water splashing in all directions as he turned his horse toward the snag. He leaned and swept up a dangling rein bobbing in the water, then tossed it back to the obviously relieved private. Within seconds, the column flowed with precision once again.

Lieutenant Glave drew alongside Reece and yelled above the din. "Colonel, sir. Doc wants to know when you want the ambulance wagons to cross."

"An hour after the main formation, right behind my supply teams."

With a hasty salute, the soldier spurred his horse around and galloped away. Reece turned back to the column, and shouted another order. The ordeal of moving a large brigade through such a narrow passage grated on him. "Keep them moving, dammit! Pull that column together, Corporal!"

Of course, riding away from Emaline did little to ease Reece's roiling discontent. He shoved aside his remorse. His heart mattered little in this equation. He would need all his skills to see him through the upcoming campaign.

Two miles upriver Emaline wrung her hands together as she paced before Shapinsay's open front door. "But why must you go too?"

Worry creased her forehead as she watched Doc push a boxful of medical supplies into the wagon bed. He turned and climbed the steps, and she moved several paces backward to allow him room.

"The colonel's ordered us across the river," he said, patting her on the shoulder as he passed. "We're to establish the hospital behind the main lines."

"But why can't you just stay established here?" She looked at the desolation across her front lawn. Established seemed such a forgiving word for the damage that sprawled before her. Fire rings gouged the terrain and hundreds of piles of pine needles and plank boards dotted the landscape, ghosts rising from the remains of the enemy camp. Garbage pits and latrines, while out of sight and thankfully covered, also disfigured her land. "Send someone else, Doc." She pulled her gaze back and stared at his retreating form. "You might get hurt."

The old surgeon shuffled to a stop, then lifted the last box of medicines near the entryway. "My dear, it doesn't work that way. We follow the regiment to be closer to the casualties."

Oh God, more casualties. More deaths.

Emaline's thoughts tumbled to the previous night. From her bedroom window, she'd spotted Reece among the thousands of new arrivals. Her heart lurched from the sheer joy of seeing him again. She waited, but he never came to tell her good-bye.

A biting wind ripped around the corner of the manor and lifted her cape into an ominous swell of black wool. Emaline pointed inside. "Who's going to care for those men in there after you've gone?"

"Captain Crowe's company will be right behind us to gather up the wounded and put them into supply wagons." He slid the boxful of amber bottles into the wagon, and then rested his ample hip against the closest wheel hub. "You know," he sighed, exhaustion carving lines across his face. "I could sure use your help where I'm going."

Emaline stared at him for several seconds before issuing a sharp laugh. "Are you mad? I can't just ride off. I've got servants who depend upon me."

"No, no. Of course you'd return once we advance further south. I only need your help for a little while with the immediate casualties. Most of my assistants don't have your unique abilities." His smile tipped upward. "And you know I would never put you in harm's way."

"I know that, Doc," she said, stifling the quiver in her lips. He was much too old to be out in these elements day after day. "I just wish things would return to normal."

"There's no normal life, my dear," he said, his shoulders sagging into a weary droop as he reached out and smoothed a hand down her arm. "There's only life."

Emaline scrutinized the devastation around her. Helping Doc with invalid soldiers inside her commandeered home was one thing. But willingly following him, even if only across the river, was an entirely different matter. How could she go with this man, however kind he might be, into the devil's lair? Then everything shifted as her thoughts moved backward four hours.

"It's your voucher exchange, Mrs. McDaniels," Major Neale said.

Emaline stared at the bundle of money he'd just placed in her hands.

"This is much more than what I thought I'd be getting." She stared at the bills, her forehead creasing in disbelief. "Who—"

"Who do you think?"

She met his eyes again and he offered a smile. "He also sends you his deepest gratitude for assisting the doctor."

Emaline's thoughts returned to the present and her eyelids slipped closed. The issue was not one of country against country any longer. In the beginning, even a month ago perhaps, she could have argued that point. But not now. Things *were* changing, the statement Reece had thrown at her that night in the library so true. The only war that existed in her life right now was the one raging out of control inside her heart. Everything boiled down to an inner battle involving just one man.

Her eyelids flew open. Doc had already stepped up into the mule-drawn wagon. And in that instant, she made her decision.

Turning on her boot heel, Emaline dashed inside the manor house in search of Euley. She found the woman bent over a patient near the back of the parlor. The ordered efficiency inside her home belied the chaos unfolding beyond its walls.

"I'm going with Doc," Emaline hollered. "Don't worry, I'll be back soon."

The old woman straightened and stared at her, but before she could reply Emaline turned and raced down the entryway, then out through the front door. As traitorous to Benjamin's memory as she knew this to be, she shouted, "Wait, Doc! Wait for me!"

Chapter Nine

The bullet caught Brennen in the shoulder. Agony exploded through him. A ragged sigh escaped as he slumped sideways and slid from the saddle. Impact with the ground crumpled him into a heap. His Morgan bolted into the forest.

Beneath his ear, the strong rumble of approaching horses replaced the fading strides of his own mount. His breath hissed out in short, static gasps. From where he lay, he watched thin beams of sunlight spill over the rim of the horizon, the distant hills brightening. The fog dispersed into wispy, serpentine streaks against the blue sky. With each labored breath, Brennen battled the repellent emptiness until he could fight no more.

Surrender became inevitable.

"I know I got him!" the sharpshooter shouted. He reined his horse to a stop near the spot where he'd seen the Reb scout fall. With the barrel end of his rifle, he probed the heavy underbrush in search of the body. "Where the hell did you go, you bastard?" he mumbled. "I know I hit you."

Frustrated, he prepared to dismount when a second trooper rode up alongside. "The regiment will be here soon. You ain't got time to admire your handiwork. Come on, we've gotta get over that ridge and make sure there ain't no more of these bastards."

"But I damn well know I got him."

"You killed him, that's all that matters. Now let's go," the man yelled over his shoulder as he galloped away. The scout shrugged, then settled back into his saddle, spurring his mount forward to join his comrade.

A half-hour later, Reece returned the sharpshooter's salute. "What's your report, soldier?"

"They're up there all right, Colonel. Just like you said. Looks like a full regiment. Maybe more, including some artillery. I took out several scouts posted near the river." He chuckled. "No doubt some of them Gray Ghosts. Hell, those sonsofbitches disappear even when you kill them." Jackson, sitting on his horse nearby, swore under his breath and the scout glanced his way before returning his attention to Reece. "And they're dug in deep all across the ridge line too, sir. Their trenches run for a good mile or more. They knew we were coming."

"Good work, private." Reece dismissed the scout.

"I knew this would happen," Jackson snapped. "Didn't I tell you? Weeks of waiting for those damn pontoons gave them all the time they needed to dig in. Jesus Christ, even Stonewall had time to make it from clear over in the Shenandoah. It'll be hell to pay to break their lines now."

Reece swept his arm toward the continuous echo of gunfire from Fredericksburg. His expression darkened. "Listen to that, dammit. The infantry's paying with their lives. We've got to make sure the Rebs don't reinforce the city." He dropped his hand, and watched the troops moving into position. "And that's exactly what we're going to do." He turned to one of the three aides beside him. "Plans have changed. Tell Hayes to bring up his regiment to the left of Colonel Adams."

"Yes, sir." The courier nudged his horse backward.

"And, tell him to be ready to move out as soon as the artillery engages." The aide nodded and spurred away. Reece directed his words to the second courier. "And you go tell Major Voelker to bring his battery into position on that ridge to the left of the river road. I want his cannonade to begin at ten o'clock sharp."

"Yes, sir." The soldier jerked his horse into action.

Reece's last order went to the remaining aide. "And you go tell Captain Gardner to bring the ammunition wagons a quarter-mile closer. We'll need his supplies earlier than anticipated."

After a hasty salute, off went the final courier.

Reece turned to Jackson. "You make sure to hit these bastards hard on their left." He pointed to a spot on the horizon hazy with smoke from the ongoing struggle in Fredericksburg. "I want you to go in there, just where that hill and wood line meet. As soon as Adams pulls back from his initial engagement, wheel your men around and drive the Rebs out of that trench." He gathered his reins tighter and stared at the swell of land lush with evergreens and hardwoods. Bare limbs towered skyward on the horizon. Even under its winter garb, this country was so vastly different from the sun-baked heat of the desert. However, by the time the sun set this evening, the splendor would be buried beneath the wicked wrath of war. "I'll give you one hour to get into position." He turned in the saddle, glanced at his friend, then scanned back over the landscape. His mouth smirked sideways. "And don't get yourself killed out there, either. You got that? I'd be hard pressed to find your replacement."

Jackson laughed. "I'll keep that in mind," he said, tugging his hat brim low. "God knows we don't want you overworked?" A split-second later, he set spurs and headed down the hill.

Reece chuckled and shook his head, reining in hard on Saguaro's bit in order to keep his horse from following.

Sixty minutes later, the first crack of artillery shells whistled through the trees, exploding with a deafening roar that sent shrapnel and case shot into the gray-clad soldiers. Mud and debris mingled with the blood of the dying.

Two hundred yards in front of the Confederate line, a solid wave of blue emerged from the cover of evergreens. Three companies of dismounted cavalry surged toward the Rebel entrenchments. Within moments, the air resonated with the din of musketry. Confederate cannons belched back, tearing huge gaps in the Federal lines. Union artillery answered with equal destruction. Iron shot and shell tore cavalrymen to pieces as the gruesome sound of lead pelted human flesh. Ranks of bluecoats rushed forward to fill the gaps left vacant by fallen comrades. And volley after volley of rifle fire rained down upon the Confederate position. The deeper, belching blasts of artillery rocked the ground. Thirty minutes into the engagement, as ordered, the Federals fell back. The lull gave the Confederates time to re-enforce their now-weakened center with men from their left flank.

Stretcher-bearers surged past Reece toward the recently established hospital in a clearing at the bottom of the hill a thousand yards away.

Raising his field glasses, he pulled his lips into a tight smile. "That's perfect," he said, watching as the Johnnies shifted their forces. His vision moved left. "Now, Jackson. Make your move."

Reece saw the top of the regimental flag through the tree line, the silk unfurling as his troops moved out from their protective cover. A split-second later, the ground reverberated with the pounding hooves of nearly nine hundred cavalry horses as they swung around the hillock and converged upon the weakened Confederate left flank. With the majority of gray-backs pulled away to support the center, the few Rebs remaining offered a brief, but futile fight. In just a few moments, the regiment overran the flanking enemy trenches.

Sunlight glinted off the saber clutched in Jackson's hand as he issued the order to regroup. As soon as headcount was established, he would press straight up the disjointed Confederates' center to help crumple their main line.

"Perfectly done," Reece mumbled, shoving the field glasses back into the case that hung around the swell of his saddle. He spurred Saguaro forward. "Let's ride, men," he hollered over his shoulder to the nearby flag bearers.

He led them down the hill toward Colonel Hayes's position.

Five minutes later, Reece spotted the venerable old soldier under a protective stand of cedars. "Brilliant job, Commander," he said, leaning down from the saddle to shake his comrade's hand. "Your troops did well. They allowed Major Neale's regiment to crush the enemy's flank. Let's give him ten more minutes to rally his troops, and then we'll hit the center with another assault."

"We took some casualties, Colonel, but I believe we can muster one more charge."

"One more is all I need. I'm riding to Adams's regiment to relay the order. We'll talk again after this is over."

The old man nodded and Reece set spurs to his horse. At the forest's edge, he reined Saguaro to a stop. Adams's regiment waited three hundred yards across the open field.

Reece glanced toward the Confederate main line.

The Rebs waited behind their fortified trench, an earthen wall four feet high and just as thick. Hundreds of long-barreled Enfields glistened in the rays of a late-morning sun.

Beside him, a flag bearer whispered, "Looks like we'll have to go around, Colonel."

Reece shook his head. "No time."

"But, sir, we're dead if we try to cross here," another added.

"You're right, if everyone attempts to cross. But a single rider, moving fast, is a difficult target. You men go around. I'm crossing alone."

Before they could voice their concerns, Reece slapped the leather reins across Saguaro's neck and dug his spurs deep into the horse's thick hide. The surefooted beast lunged forward, bolting into the clearing. Strong muscles bunched under his impressive speed. Reece leaned low in the saddle.

"Come on, boy. Faster. You can do this." With the swiftness of a tempest, his buckskin stormed across the terrain. Each thundering stride brought them closer and closer to the towering row of pines in the distance. Dirt clods churned up from the ground under Saguaro's forceful power. Popping reverberations obtruded from the trenches to his left.

A sidelong glance revealed puffs of smoke pouring from a multitude of discharging rifles. A second later, Minié balls whistled past his ear.

"Come on," he yelled, melting against Saguaro's lathered neck as perspiration tracked in rivulets down Reece's face. He concentrated only on the blowing sounds of the animal's heavy breathing.

The ground flew past them. Deadly missiles zipped around him. Yard by precious yard, they closed in on the protective tree line.

Just as he brushed past scented evergreen branches and plunged into safety, Reece felt a stinging burn across his forearm. He pulled back on Saguaro's bit and glanced at the jagged rip across his coat sleeve. Only then did he feel the warm spread of blood.

Brennen jerked awake. Beneath him, the ground shook with artillery explosions. The pain in his shoulder lanced deeper. How long had he been unconscious?

A few minutes? More? He rolled onto his back and groaned when a new wave of pain spilled from his body. He refused to die like this.

Goddamnit, get up.

He shifted, struggled onto an elbow and peered down at his wound. Blood saturated the left side of his shell jacket and turned the gold double braiding on his sleeve into a mud-colored tawny swirl. He wasn't a doctor, but from the look of things, he damn well knew he needed one. And fast. A mile into enemy territory and with the battle underway, he wouldn't be going back the way he'd come. But, where could he go to get out of this damnable cold?

Shapinsay.

Unless the Yanks burned the house, Em's was his closest option. Brennen pushed into a sitting position and five agonizing minutes later, he climbed into a wobbly stance. Despite the breeze off the river, perspiration coursed down his face.

He stumbled from the undergrowth. The faint popping of musketry filled the air. The ground beneath his brogans vibrated from nearby explosions. Brennen saw the tell-tale signs floating just above the treetops; smoke shimmered in hazy circles, strong testament of the ongoing battle beyond.

He staggered forward. Shaking fingers worked to unbutton his coat as he slipped down the embankment toward the U.S. Ford. Since he was on the backside of the enemy, he'd shuck the gray outer garment, ease into the water and blend in with any other Yanks splashing across the river.

Chapter Ten

Emaline pressed the cotton wad into the wound across the soldier's chest, trying to staunch the flow of blood until Doc arrived. She assessed the instruments lined across the table, making sure the surgeon had everything he would need. Forceps to extract the iron shrapnel. Tenaculum to seal the artery and prevent internal bleeding. Needles to sew a neat seam. She'd removed the implements from the boiling pot a few minutes earlier and hoped they'd be cool enough for him to handle.

A half-emptied bottle of ether sat at the end of the table, along with the glass vials of opium, turpentine and quinine. All were running low. Would the supply wagons from the rear arrive in time? The cotton beneath her fingers darkened with blood. Emaline pressed harder. A great many if's stood in the way of this man living. She chanced a quick glance toward the operation that took place on a nearby table.

Doc bent over a battered body and the assisting steward near the surgeon's elbow possessed the same determination. Blood smeared in darkened streaks across the front of their aprons and both men more resembled butchers cutting beef than medical professionals. She closed her heart against the agony of their decisions, hastily made in the face of so many injuries. The doctor's soft voice drifted to her above the moans of the wounded.

"...the shrapnel broke the bone near the knee," he instructed. "Look, Jeremy, do you see where it protrudes just below the muscle?" With bloodied fingers, he brushed aside pieces of uniform and bits of metal imbedded in the wound of the now-unconscious soldier. The upcoming prognosis settled over Emaline in a wave of misery. She'd heard it at least a half-dozen times today. "Take the leg. Do what you can to seal the flap once you've removed the limb."

The assistant nodded and took over the procedure as Doc shifted sideways to join her. Emaline peeled back the saturated cloth to expose the jagged wound. Two minutes into the operation, the need to continue vanished along with their patient's soul.

"Loss of blood," Doc mumbled, fishing into his apron pocket to remove a pencil and a small journal. He scribbled his diagnosis beside the man's name.

Emaline stepped aside while stretcher-bearers removed the body.

From just beyond the tent's entrance, a loud commotion disturbed the onward march of death.

"It's a damn scratch. The bullet only winged me."

Emaline turned toward the tent's opening. She would remember the sound of that voice forever.

"Dammit, I don't want to take up their time. This is nothing." Several soldiers pushed the daunting form of Reece Cutteridge inside, one of them bellowing for the doctor.

In seconds, the surgeon appeared and made a hasty examination of the wound. "This won't take long, Colonel. The Minié just creased your muscle. But since you're already here and to appease your men, let's just get it cleaned and bandaged."

Reece agreed and then turned to speak to the closest soldier. "As soon as you get the prisoners assembled have Captain Wells check with the Provost to see where he wants them held. And have Lieutenant Glave form a company to collect the scattered equipment and get burial details organized. Make sure they identify the dead on the battlefield too. And give the list to Major Neale." The soldier nodded and vacated the tent.

Doc pulled Reece deeper into the enclosure, leading the way toward Emaline.

"She'll take care of this, Colonel," he said and then hurried back to his patients.

When his gaze met hers, Reece's eyes darkened into twin caverns of discernible fury. Only a heartbeat passed before his rage ignited into voice. "Em—Emaline?" The word jackknifed into her with a biting hiss. "Wh-what... Jesus Christ, what the hell are you—how long have you been here?"

Even though his raw anger spiraled through her, Emaline's face warmed. Her fingers, sticky with blood, curled around the edge of the table for support. She forced herself to breathe. And to remain calm. "Long enough," she replied, her words as thick with emotion as the morning fog had been earlier. "I'm helping Doc."

Reece loomed closer, his body dwarfing hers. "You're helping? Are you insane? Have you no idea the danger you're in?" His hands snaked out to encircle her upper arms and he jerked her toward him, no softness anywhere in his touch now. "Who brought you here?" he snapped.

"I rode over with Doc this morning."

"This morning?" His sharp exhalation moved the wisps of hair at her temples. "You could've been killed. My God, anything could've happened to you."

There was a potent danger to this man now—a dark power that enthralled her as much as overwhelmed her. She summoned the strength needed to pull from his grasp, then tamped down the rush of emotions. "But it didn't. And I'm fine." Reaching into the box of supplies, Emaline withdrew the necessary medicines she would use and then lined them across the table.

Warm breath brushed over her as she concentrated on his wound, his nerve-wracking silence nearly her undoing. Were her lips trembling as much as her legs? Like a lifeline, Emaline clung to her task until she placed the finishing wrap. "I've soaked your bandage in belladonna. It'll help ease your pain." She captured her bottom lip between her teeth to stop its quiver.

Then raised her head to meet his eyes.

When their gazes met, a surprising rush of desire replaced Reece's comfortable anger of moments before. Fear for her safety tore a hole through his heart, so overpowering and raw he thought he might vomit.

"There's no pain," he growled, pushing the words past tight lips. His pulse thundered in his ears, yet he allowed himself a slow breath, lifting her ephemeral fragrance deeper into his lungs.

She exuded an unbelievable brightness amid the hellish darkness of this day.

The pace of their breathing matched the expectancy in the air. The circumstances around Reece disappeared. He could not stop his hand from rising, from slipping around the back of her neck—couldn't stop the pad of his thumb from seeking the hollow of her throat. He stroked the spot as if it were the softest thing on earth.

Her eyes reflected pain, and weariness. And then, he saw something more, something hot and integral. Something he'd seen in the hazy twilight of the stable weeks before. Reece couldn't stop himself. He bent his elbow. And then his head, drawing her toward him. Every single part of him focused on reclaiming her lips.

"Excuse me, Colonel Cutteridge. This just arrived from headquarters."

The harried voice shattered the moment. Reece pulled away, releasing his hold. Gathering his response to her into a hard knot in his stomach, he turned to the courier standing near the entrance of the medical tent.

Reece stepped back and shoved his bandaged arm into the sleeve of his frockcoat. He moved toward the soldier, his stride lengthening until he reached for the correspondence. A heavy weight engulfed him as he scanned the dispatch. "Sonofabitch," he scowled as his already frayed emotions darkened further.

"Give me something to write with, Christopher."

The courier complied and pulled out a dispatch book and pencil from his satchel and handed over the items. Reece scrawled his response as he spoke. "Tell Colonel Adams to move the brigade back across the river and set up camp. I've been summoned to Falmouth for a meeting and I'll be back as soon as possible. Here are the orders I want you to give him." Reece ripped away the correspondence from the leather binder and then shoved both items back to the waiting hands of his courier.

The man nodded, pushed aside the canvas flap, and then disappeared from view. Disheartened that the infantry could not break the Fredericksburg defenses, and even more frustrated that so many of his men had now died in vain, Reece needed a target to vent his anger.

He turned to face Emaline and found one. "You're finished here," he snapped.

"I can't leave, now. Doc needs me—"

"We've been ordered to pull back."

She crossed to him and rested her hand on his arm. "But, these men can't be moved."

"They'll all be moving, and quick." Reece knocked aside the canvas flap and stepped from the tent, pulling her with him until they reached the huge campfire in the center of the encampment.

He stopped a passing soldier. "Saddle my horse and one other and bring them back to me." The private nodded and rushed off to fulfill the command. Reece shifted his weight and turned back to face her. "Take a good look around. This is war, and neither side is spared."

Her chin lifted. "I'm not afraid to face this."

"I'm afraid for you." He pulled on his gauntlets. "You're through with involvement."

"You're a bit too late, Colonel. I've been involved ever since you rode into my life." Firelight illuminated the moisture glistening in her eyes. "How can you act so calloused? Don't these deaths bother you?"

"Does death bother me?" A wicked laugh ground from his lips. "Good God, woman, death nearly destroyed me!" In a valiant effort, Reece searched his memory for his wife but could only recall a hazy, obscure image. In her place stood this hellion, an unprimed rifle pointing at him. This angel bandaging his soldiers and crying oceans of tears for the dead. This bewitching, bewildering woman wrapped in his arms, her intoxicating taste forevermore burned into memory. The muscles in his throat tightened and he issued a guttural curse.

He didn't want to care about her.

The wrangler rushed into view leading two horses. Beside him, the colonel's aide-de-camp followed.

"Sir, I understand we've been called to Falmouth to meet with the general, is this correct?"

Reece stalked over, retrieved the reins from the soldier, and then turned to face his young aide. "Yes, the infantry's assault on Fredericksburg failed. The general has called for a strategy meeting with his brigade commanders to decide their next move." Putting his boot into the stirrup, Reece pulled up onto Saguaro's back. The leather creaking, he settled himself into the saddle. Once mounted, he continued, "I've placed Colonel Adams in temporary command.

I want you to take a detail of men and head to Falmouth. Get started on the resupplies for our brigade. In the meantime, I'm escorting Mrs. McDaniels back to her plantation, but I'll meet up with you later tonight in town." Turning back to the wrangler, he ordered, "Help her mount up."

Emaline didn't budge from her position on the opposite side of the campfire even though the soldier waited beside the Morgan to assist her.

Reece fixed her with a sharp glare and pointed to the animal. "Get on. You're ridin' with me."

Her hands curled into fists and then rose to her hips. "I'm not going anywhere with you. I'm staying here to help Doc."

Reece glowered down at her across the flickering flames. "Get on the horse, Emaline."

"No." The campfire's light reflected the determination in her eyes.

Reece straightened, his breath sliding out in a slow exhale.

He noticed the bodies of a dozen soldiers lying near the medical tent. Arranged in two respectful lines, they looked as if they were napping. His gaze tracked back to hers and he stared at the barely perceptible clench in her jaw.

"I'm finished playing games with you. Climb up on that damn horse right now or you'll be straddling mine."

Without another word, she spun on her heel and stomped to the other Morgan.

Chapter Eleven

Brennen slipped from behind the stable.

Evidence of a recent Federal occupation marred Shapinsay's rutted grounds. An upturned wagon lay in a broken heap near the hen houses, and off to his far right, hundreds of small piles of hay littered the ground, outlining the remains of company streets. Nothing stirred inside the mansion, as near as he could tell. A grimace creased his face and he staggered toward the back of the house.

Are all the slaves gone too?

Furrowed ruts gouged the ground and Brennen fixated on placing one foot in front of the other. A bracing wind whipped the area and sent a shiver through him. Did he catch a flicker of candlelight spilling from one of the empty shanties? Was his mind playing tricks on him?

A fever held him fast in its grip and he wasn't sure of anything now.

Brennen tripped up the back steps and slumped against the square column. Blood-slickened hands wrapped the post for support. He gulped in air. Soaked in perspiration, his shirt clung to him as lovers in his past used to do. Another bone-jarring shudder ripped through him. He squeezed his eyes against the pain and shoved from the post.

The back door loomed into view.

Under the darkened overhang of the porch, the oppressive shadows stole his bearing. He didn't see the bucket that stood in the way of his immediate goal until his foot slammed into the upturned pail, rupturing the silence and sending an ear-shattering clatter into the night.

Brennen propelled forward in frantic, shuffling footsteps. His hands flailed outward in desperation seeking any handhold. Seconds later, he slammed into the brick wall beside the door. The impact forced breath from his lungs in a pain-filled whoosh of air. Each frantic heartbeat that pummeled his chest brought the blackness ever closer. Death's embrace waited, taunting Brennen with a wretched, metallic scent of blood.

He lowered a shaking hand to the doorknob and the metal's icy bite met his fingertips. Sweat coursed down his face, the salty moisture leaching into the corners of his parched mouth. A deep inhalation supplied him just enough stamina to shove open the door.

With the last of his strength, Brennen fell through the opening...and straight into someone's waiting arms.

The horses methodically plodded through the night.

Overhead, dappled moonlight shimmered in streaks through the canopy of branches. A brisk wind rattled bare limbs. Emaline tried to ignore the exhaustion that permeated her bones. She pulled the collar of her cape closer around her ears and stared at the hulking silhouette of the man who led the way to the river.

Heavy silence rode between them.

His wordless animosity wrapped around her like an invisible tether. Emaline's frustrations rose until she could no longer contain her words.

"Why are you so angry with me?" Only the monotonous thudding of hooves against the mossy ground answered back. Emaline sighed, and then added, "I've done nothing wrong, Reece."

"I thought I left you back at the plantation." Harsh and heavy, his words were a blow against her ears.

"Doc asked for my help."

"He should've checked with me first. I'll make certain he does in the future."

"But I wanted to help. I mean, since you got me the money and all." She didn't know how to thank him and felt overwhelmed for even feeling the need to do so.

He straightened in the saddle, but refused to turn around. "That's irrelevant."

Irritation coursed through Emaline. Her cheeks burned. "Irrelevant? Did it occur to you, even once, that I might've wanted to see you before you rode away forever?" The truth flopped from her mouth and lay between them like so many fish on a riverbank. She refused to reel back her words. "Why didn't you bring the money to me, yourself? You denied me the opportunity to…thank you."

He reined his horse to a stop. Her mount stopped, as well.

Reece turned in his saddle and finally looked at her.

"That's right," she continued, her voice rising above the gusting wind. "You just rode away, Reece. After all that's happened between us, how could you just—"

An ominous crack resonated above her head and stopped her flow of words. Simultaneously, they both glanced up.

"Come here," he ordered, still looking upward into the trees.

Emaline nudged her horse forward, and then reined to a stop beside him. "What is it?" she whispered, scanning the ancient canopy of oaks and hickories.

"Most likely the wind." Concern darkened his features and the scowl across his face deepened. "I want you to ride up here with—"

Another splintering crack preceded a portentous, swishing sound. Slivers of bark rained down upon them. A moment later, a massive limb crashed through the canopy and plummeted to the ground nearby with a heavy thud. Both horses reared in fright.

Reece struggled to calm Saguaro, while helplessly watching as Emaline tried her best to contain her own mount. The wild-eyed beast beneath her reared again sitting back on its haunches. Emaline frantically sawed on the reins.

Another branch fell through the canopy, this time striking across the rump of her Morgan. The horse shrieked in terror, nostrils snorting great, heaving spurts of air. Strong leg muscles bunched and brown eyes rolled back into its skull, exposing white. Then the beast's forelegs hit the ground in a heavy thump.

"Emaline!" Reece bellowed, lunging for the horse's headstall in an attempt to contain the animal. He slapped a grip around the throatlatch, but the motion nearly wrenched him from the saddle. A nervous Saguaro sidestepped and Reece lost his hold on the strap. The Morgan surged past him, its hooves drumming over the mossy earth until the black morass of forest finally swallowed the sounds.

The fall from the horse stole Emaline's breath.

Stunned from the impact, she lay gasping for air. Her shoulder throbbed where a low-hanging limb had swept her from the saddle moments before. The horse hadn't bothered to stick around.

Emaline rolled onto her stomach. Other than a few scratches, and the bruised place where she'd fallen, she didn't think anything was broken. *At least I landed on soft ground.* She patted the bed of pine needles, and the crispness of balsam puffed upward.

She lowered her forehead to her outstretched arms. How far into the forest had she come? Could Reece find her? Would he even try? His anger forced tears to well behind her lashes and she rolled onto her back again to stare up at the swaying pines. Caught by the wind, they whirled their ruffled limbs with a ballerina's grace.

A cloud skittered behind them, a puff of pulled cotton across the blackness of night.

She blinked back the tears and packed her lungs with air.

"Reece!" Her shout filled the forest, the echo of his name carried deep into the shadows. Exhaustion from her emotionally draining day compounded an irrational fear. Surely, he would look for her.

Wouldn't he?

Twice more, she called for him, then strained to listen. She heard nothing. Her head lowered back to her arms.

"Reece, where are you?" she whispered, fighting back a sob. Just as she started to push upward with her elbows, she heard the unmistakable chink of a bridle from a horse moving through the undergrowth.

Aided by moonlight, Reece tracked through the forest, searching the bushes for any signs left by the runaway horse—a broken twig here, depressions in the mossy ground there. Reece missed nothing in his search for Emaline. And then, he heard his name. Frantic and frightened, the cry seized him, and an agonizing eternity later, he finally spotted her. Flat on her back on the forest floor, she resembled an offering to some woodland spirit.

He reined Saguaro to a hard stop. In one fluid movement, he leapt from the saddle. His spurs chinked when he hit the ground. A quick tug on the leather ties behind the saddle's cantle released a rolled-up blanket. Emaline pushed up to rest on her elbows when he dropped to a knee beside her. The gray wool drifted over her body.

"I'm surprised you actually came for me," she whispered.

"Of course I would." Reece tugged off his leather gauntlets and dropped them to the ground. "Did you think I'd just leave you out here?" She shrugged and he glanced down the length of blanket and back. "Is anything broken?"

"Only my pride."

He worked to calm the staccato beat of his heart. "You're lucky. You could've broken your neck." He peered off into the darkness. "Looks like your horse kept running, damn fool beast." Her sigh brought his gaze back and he saw the unshed tears that spiked her lashes.

"I'm more than a handful, aren't I?" she muttered, her mouth thinning.

"A handful?" The corner of his mouth lifted. "No. You're more like a damn bucketful of trouble."

"Well, you're a hero—whether you want to be or not." The nervous laugh that followed surprised Reece. He stared at the smile that touched her lips. Her gaze darted away, then slowly returned to his. "Riding after me like that, I mean that's what heroes do."

"I'm no hero."

Her words taunted Reece, though, reaching deep inside until they wrenched apart the shell that covered his heart. The relief of finding her safe became lost under the mesmerizing truth—they were alone for the first time.

Truly alone. No one and nothing could barge in on them. Not the war, nor his responsibilities. Not one dammed thing stood in the way of... He flexed his stomach muscles in a futile effort to refuse the intoxicating summons.

"It's idiotic, all of this," he stated. "First you endanger yourself at the field hospital and now you barge through the forest in the dead of night. Good God, you're just beggin' to get hurt." He scanned the area again, but saw no signs of the enemy, no dangers lurked. Nothing moved around them except the moon-drenched canopy of pines above their heads.

And the escalating thumping in his chest.

The aroma of evergreens melted his anger and burrowed into his lungs.

All around him, unseen spirits seemed to whisper of new beginnings. His ribs ached from the forceful beat, each pound bringing him closer and closer to the unbelievable truth that he could actually care for someone again.

Reece struggled against accepting what seemed to be the inevitable. "Do you think you can stand?"

Only silence answered.

He looked down. A moonbeam laid gossamer softness across Emaline's head, illuminating her pale, oval face. In the depth of her eyes, the flicker of desire had returned.

His breath caught in the back of his throat.

"I will if you want me to," she whispered, reaching up to touch his arm—just above the wound she'd so tenderly cared for back at the tent. "But I want to thank you first for giving me the voucher money. I never expected to see any of it."

His head tipped back and Reece inhaled, her soft, sweet words pushing into his soul. He stared at the arch of stars overhead. In one long exhale, he closed his eyes and finally surrendered to the all-consuming desire for this woman. The need poured into every cell in his parched soul as he welcomed back the passion.

The feeling thickened and grew.

And he allowed it.

Reece lowered his head, and stared at her dark braid. Bits of weathered pine embedded the silken plait draped across her shoulder. He leaned close enough to smell her skin. Close enough to see the fluttering pulse in her throat where his thumb had caressed an hour before. Close enough to feel hope swelling beneath his band of loneliness.

He pulled a pine needle from her hair and let it float from his fingers in a swirl of silver to the ground. Beneath winged brows, her eyes widened, shimmering up at him.

Before he could call them back, the god-awful truth fell from his lips. "I'd give you the world, if I could."

"Reece," she said—his name a desperate plea that washed over him with all the warmth of summer. His hand wrapped her braid and he pulled hard enough to draw her into his arms.

And then…she was there. "You should've stayed home," he rasped against her lips, his breath ragged. And in the next moment, he covered her mouth with his. Heat blazed up his spine when she responded, wrapping her arms around him. Her fingers dug into the tautness that strained across his back. Like a madman driven by some unstoppable force, Reece swept her closer and deepened the kiss. Demanding from her, he won, and sent his tongue into her mouth in an insistent taste. A wildfire burned through him, unrestrained and forceful, pushing him to take what she offered, to lose himself inside her, to forget the horrors of war and the responsibilities of command that had so long controlled him. Where his hands stroked, she responded. Arching against him, she cried out for his touch. Their moans filled the forest, the taste of her skin igniting him. She pressed closer, her body demanding from him what he desired more than life…and knew he dared not give.

The years of experience in divining truth amid lies, good against bad, reared its noble head, declaring even above his passion that taking Emaline McDaniels in this manner would be a tragic mistake.

And if he didn't stop this, he would end up making love to her. He knew this truth as clearly as he knew he wanted her. But how could he be so damned selfish? How could he use such a special woman and then simply walk away?

And he would. He must. He had no right to bury himself inside her, to brand her his. She deserved so much more than this frantic coupling on the cold, hard ground.

The control must come from him.

Goddamnit...let her go.

When the warmth of his mouth left hers, her disappointed gasp speared Reece to the core.

His words twisted raw with torment. "We must stop, Emmy. Now." He nipped the kiss-swollen lushness of her lips, salving his sorrow with the weight of his righteous words. But inside, he was dying all over again.

She stared up at him, her eyes aglow with need. "But...I want you," she brokenly whispered, her breath caressing his face.

"And I you. But not here. Not like this." He watched her tears slip in a silvery path down her face. Reece reached out and captured a precious drop with his fingertip. Bringing the sweetness to his mouth, he tasted the measure of her despair.

She's already suffered enough.

He cupped her face between his palms. "What you're offering is a priceless, precious gift. I won't tarnish its value like this." Her lashes fluttered shut and he cradled her against him, inhaling the fragrance of her hair.

Her breathing slowed into a soft exchange of air and his heart twisted. Reece was loath to separate them, but finally did, drawing her to her feet. She swayed and then buried her head against his chest once more.

I'm nobody's damn hero... And certainly not hers.

Chapter Twelve

Euley emptied the basin of scarlet-stained water into the bucket. Behind her, a fire roared into life, dry tinder popping and crackling as the flames brought much-needed warmth to the room.

Israel dumped his last armload of split logs into the copper bin beside the hearth and then brushed off the lingering bits of debris and wood shavings from his woolen jacket and forearms. He moved to the foot of the bed and slipped his fingers around the wood. Carved from the finest mahogany, the headboard and massive four-poster had been shipped all the way from South America to become Master Benjamin's wedding bed. The rich wood grain now glowed under the splash of firelight. And at the center of the great berth, the feather-filled mattress cupped the sounds of ragged breathing.

Emaline's only sibling fought for his life.

"I done all I can for him but I don't know if he'll make it," Euley whispered. She offered a fragile smile to her husband.

Concern etched the angular planes of the old man's weather-beaten face. "He don' look good, dat's for sure."

"Well dat's how a dyin' man looks," she complained, frustrated at the inability to do more for Miz Emaline's brother. He'd been a gambler, a dandified rover, before the war, but Euley had always liked him. He possessed grit and determination and whenever he came for a visit, he never failed to compliment her on her cooking—his favorite dessert, cobbler made from the best apples picked from the Macintosh grove behind the stables.

Euley tossed a bloodstained rag into the nearby basin. "Bullet went clean through. But it took a chunk of his shoulder with it." Blotches of blood smeared the front of her blue-and-white bibbed apron. Her hands buried into the soiled folds as she wiped them dry on the cotton. She looked down the length of patchwork that covered Masta' Brennen's form until her gaze came to rest upon her husband.

Large black hands, gnarled from a lifetime of working tobacco, gripped the post of the bed. Cream-colored knuckles seemed to glow in the subdued light of the fire. A faded gray shirt and pants had seen a dozen years worth of washings, and leather suspenders held woolen britches in place over narrow hips. He resembled a fence post, battered and lean, and yet, still standing strong against years of adversity. Love filled every chamber of her heart. She moved to the end of the bedpost, and slipped her hand over his. Her head rested against his chest. He smelled of tobacco and the brisk bite of winter. "He's restin' in da Lord's hands now."

Israel pulled her closer, placing his chin on top of her turbaned head. "You done good, suga'pea." A long silence filled the room, broken only by the occasional pop of the firewood and the ragged breathing that emanated from the bed. "Dem Yankees be fightin' for us, you know," he whispered.

Euley nodded and then pulled back to look at him. "Won't change nothin'. They'd be fighting over somethin' else, if'n it wasn't us."

"Maybe we oughta leave too."

"And go where? Dey'd just snag you up in da war. You want to dig latrines?"

He sighed and shook his head, then said, "Moses told me he's goin' north after da winter. He says Miz Emaline can't keep him here if'n he wants to go."

"Moses is a fool. Dere's a roof over his head here an' food in his belly...what little dat's left. You and me, Israel, we's stayin'. We's earned our keep. And, Miz Emaline, she's been good to us ever since Masta' Benjamin died. She even took da time to school us when no one else even cared. I love her, an' we's not gonna desert her." She patted his back and then slipped from his embrace. "Come on, hold da light fo' me while I mop up da blood we trailed luggin' him up here."

Israel lifted the oil lamp from the side table near the bed and held it high while he followed Euley into the hallway. "When do you think Miz Emaline be back?"

Euley kneeled on the floor of the upper landing. "When she's good 'n ready, dat's when." She pulled a damp cloth off her shoulder and wiped up the crimson splatters. "Our job is to keep her brother alive an' hidden 'til she returns."

The front door opened, and Euley paused.

Israel leaned over the banister and held the lamp higher to look down into the shadowy entryway. Tacker stepped inside, dusting snow off the arm of his jacket.

"Any more soldiers?" Israel asked.

Tacker shook his head. "Dey's all gone now, even dose along da river. And it's startin' to snow. Really pilin' up too." He draped his coat over a nail rammed into the wall beside the front door, then stomped his boots, before climbing halfway up the stairs. He then slumped against the wall to watch Euley finish her task.

"Wherever Miz Emaline went with the doctor, she didn't take her horse. I fed da mare but dere ain't much grain left."

Euley rested on Israel's arm and he helped her stand. Her knees cracked when she straightened. "Well, one thing's for sure, ain't nothin' gettin' done while you's all stand around here gabbing." She headed toward the master's suite, throwing her words over her shoulder. "Bring me up two more buckets o' water, Israel. And Tacker, you git down to da linen press an' bring me up some more cloth so's I can make more bandages."

Chapter Thirteen

Reece allowed Saguaro to set the pace along the path through the forest toward Shapinsay. Emaline sat before him sharing the saddle. With her back pressed against his chest, the gentle motion of the horse had lulled her to sleep a half-hour earlier.

His arm tightened around her.

Overhead, clouds lumbered across the sky, sluggish and opaque, blocking the moonlight and stars. Snow waited. Reece could smell it in the air, and when the flakes began, he tucked the cape closer around Emaline. A shiver of cold raced through him, the iciness having more to do with his thoughts than the inclement weather.

As warm and healing as their interlude had been, he knew there could be only heartbreak for Emaline. "*You're a hero.*" Her words taunted him. Had there been no war, no pull on his time or his conscience, he wouldn't have been so damn heroic. He would've taken her right then and there. The beast inside him wore no colors and bore no loyalty to the flag.

To love means to lose.

All too well, Reece knew this to be true. If the past five years had taught him anything, they'd taught him how to survive inside his emptiness. He couldn't remain at Shapinsay, and he would never take Emaline to the battlefield.

The manor house loomed into view at the end of the long lane. Dammit, he needed to get back to his responsibilities—back to living without hope. They were expecting him in Falmouth for commander's call by midnight.

Reece roused her. "Emmy, you're home," he whispered in her ear.

"Umm," she murmured, stirring against him. A snowflake drifted to her cheek. Her eyes opened. "It's snowing," she said.

She turned to look over her shoulder. In the several weeks since knowing this man, she'd learned far more about herself than she'd garnered from all the years that went before. Indeed, in the past few hours she'd uncovered emotions she'd never known existed between a man and woman. Before the war, her life had been lazy and gloatingly arrogant. Her tongue slipped out to dampen her lips, still tender from the incredible warmth and pressure of his kisses.

"It's been snowing for the past hour," he replied. "You've slept soundly."

She leaned back against him again, her eyes slipping closed. How could she climb off his horse now and amble up the front steps as if his presence in her life didn't matter?

How can I let you go?

"I wish time would stand still," she whispered. He rested his chin on her head, his hold tightening around her.

"That's the third time you've mentioned that tonight."

"Well, I do." The heat of his body penetrated the layers of clothing, radiating life into her dying heart. She turned to face him. Her lips trembled as she held back her tears, her fingers lifting to trace a path across the dark bristles of his beard. His lips pursed, and he captured a fingertip as it passed over his mouth.

"What should I say instead?" she asked. It was so hard to face this.

He released her finger and her hand slipped down the front of his coat.

"You say good bye."

The words fell like a blow against her ear and she swallowed, feeling a sharp rush of panic. "Come inside first. At least warm up a bit."

His head shook no and the incredible ache inside her swelled.

The front door creaked open, and they both glanced toward the house. Light from a hand-held lantern punctured through the whirling snow. "Who's out dere?" Euley's stern voice cleaved the darkness.

"It's me, Euley," she shouted. "It's Emaline."

The servant's quick intake of breath precluded the wider opening of the door. "You all right, Miz Emaline?"

"Yes. Yes, I'm fine."

Euley stepped onto the veranda, grasping her shawl around her shoulders. "Get out of this mess. Who you got dere wif you?"

"The colonel. He brought me back."

"Well get inside, both o' you. Snow's startin' to pile up."

Emaline shifted sideways, but Reece tightened his hold around her waist. He leaned forward and buried his face in her hair. "I wish things could be different too," he said, his voice nearly an inaudible murmur. "A different time and place."

He shifted, his muscles tensing.

A second later, Emaline felt herself lifted from the saddle. Slowly, Reece lowered her to the ground.

Snow accumulated around her feet. She stepped back from his horse, her gaze lancing upward to lock with his. A new and equally horrific fear, worry about his safety, began to gnaw at her, a repellant, snaking sensation that coiled around and around into a raw knot in her stomach.

"Please come inside, Reece." Her hands wrapped his leg. She felt his muscles flex beneath his woolen pants. "If only for a moment."

"You know I can't."

Her fear escalated, the bubble of despair hitting the back of her throat. "You can't?" she whispered. "Or you won't?"

A dark, knowing chuckle reached her ears. "Both." He gathered the reins in his hands. "Take care of yourself. And thank you. For everything."

Emaline turned away, her footsteps flying over the ground. Soft pillows of snow bunched beneath her boots. Her cape caught the wind and whipped around her body. Her stomach churned as the fear expanded.

She would never see him again. It was as simple as that.

When she reached the front steps, Emaline staggered up them and bumped into a column. Her breasts still smoldered where he'd cupped them in the forest.

Blood drained from her face in an icy rush.

The imminent blow of loneliness waited—hovering at the edges of her mind. Puffs of white air blended with the flakes as her choppy breath melded with snow. A slight shudder shook her shoulders and she turned back to face Reece.

He remained astride his horse, watching her.

He more resembled a statue now, solid and staunch and chiseled from stone, the image haunting against the milieu of snow. Emaline turned from his impressive form and moved toward the front door.

Don't look back! She followed Euley inside. *Now close the door.*

Close it!

The slamming of the heavy wood echoed through the darkened interior of the house.

"Ain't he comin' in?" Euley asked, setting the lamp on the second step of the staircase.

How could her heart keep beating under such incredible pain? By some miracle, she managed to answer, "No, the colonel has accomplished what he set out to do." Then Emaline swayed. Her knees buckled. Euley sidled up next to her and wrapped an arm about her waist to steady her.

"You all right, Miz Emaline?"

Emaline nodded.

"Don't he know dis weather's gonna get worse afore it gets better?"

She managed another wobbly nod. "Yes. He knows."

Together, they shuffled to the stairs and Euley motioned to the second landing. "Well, go on up there. Someone's waitin' in Masta' Benjamin's room."

Emaline slipped her hand over the wooden railing for support. "W-What?"

"Go on, you'll see."

When Emaline stepped into her late husband's spacious quarters, a soft glow greeted her. In the past five years, she'd rarely entered the room. Her vision swept over the low-burning candles lined up across the mantel. A small fire flickered in the grate, yet the warmth produced by the flames could not penetrate her broken heart.

Long shadows stretched across repeated patterns of ring-necked pheasants draped in the mouths of liver-colored hunting hounds. She'd always hated the wallpaper's somber tones and grotesque cruelty. Her gaze shifted sideways and she spotted the large body occupying the center of the enormous bed.

Her breath caught in her throat.

Euley moved up behind her. "It's yo' brother," she said, her voice barely audible.

"M-my brother?" Emaline's heartbreak withered and she rushed across the room. "Dear God, what happened?" She stared down at Brennen's gaunt face. A sickly pallor blanched his once-striking features. Her hands rose to her mouth to stifle a cry. She silently begged for his chest to move. The bandage plastered across it glowed rusty red. "Is…he dead?"

"Not yet. He stumbled into da house near late dis morning an' I fixed him up as best I could."

Brennen's chest rose with his erratic breathing. Emaline rested her hand on his shoulder, then fluttered shaking fingers up to his face. "W—will he live?"

"Don't know. Da bullet went clean through, though. So dat's good." Euley pointed to the bandage across the top of his shoulder. "But he's lost a lot of blood an' a fever's taken hold. Dat ain't so good."

Emaline leaned forward, burrowing her fingers through the sweat-soaked, cinnamon-brown hair spread across the pillow. She completed a frantic sweep of the room, but saw no supplies. "He needs medicine. Bring some from the cupboard."

"Dere's no medicines, honey."

Emaline speared Euley with a pointed glare. "Why not?"

"Yankees took everythin'."

"Well, I'll send Tacker to fetch Doctor Bishop. Surely he has some."

"Da doctor's gone, Miz Emaline. As soon as Masta Brennen stumbled into da house, I sent Tacker to da Bishop's, but the neighbor said da whole family done moved to Richmond.

Emaline's eyes widened. "What about Doctor Harmon over near Berea? W-we could get him."

"Dat ol' man's been dead a year now according to his widow. Ain't no other doctor left near here."

Fear bloomed inside Emaline's chest. Her brother would die without medicine and proper care. She paced beside the bed. She had to do something. *Think. What doctor is left?*

She stopped in midstride and swung toward Euley. "I'll send for Doc Evans." Heat seared Emaline's face. "Surely he'll help me. I mean, I've spent the entire day assisting him, I can't imagine him saying no."

"But, yo' brother's on da wrong side. Why would da Yankees want to keep him alive?"

Emaline issued a sharp gust of air. "Well, we won't tell anyone besides Doc. If the Yankees find Brennen, they'll take him. And with a wound this severe, he'd die in their prison." The tears held at bay since Reece's departure swelled in her eyes. "But he'll surely die if we don't do something. I'll send Tacker. Doc was just across the ford when we left earlier."

"Snow's piled up thicker than a cotton bale out dere, Miz Emaline. Tacker's too old to go out in dis mess. I'm afraid he'd not make it dere and back."

"Then I'll go." Emaline spun toward the opening and then gasped. Reece filled the doorway.

A helpless, hope-filled sigh spilled from her mouth. The joy of seeing him again briefly flashed only to disappear under the enormous weight of the moment. "Thank God you haven't left yet." She rushed forward and grabbed his hand, tugging him into the room. "I need your help. Please." She bent over Brennen, panic flooding her voice. "He's hurt and burning with fever. H-He needs medicines. And there's no available doctor." In great streaks of sorrow, tears fell from her eyes, plopping in dark splotches onto the quilt that covered her brother. "Please help me…I've nobody else to turn to."

Reece stared at the man, searing the face into memory.

Near thirty-five years old, he guessed. A strange jealousy engulfed him. His gaze settled upon the bandage across the man's shoulder. The amount of blood staining the cloth testified to a serious, possibly mortal wound. He looked at Euley, who stood at the foot of the four-poster, before settling his gaze once more upon Emaline.

"I've no medicines with me," he said.

"But surely you can get some. I mean, after all we've…I mean, since we've…" She searched frantically for words. "He's my brother, Reece."

Her words nestled deep and the bewildering jealousy drifted away from Reece like a column of smoke on the wind. Reality, however, reared its insufferable head once more to shove aside the short-lived comfort of her presence.

Any noble thoughts he'd harbored—wanting to seek her out and explain his fears of love, his uncertainties about keeping her safe, his desire to return to her after the war and asking her to wait for him—everything dissolved beneath the ragged breath rattling from the man in the bed.

Truth's wicked blade carved apart his dreams to remind him of his foolishness. The war severed them far more than his silence ever could. Her brother pledged allegiance to the South and Reece had been killing these traitorous sonsofbitches by the hundreds. He buried his sorrow beneath a mask of stone as his gaze met hers.

"Please Reece," she begged. "He's the only family I have left. Can't you do something to help him?"

"I sympathize with you, but there's not much I can do tonight." His fingers wrapped the bedpost in a tight grip, his knuckles straining white against the wood. He refused to allow the torment coursing through his veins to reach his face.

Emaline's anguished words spilled from her lips in a desperate plea. "You could bring Doc back here."

Reece struggled to ignore the pain clouding her eyes.

She rounded the bed and gripped his sleeve, her fingers digging into his arm. "Please let him come. I'll go fetch him myself and that way you can continue on your journey to Falmouth."

"It's too dangerous for you to go out in this weather."

A heart-wrenching plea slipped from her lips. "But I'll be fine. I know right where Doc is…I could find him easily. We could be back here in less than three or four hours."

Reece shook his head. "The regiment will have moved farther south by now. If you should even be able to find him, he'll be up to his elbows with wounded soldiers. He won't leave them to come back here."

Reece scanned her face, her body. The braid draping her shoulder still trapped a pine needle and the reminder pierced his heart.

Her chin lifted and she stepped closer, her tear-swollen eyes narrowing. Her fingers dug into the muscles of his forearm. "I'm begging you. I've spent this entire day wading through rivers of *Yankee* blood to help Doc heal *my* enemy. And now I need him so very much to heal one of yours."

The fire's glow illuminated her tormented features and his anguish deepened.

"It's not that I don't want to help you. But my hands are tied. I've no medicines with me and Doc isn't available, and I've got orders to report to Falmouth." He paused, and leaned against the bedside table. "You're asking me for something I'm unable to provide right now."

Despair radiated from her eyes as she released her grip on his frockcoat and staggered back several steps. Her hands lowered to the sides of her dress, crumpling the bloodstained material beneath her shaking fingers. "I don't care about your orders. All I care about is my brother."

"I'm so sorry, Emaline, but I can't allow Doc to come here to treat a lone Reb." The remorse in his voice finally slipped out. "And if I did and one of my men should die in his absence? I can't let that happen either." He stepped closer, throwing shadows across her face. "You understand this, don't you?" He reached out, but she shuffled backward another step.

"What I understand is the unfairness of this war."

"Yes, it is unfair." He took a deep breath and then exhaled on a long sigh

"What I can do is take your brother with me and turn him over to one of our brigade doctors—if you want me too that is."

"H-He can't leave. He would surely die in this weather." She stalked to the hearth, pacing before the fire. "I cannot believe this madness." She speared him with a burning glare. "The very least I was hoping for was your help. I mean after *everything* you've taken from me. My food, my livestock…the kisses." Her jaw tensed. A small vein in her neck pulsed.

Caught between frustration and pain, Reece traversed the room and stared down into her widened eyes. Her lips trembled and he pulled his into a taut line. Knowing he was about to break her heart forever. He had no choice. "You're right about the food stores and your land's riches. I did take those things and I paid you double their worth." His heartbeat rattled in a rapid volley high in his throat. "But, if I recall correctly, it was you who begged for my lips."

"How dare you treat me this way!" Tears ran unchecked down her cheeks now.

The damning goad, as he expected, had irrevocably broken their bond.

She pointed a shaking finger toward the bedroom door. "Leave my house this instant."

"I am sorry about your brother's injuries and I do hope he lives." He turned on his boot heel and strode to the door, stopping one last time to look at her. "And for what it's worth, Emaline, I'll guarantee his freedom as long as he remains in this house."

With her finger still pointing, she shrieked, "Get out!"

The depths of his heartbreak nearly caused him to stumble as he surged past the doorframe and enter the darkened hallway.

Emaline jerked when, moments later, the slam of the mansion's front door rattled the glass panes in the bedroom. She darted to the window and shoved aside the curtains. Snow swirled in wicked white streaks, but in the eerie light, she watched Reece pull up into the saddle. He paused and looked back. Despair painted a clear picture across his features. As quickly as she saw the regret, Reece set spurs to his horse and faded from sight.

She turned around and faced the room, her right hand still clutching the lace panel. Like an ebony apparition, Euley shimmered into view. Emaline's left hand rose to cover trembling lips.

The old woman heard every one of their damning words.

Emaline dropped to her knees as wracking sobs bunched her shoulders. "Oh, Euley, what do we do now?"

The servant stepped from Brennen's bedside and shuffled across the room. Defying a lifetime of social division, she lowered to the floor beside Emaline and pulled her into a tight embrace. The fire's glow fell over them as the old woman rocked her in an age-old and comforting sway.

Chapter Fourteen

Twelve hours later, a loud pounding on the mansion's front door forced Emaline from Brennen's bedside. Leaden feet carried her down the stairs. She eased open the heavy barrier to encounter a blinding, snow-white dawn.

A half-dozen Federal soldiers stood before her on the veranda.

One man pointed to six mules ground-tied at the bottom of the steps. "We've been ordered to bring these animals to this plantation and give them to a widow McDaniels. Is that you, ma'am?"

"Yes, I'm Mrs. McDaniels." Emaline squinted against the whiteness of the new day. Her gaze darted from the men to the pack-mules, their pewter-gray backs burdened under massive crates.

Her attention returned to the young courier. "What's all this about?" she snapped, the blistering wind penetrating her work dress. She opened the door and stepped onto the veranda, wrapping her arms across her chest in an attempt to ward off the chill.

"Compliments of the United States Army, 6th Ohio Regiment, and Colonel Reece Cutteridge, ma'am. He thanks you for your heroic endeavors in aiding his wounded during the engagement at United States Ford." He paused briefly to withdraw a printed form and a pencil from under his greatcoat. He handed the items to her and shaking fingers accepted them. "I'll just need your signature, ma'am, and then we'll be on our way."

Murmurs in the hallway caused Emaline to glance over her shoulder. Euley, Israel, a wide-eyed Tacker and Moses filled the door's opening. She turned to the soldier again and scrawled her name across the document before handing the items back with a mumbled thank-you. The men tromped off the veranda, remounted, and rode out of sight.

Tacker and Moses surged past her and descended the steps. Her gaze followed them as her lips pulled tight.

He's trying to compensate for his appalling behavior. She snorted. *A little too late, Colonel.*

The man was nothing but a contradiction. Last night he spewed such despicable words. And this morning he delivers the goods? Emaline stared in bewilderment.

In less than five minutes, the men had stacked all the wooden crates inside the empty parlor.

"I'll go stable da mules and be right back," Tacker said. "Come on, Moses. You can help me."

Euley started a fire to chase away the nip in the air. A few minutes later, an odd silence permeated the room as they all stared at the box collection.

"Well, somebody should open one, I suppose," Emaline quipped. She crossed her arms and stared at the bare floor, anger toward Reece still percolating inside her despite his gifts.

Euley unbuckled the straps on the largest crate and then pushed aside the lid. Her gasp filled the room as her hands clapped in front of her. A moment later, she reached inside the container. "Will you look at dis," she said, lifting out a heavy cloth sack, the word *BEANS* stamped in black ink across the muslin.

Another bag stamped *RICE* followed.

"And look…" Israel scooted over to join her, pulling out several more canvas-wrapped packages to reveal bacon and hams. They mounded them on the floor beside Emaline's feet and Euley glanced up, smiling. "He's given us back our food."

"And mo' besides," Israel added.

Emaline swallowed. She was thankful Reece had done the right thing in replacing the supplies, but she nonetheless could not forgive him for his reprehensible behavior regarding her brother who still hovered near death upstairs.

I deserve an apology, if nothing more.

Dozens of potatoes, both sweet and white, and carrots, some still with their tops dried in place, piled up around her. She finally unfolded her arms and peered into the box. A veritable bounty still filled the interior. And this was just the first container. What did the others hold? Emaline nudged aside the vegetables near her feet and sunk to the floor to help.

Together, they removed muslin bags stuffed full of coffee and stacked them into swaying towers beside the vegetables. Sacks held flour, sugar and several bundles of fresh bread. Each one carefully wrapped in cotton toweling, piled alongside everything else. Chunks of salt-pork, preserved for the winter, mounded into another pile beside the spuds. Jars of preserves and meats reflected the fire's light.

A half-hour of discoveries later, all the crates were empty.

"What's dis?" Euley asked, pulling out a large portmanteau from the bottom of the last one.

Dropping a ham to the floor, Emaline scooted over beside the woman and took the leather chest. Settling it across her lap, she opened the latch. A letter rested atop a collection of amber bottles.

She broke the wax seal on the envelope and withdrew the letter. Her stomach wobbled as bold handwriting swirled before her eyes.

She began to read:

My Dearest Emaline,

Please forgive me for my behavior last night. I am so sorry I hurt you. You did not deserve such callous treatment. I know you don't understand the responsibilities that I face, and unfortunately, they far outweigh any personal feelings or desires I possess. I hope one day you will come to understand this and find it in your heart to forgive me. Inside the case is a collection of medical supplies, including several potent drugs. Doc has assured me these will help your brother regain his strength. And contrary to what you now believe, I do hope he recovers.

I will never forget you or the courage you have displayed. The brief time we spent together will forever remain in my heart.

I am eternally in your debt,

Reece

The tears blurred beneath Emaline's lashes and plopped onto her hand. She swiped them away with a dash of her fingers, then refolded the letter.

"Well? What'd he say?" Euley asked, peering into her face.

"H-he sent medicines for Brennen. And..." She paused, then whispered, "He also says he's sorry."

"Well he oughta be," she snapped. "Here, let me take a look at what's in there." She pulled the case off Emaline's lap. "It sure is a fancy kit," she said, touching the bottles as if they were pure gold. "Here's chloroform, and laudanum, and morphine." She reverently skimmed over each one. "And look. Here's some quinine and fresh bandages too." She smiled up at Emaline. "Yo' brother might just have a fightin' chance, now."

"Yes." Emaline nodded, clutching the letter against her chest. "Yes, he might."

The old woman clucked her tongue. "Da colonel still cares 'bout you, Miz Emaline. Why else would he—"

Emaline climbed to her feet. "This is the last time I want his name mentioned in this house," she announced, shoving the letter into her apron pocket. "Now hand me the case, and you all start putting away these things."

With the cumbersome medical kit secure in her arms, Emaline headed toward the hallway. As she passed the men kneeling near the crate of grain for the mules and her mare she asked, "And will one of you please bring me a fresh pot of water?"

She disappeared up the stairs.

Chapter Fifteen

Reece glared into the ashen face of Major General Ambrose Burnside. "With all due respect, sir, I refuse to send another man or animal into that wallow." A roll of thunder nearly drowned out his words.

"I concur with Colonel Cutteridge," added General John Cochrane, his thin mustache pulling taut over his lips. "Surely you realize the foolishness of continuing this course in these conditions, General."

The bushy facial hair that swept both sides of Burnside's countenance twitched as he leaned over the maps spread out on the table. "We've just gotten rid of McClellan and his foolish failure to pursue General Lee after Antietam, gentlemen." His reluctance to lead reflected in his voice. "Even though I'm inclined to agree this is not the same engagement we faced a month ago, this shift around our enemy's flanks is vitally important to break the stalemate. It is in our best interest to continue despite the weather. We certainly don't want to lose our momentum."

"What momentum?" Reece grumbled. "There's no way we can move in closer." He cut his gaze to the Cavalry commander, George Bayard, a friend who'd requested Reece's attendance at this meeting.

General Bayard nodded. "I agree with Cutteridge, as well. The rain is relentless and the mud is too deep. We've lost our element of surprise. Hell, we can't even shift around Fredericksburg—"

"The damn Rebs know our plans anyway. This is all a waste of time," Reece interjected.

Burnside shot him a pointed glare, and snapped, "What's he doing here? This meeting is only for my generals."

"I asked him to attend because he's already inspected the route you're suggesting," Bayard said. "And he knows what he's talking about, General, so I recommend you listen to him."

Burnside grumbled, stubbed his cigar into the ground near his boot, then returned to the maps. "I refuse to allow this type of insubordination. When I assumed command, I promised President Lincoln we could accomplish his request to capture Richmond. Since we can't go through Fredericksburg, by God, we will go around it. I'm honor-bound to try."

Reece mumbled under his breath. "Honor-bound, my ass." He turned back toward the group. "Look, my scouts report Lee is already shifting troops along the river to parallel our every move. We'll be cut off again, and more men will needlessly die." Reece scowled at his immediate superior. "This is all bullshit, George, every bit of it."

Reece spun on his boot heel and moved to the entrance of the large tent. He stared out at the pouring rain. His frustrated thoughts retraced the fiasco of the past three days.

The first morning, General Burnside proclaimed to his troops that the auspicious moment had arrived to strike the mortal blow to the rebellion. Under cloudy skies, he ordered the Army of the Potomac into massive columns. In majestic pageantry, he sent infantry, artillery and cavalry up the river from Falmouth in order to flank Fredericksburg. The campaign began with high hopes, the soldiers enthusiastic and eager to thwart the enemy and avenge their fallen comrades of a month before.

By late afternoon, however, fog rolled in from the Rappahannock.

By nightfall, the torrential rain began, soaking more than a hundred-thousand soldiers in a matter of seconds. As the night progressed, the Army of the Potomac resembled little more than a suffused and shivering mass of

Union blue. Soldiers feverishly pitched tents that evening in an attempt to seek some type of shelter from the drenching onslaught. The biting sleet that followed brought the already-weary infantrymen to their knees. Relentless claps of thunder split the night as the deluge continued. By dawn of the second day, the roads had deteriorated into mud bogs.

A slamming fist to the table behind him drew Reece's glare.

"There's got to be a way around these bastards," the Major General snarled, intending to push his weary soldiers onward.

Reece sighed and shook his head again. Burnside simply followed in the wake of a half-dozen other generals who had failed to perform to the high expectations as Commander of the Army of the Potomac. And this morning, he began the offensive again. The first regiments of infantry finally slogged their way through the mud and muck to reach the river. Their incredible endeavor, however, proved short-lived. The pontoon and artillery trains, which would have given them access across the waterway, had been ensnared within a two-mile-long quandary and their wagons sank in mud up to their wheel hubs. Cannons mired so deep that neither twelve-horse teams nor groups of men hauling on ropes could move them. Wranglers watched as teams of mules sank deeper and deeper in a vain attempt to extricate the wagons.

Throughout the appalling afternoon, dozens of horses and mules died of exhaustion. Soldiers hooked heavy chains around the necks of leading mules to try to free them, but the unbearable suction of mud pulled the life from each animal. Instead of freeing the teams, the wranglers only succeeded in breaking the necks of the stalwart beasts.

Spirits plummeted, as did the confidence of the junior officers toward their commanding general. Infantrymen fell by the thousands into the mucky chaos, their shoes literally sucked off their feet by the quagmire.

Reece turned to face the ongoing argument again.

His voice carried above the din. "This whole damn thing has been a disgrace from the start. We haven't had a victory since Antietam, nor have my men been paid in six months. And now, you're asking them to continue in this demoralizing muck, not to mention risk more good mounts we can't afford to lose. And for what?" He glanced at his commander. "I'm calling my men out, George." His words echoed above the driving rain that pounded the tent.

General Burnside lifted bushy eyebrows and stared at Reece. "Are you disobeying my direct order, Colonel Cutteridge?"

"Call it what you want, sir. Frankly, at this point, I don't care." Reece slapped his gloves against his thigh and jerked his gaze away in frustration. Another clap of thunder rocked the encampment. The general issued a deep sigh and paced the room.

General Sumner, commander of the Right Grand Division, shouted above the noise. "They already know our plans, Ambrose. Cutteridge is right about that. Let's just wait until the rain eases up a bit. Then we can try again farther downriver."

Burnside smacked his hand against his thigh, his lips compressing. The air around the men vibrated under the tumult. "Well, apparently even God is behind all of you." Rain dripped from the canvas ceiling into a puddle in the center of the map, underscoring his words. "Fine. I'll halt the advancement and leave for Washington in the morning to share my report with the President. In the meantime, gather your men and bivouac where you can until you receive further orders from me."

With barely a salute to their commander, the officers dispersed into the rain-soaked afternoon to begin the monumental task of collecting their mud-covered troops.

Chapter Sixteen

Brennen narrowed his eyes and ground his words toward Emaline. "Don't you understand? I've got to go back." His injury had left a gruff tone to his voice along with a persistent niggling cough.

She shoved her chair backward and surged to her feet. "Two and a half months ago you nearly died. And it was just three days ago that you finally stood without help."

"I can't sit around here when my boys need me. Every day, more Yanks ride by. If I'm to go, it's got to be soon."

"I refuse to listen to any more of this nonsense." She gathered up the empty dinner dishes and crossed to the swinging doorway. A carefully placed hip shoved it open, and she entered the kitchen. Using a cane for support, Brennen trailed behind her.

"It's a matter of honor, Em," he said, the wooden tip thumping against the floor in cadence with his shuffling footfalls.

"Honor, my eye. There's no honor in dying for a lost cause."

"We've not lost yet, not by a goddamn long shot. And as long as Jeb Stuart rides, I too shall fight."

"Don't curse in front of me." Emaline knew her brother would clamor to rejoin the war as soon as he could walk unaided. She just didn't expect his fervor to return this soon.

I'll guarantee his freedom as long as he remains in this house.

As if he had spoken the words only yesterday, Reece's statement blistered into recall. She knew he'd referred only to Brennen's *healing time* at Shapinsay.

Emaline had lost so much already. The thought of losing her brother now drove a knife through her heart. "Haven't you had enough of this ridiculous war? Just look at you. You can barely walk without a cane."

Brennen leaned against the table and draped his arm over her shoulder. "I know you don't understand. I don't expect you to understand."

"No, I don't understand any of this." She sidestepped away from him. "I don't understand why men butcher one another, or why they think something will be solved in the doing of it." Scenes of wounded men, dying men, men who'd never see their loved ones again surged into her mind.

Brennen folded his hand around her braid as he'd done those many years ago in their youth. Only two years separated them in age. "Sometimes I still see you as my baby sister, chubby cheeks and all." Soft chuckles gave way to another coughing bout. Emaline reached for a chair and carefully lowered him onto the seat. She splashed water from the pitcher into a cup.

He gasped for air, the ordeal over.

"Here drink this, you silly goose," she said, raising the glass to his lips.

He swallowed and then leaned his head back against the chair. "Well, I thought I was getting better." A shallow smile tugged at his lips.

When she saw the grin, Emaline's expression softened and she gently batted his arm.

Then they heard hooves pounding the hard-packed earth.

Horses.

Emaline rushed to the window and raked back the curtain. At least twenty Union soldiers appeared between the veranda and the shanties. Several already had dismounted and were striding toward the door.

"Yankees!" she hissed.

Whirling, she pulled Brennen toward the servant stairway beside the back door, and shoved him onto the small landing just as one cavalryman banged a fist against the wood. The window glass rattled under the blow.

"Open this damn door!" a gruff voice bellowed on the opposite side.

"Hurry," she whispered against Brennen's ear. "Get inside Euley's trundle bed." They'd hidden him the same way twice before in recent weeks.

Just when her brother began his assent, another wracking cough doubled him over. He slumped against Emaline, pulling her down onto the darkened landing with him. She glanced over her shoulder to the back door. Less than five feet separated them from the Yankees.

Scrambling to her feet, Emaline stood over Brennen's tormented form and tugged on his good shoulder. "Get up," she pleaded. "They're going to break down the door."

He didn't budge.

A rifle butt exploded glass and Emaline's fear along with it. Late-afternoon sun silhouetted a hulking shape as crystalline shards glinted in the rays of light that split around him. Emaline dropped her hold on her brother and stretched sideways. Shaking hands rose to hold the door's safety bolt in place. Boots thumping on a hardwood floor echoed from the dining room as more soldiers entered by way of the front door.

Pounding footfalls moved closer and closer.

Emaline's frantic heartbeat resonated in her ears, nearly drowning out Brennen's ceaseless coughing. An agonizing second later, the dining room door swung open as the enemy spilled into her kitchen.

Her grip fell from the bolt. Straightening, she swept the hem of her work dress over Brennen's huddled form. Several soldiers advanced toward the landing, knocking over a chair near the table in the process.

They loomed over her, their faces blurring into sneering demons.

Emaline's fears multiplied into a harsh shriek when a Yankee reached for her arm. Her hands rose and she raked her fingernails across his face.

A hell-spawned yelp met her ears. "Sonofabitch." The man snared her wrist and hauled her toward him. "This bitch is wilder than a goddamned hornet..."

The sentence disappeared under the ensuing scuffle as the man jerked Emaline away from the landing. Responding to her cries, Brennen managed to reach out for her ankle, but another bout of coughing seized him and he lost his hold. A hand snaked in through the slivered opening on the backdoor to search for and unlock the bolt.

"She's a damn hellcat. Somebody get over here and get her off me!" Several soldiers sprang forward and a half-dozen pairs of hands pulled her away, their fingers digging into the muscles of her upper arms. Emaline twisted in a futile attempt to flee their hold. Dying sunlight poured into the kitchen from the fractured doorway and outlined five more Yankees.

They loomed over Brennen's stricken form.

"Well, lookie what we've found." One burly soldier, his face covered with scrubby whiskers, poked Brennen with his rifle barrel. "Do you think we've got us a real live Johnny here?"

Another quickly added, "Kill the sonofabitch."

"Noooooo, please don't." Emaline's pleas ricocheted around the room.

A lanky soldier squatted near Brennen. Grabbing the back of his shirt, he flipped him over. "Maybe he's a deserter. Wounded too." He dragged Brennen from the landing, past the back door, and deposited him in the center of the room. The scrape of glass against wood rode with him.

Emaline frantically scanned the soldiers for the man in charge. Three yellow slash marks on the coat sleeve of a barrel-chested man told her she faced a sergeant. She glared up at him. "Please leave him alone."

"He's hurt. Bleedin' too." Lanky pointed his carbine to the slow spread of blood permeating Brennen's shirt near his shoulder. An infection that just wouldn't heal had caused the wound to reopen more than once. A trickle of red also glistened near the corner of her brother's slack mouth.

Emaline broke free and rushed to him. She bent to assist him in sitting up. Her rage became a ruthless inferno. "How dare you burst into my home."

Burley cocked his head to the side and peered at her. "Well pardon me all to hell. I guess no one told you there's a war goin' on out yonder?"

"You have no right to barge in here like this!"

He rolled back on his boot heels and laughed. "Well, now, my cap'n gave me the right, ma'am." He glanced at his comrades and they nodded in agreement, grins etching their faces. "Ain't that right, boys? The cap'n gave us permission to just barge right on in here like this, didn't he?"

Burley grabbed Emaline's arm, righted the chair, and then shoved her into it. Behind her, four soldiers pulled open the pantry and ransacked the small area.

"What do you want?" she snarled.

A smile broke the bushy beard in two as Burley revealed a row of large teeth. "We're on a foraging mission, ma'am."

"You Yankees have been here before. There's nothing left!"

All eyes stared down at Brennen sprawled across the floor near her feet. "Well, it appears them last ones must've forgotten about him."

"He's hurt." Fear spiked her voice. "Surely, you can see that."

Bending down, Burley peered into her eyes as he reached sideways to pat Brennen on his head like a child. Her brother attempted to slap the calloused hand away. "You know, these Johnnies have a remarkable way of gettin' better and healin' up. That causes us some concern because we can't kill them fast enough."

Behind him, the other soldiers resumed rummaging through the cabinets.

"He's a far cry from being healed up and in fighting form," Emaline snarled.

Burley pointed a finger in her face, his dirty nail grazing the bridge of her nose. His eyes narrowed into slits. "I'm in charge here, lady, so why don't you let me make them decisions, all right?"

Brennen struggled to rise. Emaline pushed away Burley's hand and bent to help her brother, angling him over to the chair beside hers.

Fortifying himself against another bout of coughing, Brennen pierced the sergeant with a steely glare. "There is no need for you to taunt my sister."

All eyes swerved toward him.

Lanky sucked in a deep breath. "Ooohweee, will you just listen to that perfect Virginny drawl, boys. Ain't no doubt this here's a real-live Reb." He waved his carbine in the air around Brennen's head.

Desperate to end the ever-increasing nightmare, Emaline stood and pointed her finger toward the pantry. "Take whatever you want and leave."

"Well now, it looks like we've found what we need right here." Lanky motioned to Brennen who slumped sideways in the chair. The rifle poked him in the shoulder just beneath the ever-widening pool of blood. "We'll just be takin' him off your hands now, missy." He nodded toward the group, then reached down and jerked Brennen up.

Emaline's intake of breath burned all the way to her stomach. Sharp words rang through the room to halt their steps. "Colonel Reece Cutteridge of the 6th Ohio Cavalry has guaranteed my brother's safety while he is under the roof of this house." The soldiers gawped at one another and Emaline could tell from their puzzled expressions that they weighed the veracity of her words. "That's right," she said, her chin sharply rising. "Colonel Cutteridge declared his safety since I lent aid to his regiment during a military engagement back in December. I helped their doctor, and in so doing gained my brother's freedom while he recuperated inside this house."

Burly inhaled and then nodded over to Lanky, a lopsided grin lifting his lips. "Well this must be our lucky day, ma'am. You see, Colonel Cutteridge, ain't our commanding officer."

Lanky dragged Brennen toward the shattered door.

Emaline launched herself at the man in an attempt to stop him, but he shoved her aside. She banged into the table and crumpled into the chair. It toppled, carrying her to the floor. Blazing pain radiated down the side of her face from her cheek's impact with the hard wood.

With reckless speed, the remaining Yankees cleared the house of supplies. They swung the canvas sacks over their shoulders, and with faces wreathed in wide smiles, tossed several mocking thank yous in her direction.

The men followed Lanky out the door and back to their waiting horses. Several others joined in pulling Brennen down the back steps and across the yard. Unceremoniously, they plopped him face down over a horse. He frantically pushed against the animal in an effort to slide from it, but a blow to his back from a rifle's butt put a stop to his struggles.

Emaline staggered down the steps after them, her sobs hysterical.

She wrapped her fingers around the horse's bridle to prevent its departure, but Lanky placed his dirty boot against her shoulder. With a quick shove, he propelled her to the ground and then set spurs to his horse.

Seconds later, Brennen disappeared from sight around the corner of the house.

Chapter Seventeen

Headquarters of the 6th Ohio
Falmouth, Virginia
February 28th, 1863

"Colonel, you in there?"

Reece tossed the map on the desk and leaned back in his chair. "Yes, come in."

Lieutenant Glave pushed open the canvas flap and peered inside. "Someone's here askin' for you, sir."

The aide-de-camp stepped aside to allow the visitor to enter the tent.

Reece raked a hand through his disheveled hair and waited while the cloaked guest stepped into his quarters. The young lieutenant dropped the flap into place and disappeared from view.

"What can I do for you?" Reece asked, remaining seated. He scanned the petite form. A woman lurked somewhere beneath the voluminous folds of a full-length Kinsale cloak.

He exhaled sharply. *Sonofabitch.* Obviously, his men thought a prostitute might be just the thing to cheer their sullen commander. He'd pay her and send her on her way. He started to reach into his pocket to retrieve a coin, when something stopped him. He leaned forward, his brows pulling together.

No prostitute on earth owned such an expensive garment.

His stomach muscles tightened.

An olive-green leather glove lifted to push the deep-ruffled hood backward and moments later, the cape swirled from the woman's body to the chair.

Blistering heat speared Reece when a thick, coffee-colored braid tumbled down her back.

He shoved upward, his chair toppling backward as he rammed to his feet. Emaline turned to face him.

"I'm in need of your help," she said, her voice shallow and strained. An ugly bruise rode across her left cheekbone, the edges a disturbing shade of violet.

"Good God, Emaline—what happened?" Her incredible reappearance into his life pierced the chambers of Reece's empty heart with a stabbing thrust.

"I had Yankee visitors. They helped themselves to my provisions."

He rounded the desk, knocking sideways a stack of papers in his haste. "You shouldn't have fought them." Even as he said them, he realized the significance of the words. She'd fought him, hadn't she? Of course, she'd fight anyone else.

"Yes. But this time, they took my brother."

An immediate recollection of the wounded man and the night of his discovery flooded through Reece. The strangled question fell from his mouth. "He recovered, then?"

"Yes, but he's still weak. The ailment lingers in his lungs."

"Here. Sit down." He jerked around a spindle-back chair beside his desk and angled the seat toward her. Emaline settled onto the wood, pulling her cape and scarf across her lap. Reece pushed aside the papers, then reached for the whiskey bottle sitting on the table. He pulled the cork, his gaze never leaving hers. "I can't believe you're actually here." Reaching into a nearby portable cabinet, he produced a small tumbler, sloshed the amber liquid into the cut crystal, and then handed it to her. "Drink this."

She studied the glass, then took it from his hand. Where their fingers touched, an instant burn sizzled. In one long swig, she downed the potent liquid. A soft cough fell from her mouth as the whiskey settled.

How in God's name had she even found him? How many soldiers had she asked before locating his camp? A hundred? A thousand? The entirety of Spotsylvania County crawled with Federal troops, and yet, miraculously, here she sat.

She placed the glass upon the desk and speared him with a pointed glare. "I've come to collect upon your promise."

His eyebrows lifted. "My promise?"

"Yes, Colonel, the ill-gotten promise I received in regards to my brother. Surely, you haven't forgotten our time together so soon, have you?" She didn't move, yet any fool could have seen the fury that coiled inside her by the color washing over her face.

Her words lacerated Reece. He deserved her animosity; regretted his cruel words every day since their parting argument. When he closed his eyes at night, she was the last image that flickered behind his lids. When he awakened, she was the first image to appear.

"Allow me to refresh your memory. You said as long as Brennen remained at Shapinsay, he would be free. Remember?" She narrowed her eyes. "Well, your Yankee heathens barged into my home and removed him—thereby breaking the promise you made to me that night. So now, I've come to collect."

Emaline sat bolt upright in the chair, yet he clearly saw the exhaustion hovering at the edge of her composure. The hurt and shame he'd forced her to feel that night raced over him again in a chilling reminder.

"Yes," he softly replied. "I remember every detail of our time together." Their gazes caught. Hers slid away. "And I also remember the promise."

Her gaze skipped back. "I need to know what you're going to do about it. And unfortunately for you, this time not a single one of your vouchers can ever hope to correct this tragedy." She tried to bolster her emotions with defiance, but the attempt failed and chunks of the armor fell away with each shaky breath she drew.

Reece swallowed. The inevitable storm cloud of remorse settled over him. He straightened to his full height and readjusted the saber belted around his waist. The joy of seeing her again swelled inside him. So unexpected. So unbelievably wonderful. Even though she now demanded something that conflicted with everything he believed in…as sure as he would draw another breath, he knew he would do whatever he could to help her.

He strode to the tent's entrance and swept back the canvas flap. "Find Major Neale and have him report to me, at once."

"Yes, sir!" the closest soldier responded, and then sprinted off.

Reece turned to Emaline again. She shifted in her chair to face him, her fingers curling around a worn wooden slat. She bit her lower lip to stop its tremble. The frantic look that followed forced him across the enclosure and back to her side. He dropped to a knee before her, the muscle in his thigh tightening.

In so many ways, it seemed, he was destined to be this woman's protector.

"I'll find him, Emmy. I promise." His breath caressed the hideous bruise and her head lowered. The tears she'd obviously held at bay for so long, pooled behind her dark lashes.

Slowly, they trickled down her cheeks. "Thank you," she mumbled.

He nodded. "How long ago was he taken?"

"Three days."

His breath hissed inward. "Three days is a long time, but I'll see what I can find out."

The canvas flap swept open.

Jackson entered the tent.

"Are you out of your damn mind?" his friend roared. "You'll lose your eagles if you're caught."

Reece stood near the supply wagons, staring across the encampment. "What good is my rank if I can't use it?"

"What you want to do is treason, you imbecile," Jackson rasped. "Plain and simple."

"Look." He speared the man with a razor sharp glare. "I've thought long and hard about this and I'm willing to take the risk."

"You're willing to lose your command and face a possible court martial? And for what? A damn woman?"

Reece clenched his jaw, his hand curling into a tight fist. "I'm warnin' you. Don't start with that again."

Jackson raised both hands. "Hey, don't blame me for feeling this way. This isn't like you."

A strange emptiness settled into the pit of Reece's stomach. He sighed and looked back at his tent. Emaline slept inside on his cot. The exhaustion of the three days she'd spent searching for him finally overwhelmed her. "It doesn't matter anymore. I'm willing to take the chance."

"Why?"

Reece slid his gaze back, a bitter taste burning his mouth. He considered not answering, in truth, because he did not want to explore the reasons behind his reckless decision. Then he sighed, and simply said, "Because I promised her."

"Promised her? Bullshit. This isn't about that, and you damn well know it."

Reece fought against the truth. His head pounded, trapped in a vise of his own making. He pulled in a deep breath; the pain inside his heart bored down with teeth and claws.

The sulfuric smell of burning wood from a thousand campfires settled over him. The regimental encampment stretched out in a canvas city nearly a quarter of a mile wide. Everything about the bivouac reflected his trademark touch—orderly and disciplined. Yet the exact opposite raged inside Reece. Since meeting Emaline, nothing about his thoughts or emotions had been orderly or disciplined. Nothing had made any sense after riding onto Shapinsay four months ago. Nothing mattered except helping her now.

"It's just that…" Reece paused and his voice spiraled down into a guttural whisper. "I spent the years since my wife's death running from my miserable life. That's the damnable truth of it all." He stared at his white-knuckled fingers wrapping the side of the wagon. "My ranch, my stock, everything I owned meant nothing. I went through the motions of living." Reece scanned the encampment again. "And then this war came along and I buried my pain under the mantle of command. Giving orders gave me the outlet I needed to ignore the detestable void. And it worked perfectly until that little hellion in there pointed her rifle at me and pulled the goddamned trigger."

He glanced over his shoulder back to his tent. No woman on earth could bring to him what Emaline represented. The softness in her eyes as she offered herself on a bed of pines, the remembered taste of her lips, and the softness of her skin. Her heartbreak when he held himself back...and her supreme sadness when he couldn't help her brother; everything tore a hole in his heart.

His sigh went gut-deep and carried his angst. "For the first time in five miserable years, I feel something." He turned to his friend. "No other woman would've sought me out like this, nor demand me to help her. Especially, not with the way I left her believing I misused her feelings."

Jackson leaned his back against the wagon and crossed his arms. "And did you?" he questioned, looking at the command tent.

"No." Reece smoothed out the word. "But, I let her think so."

"If you truly care about her, why did you push her away?"

"You said it yourself, remember? Back at Shapinsay. This wasn't a good time to fall in love, and the same war which brought her to me will only pull us apart." A scattering of pictures, words, and feelings raced through Reece's mind. For a brief moment, a flicker of hope flared, only to be lost in the next. "And I told her that same thing in so many words that night I found her brother." He dropped a lasso around his sadness, reining in the torment. "But, that doesn't mean I can't help her now. If finding Brennen will ease some of the pain I've caused her, then I'll do everything in my power to help her. I owe her that much."

Jackson raked his hand across his face and glanced back. "Hell's fire, Reece...at least send someone else. A patrol, maybe, or a few handpicked men."

"No. I won't endanger anyone else. Since I'm choosing to help her, it's my responsibility."

"A colonel and a woman? All alone doing God knows what? Damnation, all you'll accomplish is raising suspicion. You know this as well as I do. Wherever the Reb's being held, assuming he's even still alive, you can't just barge in there and ask for his release." Seconds passed in strained silence until a harsh curse fell from Jackson's mouth. He finally said, "Since you're so damned determined to do this, I'm coming along."

"No. You'll need to take my command in case something happens."

"Look, pal," he snapped, "if you're thrown into the brig, we both know I've absolutely no desire to be in charge. So shut the hell up. I'm going along whether you like it or not."

A lopsided smile lifted Reece's lips. "Well, don't blame me then when we're both rotting in prison." He extended his hand.

And Jackson's firm clasp met his. "Deal," he said, then released his grip. "But first, we need to find out where her brother's being held."

Reece nodded, leaning against the wagon. "And I've got an idea about how we can break him out when we do. Tell me what you think about this…"

Chapter Eighteen

Evening mist settled over a cluster of warehouses that lined the pier at Aquia Creek Landing. Reece surveyed the area before him. Light emanated from the dirty windows of several outbuildings. A soldier slumped against the wall of the nearest clapboard shack and tugged his coat tighter to ward off the chill. Beside him, an Enfield rifle rested against the weathered wood.

Good. Caught him off guard.

Reece turned in his saddle, and peered at the ambulance wagon behind him. Jackson and Emaline perched atop the seat of the two-teamed rig. He nodded toward them, tugged his slouch hat lower, then spurred Saguaro forward into the clearing. When the wagon lumbered over the railroad tracks, the guard lurched into a stand, grabbed his weapon, and turned to face them.

Light from the closest window laid a glint across the embroidered threads of the medical officer epaulets that now graced Reece's shoulder. He rode straight toward the young sentinel and reined to a stop. The soldier stood straighter, and offered the obligatory salute.

"Where are they keeping the prisoners, son?" Reece asked, returning the gesture.

"In the warehouses, sir." He angled his head. "Behind me."

"And your commanding officer?"

The private pointed to the shed where the lamplight glowed. "He's inside there, sir."

Reece motioned to the building and Jackson nodded, rolling the vehicle to a stop in front of the structure. A moment later, they all dismounted and entered.

The wintry air that followed Reece into the dimly lit room swirled cigar smoke into a shifting cloud. He peered through the rippling glow at four soldiers playing cards around a small wooden table. Fat cigars clenched between their teeth generated the thick haze.

Behind him, Emaline's delicate cough interrupted their game.

A scrawny captain leapt to his feet, followed by the other three men. They laid aside their cigars and offered quick, sloppy salutes.

Reece stifled a smile.

As he hoped, arriving late at night had caught these boys off guard too. A glance at the ante in the middle of the table revealed a dozen greenbacks, two seated liberty halves, and a shiny one-dollar gold piece. With a pot that large, these men would want to return to their game as soon as possible.

Good.

The soldiers scanned his felt-green shoulder bars, before dropping their gaze to his emerald waist sash. Reece read their minds: *Medical. No big deal.*

The smile threatened his lips again. He returned their salute.

Infantry are so predictable.

"Who's in charge?" he asked, his voice slicing through the gloom.

The young officer stepped forward, extending his hand for the customary shake. "I am, sir. Captain David Wiggins."

"Major Stevens," Reece replied, returning the soldier's greeting. The name was too nondescript to set anyone on alert or lead to any questions later. "I'm afraid we have a problem, Captain." The straightforward approach would intimidate the young man. And indeed, the soldier stood a bit taller, sucking in his stomach.

"What's that?" Captain Wiggins looped his thumbs in the waist pockets of a dark-blue vest.

Reece sighed and pulled off his gauntlets, tucking them into the waistband of his saber belt. "I need to assume responsibility for one of your charges."

"Now?"

Reece impaled him with a glare. "Yes, Captain. Now. I'm a busy man. I don't have all night."

A quick wave of the man's hand indicated the small office near the back of the room as he glanced at his card-playing comrades. "Give me a few minutes here, gentlemen, and help yourself to the brandy. I'll be back soon enough to take this money off your hands." The soldiers nodded, laughing as they reached for their cigars, one man lifting the half-emptied bottle sitting on a side table.

Wiggins led the way to a battered oak desk. He scanned Jackson and Emaline, then offered them the empty chairs against the wall. He shrugged his shoulders when they refused. "All right," he said, rounding his desk. "What's all this about, Major?"

"I understand you have prisoners awaiting incarceration at Point Lookout. Is that correct?"

"Yes. A hundred and fifty." The man shifted his gaze to Emaline. The left side of her face still sported the fading bruise. Would he be curious enough to ask why? From the corner of his eye, Reece saw Emaline step back into the swirling shadows and lower her head, clasping her hands in front of her as if in prayer. The cape she wore swathed her from head-to-toe, and bruised or not, she sent the clear message she wanted no part of the captain's appraisal.

The young man dismissed Jackson with a curt nod before planting himself in the spindle-backed chair. He leaned backward and clasped his hands behind his head. "The transport picks them up at dawn tomorrow." His gaze resettled on Reece, and a flicker of suspicion surfaced. "Why do you want to know?"

Reece pulled a folded letter from the breast pocket of his frock coat. Forging General Hooker's signature across the bottom of the document took practice, and he'd spent the better part of an hour drafting the request. He snapped the paper open with a sharp rustle, then passed the orders on to the captain. "One of them has cholera."

Wiggins dropped his mouth open as the chair legs hit the floor. "Ch— cholera?" He reached for the correspondence. "Christ Almighty. Are you certain?"

Reece nodded, waiting while the officer scanned the letter. The youthful features shifted from shock and fear to pulse-pounding anger. He dropped the missive to the desk and glared at Reece, his eyes narrowing into slits. Protocol flew straight out the window. "Why in God's name would you people send me an infected prisoner? You know better than that, Major."

Perfect.

Reece retrieved the letter and slid it back into his breast pocket. "We didn't realize he was a carrier until a few hours ago." He pointed his thumb back over his shoulder toward Emaline. The captain's gaze abruptly shifted. As planned, she nodded appropriately. "Mrs. Smith discovered the problem when two of his companions under her care at the hospital died earlier this evening. She immediately brought it to my attention." Reece leaned forward, resting his hands on the desk. "And I've moved some pretty big mountains to get here as soon as possible, Captain. So I'm not interested in a debate of the lesser details." He straightened, settling his hand over the hilt of his sword. "We'll need to remove him from your population of prisoners. He's to be quarantined for further treatment."

"What if my men come down with this malady? Did you people think of that?"

"I believe we've caught this in time. That is, if the prisoner is still here."

The captain jerked open the desk's drawer, retrieved his ledger, and dropped it on the desk. "Well...give me the damn name," he hissed.

"Benedict. Captain Brennen Benedict. We believe he's part of Stuart's cavalry—Jackson's division. Captured sometime around the first part of this week over near Falmouth."

Captain Wiggins flipped open the prisoner list and began scanning the record. Fear of plague shoved any military code of behavior to the back of the man's mind, just as Reece knew it would. This dandy's loyalty only went as far as delivering prisoners to their transportation point and making certain they got on the ship.

It did not include dying.

The chink of glasses and ribald laughter reached out to Reece. He stifled another smirk when Wiggins looked up.

"Oh, shit," the captain groaned. "Yes. He's here…in the warehouse across from the livery. They brought him in yesterday."

"Does anybody know his condition?"

"I haven't heard anything out of the ordinary—at least there was no mention of any of them dying yet when rations were handed out this afternoon."

"Excellent. Then we've reached him in time. I've brought an ambulance wagon."

"I sure as hell ain't going to get him," Wiggins growled, scribbling the release information in the ledger. "I'll have one of my men take you over." He shoved the discharge form across the table. "Sign this and then get that bastard out of here."

Reece scrawled a name across the indicated line. Then they all crossed to the door, the captain following only as far as the gaming table. He nudged the closest man. "Sergeant Brown, escort these folks to warehouse number three. They're here to claim a prisoner." Wiggins turned back to face them, his lips pulling tight as he offered a thin smile.

Reece nodded, sliding on his gauntlets. He worked the leather down each finger. "Thank you for your cooperation tonight, Captain. And let's just keep this quiet. There's no need to alarm others unnecessarily." The last person out of the building, Reece pulled the weathered door closed behind him with a thump.

And then, he finally allowed the smile.

The smell of unwashed bodies wafted around Brennen as a penetrating chill seeped in through the weathered boards of the enclosure. One hundred and fifty men confined to a thirty-by-sixty-foot room.

No windows.

No ventilation.

He leaned against the wall and willed the pounding in his chest to slow. His shoulder throbbed and yesterday he'd lost all feeling in his right arm. If he lived long enough to see a surgeon, they'd probably end up lopping the damn thing off. The door creaked open and a rush of fresh air swept into the small interior.

He glanced to the opening.

They weren't due food rations until tomorrow morning.

A Yankee sergeant's voice boomed above the murmured din. "Captain Benedict. I'm lookin' for a Captain Benedict. You in here?"

Brennen stiffened.

Good God, what now?

The crowd parted to allow him room to stagger forward.

"You Benedict?" the sergeant growled.

Brennen nodded, fighting back another spasm that gripped his chest and threatened to spill out in another gut-wrenching cough. He swayed where he stood. Bile surged upward to burn in his throat.

The sergeant turned to face a tall, dark-haired officer looming just outside the door. "Here's your man, Doc."

"Thank you." The medical officer offered a thin smile.

Brennen's gaze swept the big Yank.

He'd seen this man before...he never forgot a face.

Medical, my ass.

He'd remain silent for now though and see what the hell unfolded with the impressive colonel he remembered from the Rappahannock River crossing.

The sergeant's voice penetrated Brennen's thoughts. "Oh yes, I remember you. The one who's got no sense of who's in charge. Let's see, boy, how many times did you try to escape on the march over from Falmouth? Two times? Three? Hell, you nearly bled to death in the process." A wave to the dried blood that stained Brennen's shirt testified the fact. The bastard turned back to face the big Yank. "You might want to remember this'n here don't got no sense, Doc. He'll bolt at the first opportunity regardless of whether it kills him or not." He gave a quick shove and laughed when Brennen staggered two steps before recovering his balance. "Good luck. He's all yours."

"I appreciate the warning, Sergeant. Where he's going, though, he's not likely to run."

Brennen shuffled from the warehouse and into the freezing night, heading toward a waiting ambulance wagon. A quick glance to the front of the vehicle revealed two figures cloaked in darkness sitting in the driver's seat. Brennen couldn't distinguish their faces.

Hell, he could barely stand.

He clambered into the wagon bed and waited while the wiry sergeant attached iron shackles around his wrists and ankles before handing the key to the officer. Brennen slumped against the wooden side of the ambulance, thankful at least to be out in the fresh air.

His gaze never left the big Yank as the man pulled up into the saddle.

The driver snapped the reins and the crisp flick of leather echoed across the backs of the sturdy mules. The wagon lurched forward, pitching Brennen sideways.

Chapter Nineteen

Brennen rolled over and braced his back against the side of the wagon. Three to one, the odds of a successful escape weren't in his favor. The warehouses grew smaller and smaller. The wagon left the wharf and rumbled over the railroad tracks crisscrossing the Union stronghold. The Potomac reached out to taunt him with its briny smell.

Freedom.

Even shackled, if he could make it to the waterway, he could disappear under the water and somehow swim to freedom.

The wagon slowed and then turned southward toward Falmouth. The stones crunching under the wheels kept perfect pace with the crushing thump of his heart. His chest ached and he stifled another cough. The mist off the river swirled around him and added to the shivers that crawled up his spine.

The entire time, the big Yank rode alongside the wagon, a well-oiled Remington pointed straight at Brennen. Another jolt from a deep depression in the dirt road sent a fresh wave of pain coursing over him.

His head lolled back to rest on the edge of the wagon.

Shimmering just above the horizon, an opaque moon skipped along with them; a luminous stone tossed across the glassy surface of night. The light that spilled forth would be enough to guide Brennen as he put one foot in front of the other. He smirked. Though wounded, he could still escape, and would do so at the first opportunity. The jagged outline of treetops eerily skimmed along the bottom half of the iridescent moon. Clumps of melting snow flanked both sides of the rutted road and resembled cotton boles left in the fields to rot. He returned his thoughts to the man holding the Remington.

What's going on here, you oversized sonofabitch?

Brennen remembered centering his field glasses on the colonel just before the bullet's impact. As if reading his thoughts, the man holstered his revolver and offered a smile.

"We're clear," he said.

The branches from a dense copse of pines swallowed the silver light. The wagon lurched to a stop. Immediately, the caped figures up front swiveled to face him. The smaller one pushed back the hood of a cape to reveal a bright, familiar smile.

Brennen's mouth dropped open. "Emaline!" he gasped, struggling to sit straighter.

His sister scrambled over the seat and dropped into the wagon bed next to him, her boots loudly thumping when they hit the wood. She settled close, her garments sweeping his legs. "Yes, it's me. You're safe now." She reached out, touching his face. Her fingers glided past the stubble of his beard. "Reece. Quick. Let's unlock him."

The iron latchkey sailed through the night and landed at the hem of her cloak.

The driver looped the reins around the wagon's brake lever and leaned over to offer his assistance.

When the metal fell away, Brennen rubbed his wrists and stared at his sister in stunned disbelief. "Good God, what's happened to your face?"

"A parting gift from the Yankees who captured you. I'm all right now. It's fading."

His gaze shifted to the big Yank still astride the buckskin. Brennen canted sideways to whisper in her ear. "What's happening here, Em?"

"You're being rescued, silly." Her lilting giggle filled the space between them. "And these men are helping me."

Brennen's eyebrows rose in startled surprise, and then shifted into a sharp line across his forehead. He leaned closer. "Why would these bastards help me?"

"These are the same officers who commandeered Shapinsay several months ago."

His gaze bounced from Emaline to one Yankee and then the other, before reconnecting with hers. "Are you in some kind of trouble?"

"No, you dolt. Colonel Cutteridge promised me you'd be safe while you recuperated at the mansion." She smiled and glanced to the outrider. Her expression softened even as her voice rose. "And I'm holding him to that promise. Isn't that right, Colonel?"

Brennen read volumes in her look. He might never know the details behind her outlandish statement, but he sure as hell knew part of the answer, and his baby sister had much more to tell him than the mere fact that this man had commandeered Shapinsay.

He stared hard at the colonel.

"She's right, Benedict." The Yank matter-of-factly offered his hand. Brennen accepted the handshake. "Reece Cutteridge. Colonel. Sixth Ohio. And up front there we've got Major Neale, my second-in-command."

The major extended his hand toward Brennen, his teeth flashing white with his grin. "I'm also a Yankee bastard," he quipped. Emaline sent him a pouting look and he shrugged. "Hey, I couldn't help but overhear you two."

Brennen sighed and finally relaxed, accepting the man's handshake. Then the second-in-command tossed the shackles under the front seat of the wagon. When he straightened again, Brennen asked, "I suppose you promised my sister too?"

A mischievous glint appeared in the major's eyes. "Nope, I just came along for the ride. This is quite risky, you know, breaking into our own stronghold to *steal away* a Reb prisoner. Hell, I wouldn't have missed this adventure for anything." He shot a quick glance toward the colonel, and then grasped Emaline under the arm to help her climb over the wagon's seat.

The colonel spurred away from the group and cantered toward a cluster of trees.

A moment later, he emerged leading a saddled horse. "This might be more comfortable than the back of that wagon, Benedict. You able to ride?"

Brennen's bemused expression shifted into a furtive grin. "Hell yes." He shuffled across the wagon bed, lifted a wobbly leg, and slid onto the back of the

Morgan. Seconds later, he settled into the saddle, cutting a smile to the Yank. "Ah…back home again. Thanks."

The colonel chuckled and tossed him the reins. "We best be ridin'. I promised Doc if he wouldn't ask questions, I'd have his damn wagon back by sunup." He looked at Emaline once more. She gazed up at him with a sweet expression on her face. Brennen threaded the leather traces through his fingers, watching the unspoken interaction between his sister and this intrepid man. "Well, Colonel. I owe you one, that's for damn sure."

The officer anchored his interest on Emaline and even in the subdued light, Brennen saw the glint of desire flickering in the Yankee's eyes.

He wants her. Brennen chanced a quick look to Emaline and saw the same reflection dancing in her eyes too.

Sonofabitch.

A multitude of questions bounced around inside his brain, but the colonel's voice displaced all of them.

"We've got a twenty-mile ride tonight. Let's move." The big Yank nudged his horse and the buckskin sprang into action. Brennen tapped his heels to the Morgan's side. The beast lunged forward into a steady canter behind the colonel. With a rattle of harness chains, the mules lurched into motion behind them.

An hour later, the group stopped near a small bridge.

"We'll part here," Reece said. "Falmouth lies about eight miles over that ridgeline."

Brennen nodded. "I'm familiar with this area."

"Your troops control the southern bank of the Rappahannock around Fredericksburg."

"Then I'll cut across the fields and loop around down near Falmouth Station."

Moonlight glinted off the metal saber scabbard that rested against the colonel's leg. He slipped his boot from the brass stirrup, stretched his leg muscle, then reset his foot back in. "Now, if it were me, Benedict, I'd want to know the Federal Army is spread all along the Rappahannock toward Mansfield going east and Richardsford west. It's no secret. Lee's been paralleling his troops with ours for miles in both directions." He paused for a long moment and then glanced to Brennen. "Who do you scout for?"

"The 8th Virginia."

Reece nodded. "Last I heard the 8th was still assigned to General Jackson's corps. We believe he's shifting his cavalry southwest in an attempt to flank us somewhere over near Chancelorsville. But, again, no secret there." Reece smiled before adding, "And again, if it were me, I'd want to know that I need to circle around and cross the river up near United States Ford. Then I'd need to light out fast for Hazel Grove. I'd cross tracks with Stuart somewhere near there."

Brennen chuckled. "Hell's fire, Colonel, the Yanks should let you lead their damn army. This thing would be finished in a fortnight." He leaned over and offered his hand. "Thanks, I'll keep all that in mind."

Their hands connected in a firm shake before separating. "And, Benedict, if none of this works out for you, we've never met."

Brennen laughed, gathering the traces tighter in his hands. "Nope, I ain't never heard of any Yankee bastard with a crazy name like Cutteridge." Brennen turned slowly in his saddle and faced his sister. He could see the tears welling in her eyes. "You all right, Em?"

Emaline nodded. "Please be careful. And have a doctor look at your shoulder as soon as you can."

"What, this ol' thing?" He shrugged his shoulder in a small circle and grinned at her. "It still moves and that's all that matters. You know me, I'm always careful!" He leaned toward her and touched her cheek, his fingers sliding over her cool skin near the bruise. "You take care of yourself, too. And…Em, don't allow yourself to get hurt." He hoped she would take his meaning. Brennen had no more time to explain the rules of love during wartime…these few would have to suffice. She nodded, turning her head to place a kiss in the palm of his hand. A moment later, the soft thud of horse hooves meeting the snow-soggy ground whispered through the night. Her Gray Ghost had returned to war.

Chapter Twenty

Emaline sat on the chair, her foot impatiently tapping.

Where is he?

An hour earlier, Reece had deposited her in this cramped hotel room and then left. He gave no explanations, no hint of when he might return, no reasons why he must go. He'd simply told her to stay put.

Stay put my eye!

Emaline stood, crossed to the small window, and peered past the dirty panes into the early evening below. Falmouth swarmed with blue-coated soldiers. Everyone seemed to be going somewhere and doing something.

And she was not.

Where did Reece go? But more importantly, why was she still sitting here waiting for him? Thoughts scattered through her mind. By now, her brother surely had reunited with his soldiers. Just exactly how long did it take for Reece to drop off Doc's wagon? Maybe they'd all been caught after all. Overwhelmed by the turn of events in the past thirty-nine hours, exhaustion crept through her impatience.

Emaline dropped the limp curtain into place.

A commotion from beyond the closed door interrupted her thoughts. No sooner had a knock sounded than a key turned in the lock and the wood swung wide.

Emaline headed across the braided rug, expecting to encounter Reece and give him her views about being abandoned in this cramped hotel room for so long. She stopped in her tracks when the form of a woman back-ended her way into the room. Beneath the layers of blue and yellow plaid, the servant's ponderous girth jiggled.

"I...I'm sorry but this room is occupied." Emaline worried her words weren't heard above the scratching resonance of metal against wood.

The woman slowly straightened, her hands pressing against the small of her back. "Yes, Mum," she gasped, struggling to catch her breath. "The colonel paid me good money to bring this tub up here for ye." She bent once more and finished pulling the large copper kettle through the doorway. Once it cleared the doorjamb, three children filed in, each one carrying steaming buckets of water in their grubby hands. They sloshed their responsibilities into the tub and then scurried back out, the last little urchin grinning at Emaline as she closed the door behind her.

Emaline stepped closer to the chambermaid. "I...I'm sorry, but I didn't ask for this."

"Yes, Mum, I know'd that, but the colonel paid for six buckets o' hot water and a half tub full of cold for ye bath."

Emaline's eyes opened wider than the Rappahannock.

The maid leaned over and swirled the water around in the tub to blend the temperatures. "If'n my man paid good money for me to have a bath, I'd say God love him, that's what I'd say." She dried her chubby forearm in the folds of her rush-colored apron. "Now hurry lass, afore ye water chills. I'll be back in, say..." she rolled her eyes heavenward before reconnecting with Emaline's and adding, "...an hour. That should give ye enough time for a good soaking too." She straightened the dust cap holding her faded red curls in tow and then winked. "You sure is fortunate to have a handsome man spend this kind o' money on ye. 'Tis a real treatin' these hard times." Two items appeared from under her ample arm. "And here's ye towels too. I'll just be puttin' them over here, dearie. The colonel paid for two. So use both!" She draped the off-white, worsted terry cotton huckaback's over the spindled chair, and then turned to face Emaline. Her hands clapped together. "Now, just settle in and relax. I'll be back later." She lumbered to the door and opened it, offering one last smile before slipping from the room.

The door closed with a soft click and Emaline shifted her thoughts to the copper tub. Enormous barely described its size. The steaming metal container occupied the space on the hearth and reflected the flickering flames inside the fireplace, orange and yellow tongues dancing around a glittering whisper of blue. Emaline couldn't remember the last time she'd taken a full bath. Not the pitcher and bowl wash downs that had been her choice during winter, but an honest-to-goodness bath.

Unbidden, a small giggle escaped her lips.

The audacity of Reece Cutteridge! Look how bold a man becomes after a woman offers him her lips.

Heat rushed to her cheeks as a wicked smile winged her mouth.

She leaned over the tub and inhaled. Tendrils of steam curled around her face and the aroma of sweet lavender settled deep into her lungs. Heavenly and inviting, the fragrance laved the wounds still lingering in her heart. Emaline spotted the bar of soap lying on the bottom knowing the maid had purposely placed it in the warm water to soften.

She glanced to the door. Since Reece had already paid for everything, what harm would there be? It would be such a shame to let the water cool without enjoying its benefits.

Decision made, Emaline unpinned the jet-and-ivory brooch at her throat and placed it on the side table along with her crocheted collar. The cameo was Benjamin's last gift to her before he died. She caressed the scalloped edge of her collar, the embroidered organdy so demure and proper.

Another sigh filled the room.

Demure and proper?

In the past four months, she'd been anything but. Her thoughts drifted to a pine-shrouded clearing. Irritation vanished along with the traveling dress from her body. The warm underslip, celadon-green and quilted, followed the garment, pushed straight to the ground to lie in a heap on top of her dress. The polished cotton that lined the slip caught the fire's glow and shimmered back at her in tones of caramel and coffee.

Somewhere deep inside the old building, someone was frying bacon. The luscious, smoky aroma curled around her hesitation. One leather-walking boot thumped to the floor, followed by the next. Balancing on one leg and then the other, Emaline rolled her white jacquard stockings downward, tucking them inside each boot. Blue ribbon garters dropped on top.

She straightened and wiggled her toes.

A soft tug on the ecru ribbon of her camisole loosened the Rosepoint lace that draped her shoulders. A second later, the delicate piece floated to join the heap of clothing.

Honed from a lifetime of practice, nimble fingers made short work of the busk closures riding the front of her corset. As each hook unfastened, a sigh of relief followed, until the steel-ribbed necessity landed with a heavy thud behind her. A knee-length chemise finally joined the sodden pile of clothes beside the tub. Emaline stared at the passementerie bodice and cap sleeves, remembering when she'd spent a month embroidering the piece while sadly watching Benjamin die.

The low flames in the hearth threw warmth into the room. She gazed down at her bare breasts, expecting to see some change where the colonel's hands had mapped her curves.

Emaline toyed with the ivory buttons that secured the waistband of her pantalets. This was the last vestige of modesty left on her body.

She stared at the door.

If Reece returns...

A shudder of excitement began in her ankles and inched upward to settle in the warm juncture between her thighs. Instantly, her nipples hardened. She cupped her small breasts in an attempt to relieve the sensation. The recollection of the colonel's calloused hands touching her through the layers of cloth brought a soft moan from Emaline's lips.

Her head tipped back. Her hair brushed the curve of her lower back and sent another ripple dancing up her spine. Emaline's gaze drifted again to the tub.

The scented water beckoned with open arms. She sighed, straightened again, and slowly lowered her hands to the button on her pantalets, slipping the cloth over her hips. The chill in the room raised goose bumps on her naked flesh. She stepped out of each leg and then scooted the crumpled batiste linen over to join the pile. Lifting her foot over the metal side, she tested the water with her toe. Heat radiated up her leg and tightened her calf muscle.

A soft gasp fell from her mouth.

Yes. I want this.

In a heartbeat, Emaline was up and over the side of the tub, her fingers gripping the warm metal. She eased herself into the enveloping cocoon. Leaning back, she allowed the glorious heat to penetrate every muscle. The smell of coffee brewing somewhere downstairs fused with the lavender steam and embraced her.

Her eyes slipped closed. The image of Reece returned. Her skin prickled where the soft rasp of his beard had brushed her neck. Where he'd licked and nipped along her throat, the reminders of where his tongue laved still burned hot.

"Reece," she whispered. His very name stoked her memory. "Thank you so much for this." Only the shadows heard her gratitude.

Twenty minutes later, Emaline completed her bath and reluctantly stepped from the water. Her fingers closed around the soft towels.

The colonel paid for two. So use them both.

Her lips lifted into a soft grin. She wrapped one towel around her head and the other around her body. Padding to the straight-backed chair beside the hearth, Emaline settled onto the worn seat. Warmed by the fire, the wood radiated heat through her bare skin and penetrated into her relaxed muscles.

Emaline blotted the excess moisture from her hair.

With no brush at hand, she used her fingers to untangle the wet strands, combing through them to separate the damp curtain of curls. A light knock upon the door startled her and Emaline gasped, clutching the towel closer to her breasts. The door handle turned and seconds later, a white cap popped through the opening. A face sporting a beaming smile followed. "Well, dearie, are you all clean?"

The thrilling sense of anticipation splintered into sorrow-filled shards. *Not Reece.* Emaline refused to allow the disappointment in her heart to reach her face when the rotund woman skimmed through the opening and closed the door behind her.

"And look what I have here." With a flourish, the maid swept a garment from her forearm and held it up for Emaline's perusal. "We certainly can't put those dirty things back on now can we?"

Emaline stared at the nightgown. Amply cut and unadorned by even an embroidered hem, the sleeping garment fastened all the way up the front with a single row of ivory buttons. Long, full sleeves gathered at the wrist by delicate white ribbons. "'Tis a gift from your man, dearie," the servant said, draping the nightgown on the bed. She turned and swept up the pile of discarded clothes. "I'll just have these brought back to you in the morning clean as a new day." She crossed to the door, opened it a slight crack, and tossed the clothes into the darkened hallway. She hustled over and clamped her hands around the metal tub. Shuffling backward, the maid pulled the container toward the door. "Sleep well, Mrs. Cutteridge."

The door closed behind her exit.

Mrs. Cutteridge?

The name settled into Emaline's bones. Had Reece said that to avoid embarrassment for her? The nightgown replaced the towel and billowed around her naked body to bring warmth and comfort to her heart.

Despite the madness of this entire situation, a strange calmness claimed her world.

Emaline lowered to the bed and bounced a couple of times to test the mattress. An errant giggle escaped when the quilt puffed around her. She snuggled into the feather mattress. The sheets smelled clean, the comforting essence of lye soap reminding her of home. Shapinsay lay only seven miles westward. Why didn't she just begin walking home now that her brother was safe? Why had she allowed Reece to lead her up those narrow stairs and isolate her in this room? Why did he pay for the bath?

More importantly, why was she staying put?

Emaline tried to ignore the questions, tried to ignore her quickening pulse. The answer hovered on the edge of her mind.

I'm waiting for him.

Emaline rolled onto her side. The muted rumble of cannon limbers and wagons rolling past in the street below, the muffled drone of voices, everything blended together into a lulling melody. Less than an hour later, her eyes dropped closed and she finally drifted off to sleep.

Reece opened the door and stepped into the room. He quietly crossed to the hearth and added more wood to the glowing embers inside the grate. Within seconds, flames sputtered to life when the residue from the logs met the blaze.

He gazed at Emaline. She was soundly asleep. Last night's activities had drained everyone. A smile creased his lips. He remembered pulling her up the stairs, her frustrations growing when he'd placed her in here. He knew she needed sleep and he'd paid good money for her to have that opportunity. His smile deepened at the memory of the irritation on the face of the young captain whom he'd ousted from the room. The prostitute clinging to the officer's arm had demanded a hefty price for services despite not having fulfilled her mission.

Reece crossed to the bed and reached for the extra blanket from the spindled foot rail. The gray wool floated over Emaline. She didn't stir. He stared down at the coffee-colored hair that fanned the pillow. Each silken strand glinted at him, its richness highlighted by the fire's glow.

He swayed, and his hand braced against the headboard. Exhaustion seized him. After two days without sleep, his body demanded retribution. Reece lowered to the edge of the bed and then carefully stretched out beside Emaline.

His arms tucked beneath his head. He listened to her breathing.

Shallow.

Sweet.

He couldn't help himself. He rolled onto his side and gazed at her. Her lashes lay like dark crescents against her face. Reece swallowed. How in God's name could he keep from touching her?

He'd waited for her to fall asleep so he could share the bed without compunction. *What a goddamned stupid idea.* Her soft breathing wrapped around him with silken tethers and the whiskey he'd drank weakened his firm resolve to avoid touching her.

He reached out and picked up a dark strand of her hair, threading the softness through his fingers, accepting the ache that coursed through him. Reece took pride in being a man in control, yet his hand slipped across her waist with a will of its own. The whiskey did the talking now. He gently pulled her against him and buried his face in her hair, smelling the matchless scent of her.

Lost in the throes of slumber, she didn't stir.

How could he wake her? *I can't.*

His eyes slipped closed. This was enough...for now. And in the precious moment just before sleep also claimed him, Reece finally realized he'd at last come *home.*

Floating somewhere in the layers of sleep, Emaline felt wondrously warm and protected. She snuggled deeper into the heat, bringing the exquisite sensations closer. The weight of something...an arm, perhaps? The contour well defined and muscular slipped over her waist.

The warmth enveloped everything and she slipped deeper, surrendering herself to the comfort and security that encased her. While the moon rode its silvery arc toward sunrise, Emaline reveled in the protective pressure of that magnificent arm.

The next morning, a heavy knock persisted, driving away her glorious dream.

Emaline sat straight up in bed. The door creaked open and a young girl appeared. She quietly entered the room and laid the now-cleaned clothes on the chair. Ten minutes later and fully dressed, Emaline stood at the window and stared down into the bustling crowd.

Had Reece deposited her in this room and forgotten about her?

She crossed her arms in front of her waist, her fingers gripping her elbows. Well, she'd accomplished exactly what needed doing. That was the end of it. He certainly didn't owe her anything more. He told her as much with his absence.

He'd kept his promise, though. Her brother was free.

Another knock upon the door forced her to turn back into the room. "Come in," she whispered, her expectation soaring. The door eased open and a young soldier stepped into view.

"Good morning, Mrs. McDaniels," he said.

He stood alone. A fresh wave of disappointment swamped Emaline.

"Good morning."

"I'm Lieutenant Lucas Glave, ma'am, the colonel's aide-de-camp. He's asked me to escort you back home and make certain you arrive safely."

Emaline blinked. "I see." Her tongue slipped out to moisten suddenly dry lips. "And Colonel Cutteridge? Will he be joining us as well?" Her mind spun around the warmth of her dreams last night. Reece, holding her tightly in his arms. Reece, caressing her and murmuring in her ear, his breath hot against her skin.

Reece, keeping her safe from the madness that swirled beyond this room.

The lad stood by the door, his hat held loosely in his hands. "No, ma'am, the colonel has business elsewhere this morning. If you're ready, we should be going."

Her heart hammered in her chest, driving the pain of Reece's evasion deeper into her stomach. Emaline nodded with difficulty. She drew her cape across her shoulders, fastened the corded loops, and anchored a smile into place. The soldier escorted her from the hotel and over to a horse near the railing that ran the length of the building. One and one-half hours later, with few words spoken between them, the young lieutenant completed his assignment. Emaline stood on Shapinsay's front steps and watched him ride away.

Tears scalded a path down her face.

Chapter Twenty-One

Wilderness Campaign
Battle of the Wilderness
May 4, 1864

The clash between the Union and Confederates came at mid-day when the blazing sun reached its apex. The Federals crossed the Rapidan River and entered the forest from the Orange Plank Road, stumbling through the morass of woods.

Reece coughed hard to push out the putrefying taste of smoke.

The pitiful screams of the dying fused with the horrendous report of enemy fire and echoed around him. Sparked by gunpowder, eons of decayed leaves became ready tinder and fires sprang up in front of his regiment to illuminate the forest in a myriad of haunting effigies. The sweeping arms of battle ensnared them all. Artillery explosions rocked the ground and everywhere Reece turned, chaos rode the winds that fanned the noxious flames until his retreating troops could determine neither right nor left, north nor south. Wave after wave of cavalrymen threw themselves into the melee. Horses shrieked above the tumult. Within minutes, thousands of trampling hooves crushed the velvety softness of a late Virginian spring. Mortar shells screeched overhead, snapped off treetops, and ripped apart his command.

More at home in this ruthless setting, the Army of Northern Virginia thwarted and repulsed his army at every turn, and the farther Reece pushed his troops into the raging inferno of tangled undergrowth, the more vulnerable and bogged down they became. The brambles of the forest seized them within a sinuous, slippery grip. Visibility dropped to less than twenty feet, leaving Reece no other option but to call a complete halt.

All the while, the fires of hell crept closer.

From under the mantle of smoke, at the point where the Plank and Brock Roads crossed, Reece and his entourage of couriers emerged onto the rutted turnpike. Three and a half years' worth of campaigning reflected in the tight set of his battle-hardened muscles and the fires highlighted his uncompromising resilience. A crease of unease crimped his forehead, pulling hard at the hollow gauntness the war had etched into his face.

His long hair lay plastered to his neck from the heat of the fires, and like many others in this god-forsaken war, he bore a permanent reminder of its stress. The horrors of Chancelorsville, Gettysburg, and Brandy Station all took their toll on him this past year and a whisper of silver now wove through his dark locks, a badge of honor he wore proudly. Tentacles of memories reached out to taunt him. Amid the chaos that encompassed his life, he only needed to close his eyes to lose himself again in the remembrance of Emaline, her sweet skin and the luscious, succulent taste of her. Nothing had changed inside him in that regard. His desire for her had never waned. And now, once again, he was so close to Shapinsay…and to her arms. Not a day went by that she wasn't in his thoughts.

An artillery shell shrieked overhead and exploded in a nearby tree. His thoughts raked back into control. He swiveled in his saddle and stared across the clearing. Easing back on Saguaro's bit, Reece searched for a way through the bedlam.

This is asinine. Why would General Hancock demand a council of officers now?

"We're too far down," he bellowed above the din. Sweat poured in rivulets down his face. The swirling smoke stung his eyes. Finally, he spotted a rutted path coiling eastward off the lane. "There's the way to the Wilderness Tavern. Come on." He spurred Saguaro into action. "Hancock's waiting for us—"

Before he finished the statement, another round of artillery screamed through the thick blanket of smoke. A split second later, the twelve-pounder shell exploded less than ten feet from where Reece and his couriers clustered.

Shrapnel flew in all directions.

The Gray Ghosts were good at their jobs and as their honored name implied, they seemed to hover in the haze above their enemy. Surrounded by the acrid cloud, they picked their way through the tangled vines.

Brennen led his small platoon into a clearing near Brock Road.

"Hey, Cap'n," a soldier yelled above the uproar. "There's a fine lookin' animal." He pointed to a buckskin near the clearing's edge. The horse, nearly sixteen hands high, stood among a cluster of dead mounts.

The soldier guided his Morgan toward it, carefully stepping over a scattering of dead Yanks in the road.

"Grab him, before he gallops off," another said.

"He ain't going nowhere. There's a foot caught in the stirrup." The man sidled up next to the horse and aimed a kick at the boot to free the beast. As the leg dropped to the ground with a heavy thud, a moan issued from the man sprawled face down beneath the animal.

"Damn, this'n's still alive, Cap'n!"

"And he's a colonel too," another added, pointing to the wounded man's shoulder straps. The group formed a circle around the big Yank and Brennen swung from the saddle.

A colonel?

Capturing one of those didn't happen often. Something pulled at his memory. He knew only one Yankee colonel... What were the odds? He tugged on the officer's shoulder and rolled the man onto his back.

Blood saturated the white shirt beneath an open frockcoat.

"Shrapnel's got him in the chest, Cap'n," a comrade said.

"He's a dead man," another added. "He just don't know it yet."

Brennen's gaze slid upward and settled on the face just to be sure. Dark hair framed the unmistakable features of Reece Cutteridge.

"Shit," he whispered—the oath a sad sigh. He'd know this man anywhere. Brennen leaned over the colonel and checked the extent of his injuries.

The closest soldier dismounted. "What's wrong, Cap'n?"

"It's him."

"Who's him?" a second man asked, dropping from his saddle to join them.

"The Yank who broke me out of prison last year. You remember, I told you about him."

"Well, your friend ain't long for this world."

Brennen agreed, but he couldn't just leave him out here on the road like this. He glanced across the clearing and calculated their position. Chancellorsville lay a handful of miles to the west.

The Orange Plank should be little more than a mile away.

That meant his sister, if she hadn't been forced from the plantation by now, was less than ten miles away. Regardless, they could make it to Shapinsay and back by morning if they rode like hell. If Emaline still lived there and if she still cared enough to want to help the colonel, she was the only chance this man would have to survive. That is, if he lived long enough to get there. Many ifs stalked Brennen's decision, but he owed the big Yank and that made his choice easier. "Help me get him onto his horse."

Emaline raised her head from the library desk, unsure exactly when she'd dozed off. Working in the garden all day, coupled with the unusually hot spring, had tapped her strength.

Darkness entombed her.

What time was it?

She stretched the tightness from her muscles. The sudden soft chiming of the mantle clock told her midnight had arrived. Apprehension controlled her world and she cocked her ear to listen to the murmur of night wafting in through the open upstairs window.

Had something awakened her?

Except for the distant and ongoing rumbles of cannon fire, she heard only the crickets singing.

Emaline forced herself to relax and leaned back in the chair, pulling the knitted shawl over her shoulder. Sometime during the evening, the wool had slipped down around her waist. Beneath the desk, her feet slid into leather house shoes. Then, the faint whickering of horses, close and defined, filtered in through the window along with the dust-infused scent of an approaching rain. Chinking bridle rings told her the noise hadn't come from her mare or the mules in the stable. Emaline bolted upright and opened the desk drawer.

She withdrew Brennen's pistol. Always loaded, the Adams revolver weighed heavy in her hands. She rose to her feet and edged around the desk. The shawl tumbled to the floor. Unmistakable scuffling of boots upon the front veranda brought her to the top of the dark stairs.

Oh, dear God…not again.

Visions of ol' Moses screamed across her memory and she again tasted the bile of fury. A pack of filthy despots had cornered her servant down by the river last fall. Taunting Moses as he fished for their supper, the renegades heckled him, robbed him of his days' catch, and then mercilessly beat the man. Benjamin's trusty servant, who had served him faithfully for more than forty years, lived only long enough to see the first snowfall in December.

Even now, the tragedy sickened her.

Damned filthy deserters!

She'd shoot every last coward herself if she had the opportunity.

Robbed of any guiding light, Emaline slipped down the main staircase and crossed through the parlor by memory. Most of the heavier furniture remained stacked in the attic and the sparsely decorated room still echoed the emptiness of her life since Reece's departure. She peered out the window. Swollen clouds stole the moonlight, and Emaline saw only the blurry outline of milling soldiers.

Were they Yankees? Southerners? Damnation. She couldn't tell.

One of them shoved open the front door and Emaline melded against the curtains. She'd have only one chance to shoot them. She had to pick the best time. The stench of sweat and horses assaulted her nostrils and she held her breath, pointing the revolver toward the group.

"I know I saw a light comin' from upstairs." A gruff voice filled the foyer as four shadowy figures entered the house. "You sure she's still here? Hell, anyone could be roaming around this big house."

Emaline hesitated.

She?

Her finger eased off the trigger.

They're looking for me?

They carried a large, bulky body between them and another voice she did not recognize whispered, "Where we gonna' put him, Cap'n? This sonofabitch ain't light, you know."

Captain?

Her heart lurched in her chest and sent a fresh wave of fear up her spine. A captain had been the one to beat ol' Moses to a pulp. The servant had managed to share that bit of information before he lapsed into unconsciousness. Had the pig returned this time with a few more of his thugs? Emaline strained forward, squinting in an attempt to see better. Nothing helped. It was too dark to decipher faces and the low roll of thunder masked their whispered words.

The load they carried was no doubt an injured comrade.

The men lumbered up the stairs and disappeared into the interior of the second floor. Emaline followed, hugging the wall so the stairs would not creak as she ascended behind them. She'd take her time and make her aim count.

Lightning split the night and illuminated the house in a silver wash. The men shuffled down the hall and finally entered Benjamin's old room. She heard a muddled mixture of mumbling and cursing, and then lamplight flooded the hallway from the open doorway.

Emaline eased around the doorjamb and peered into the master suite. Her nostrils again flared. The musty odor of the room's neglect mingled with the bite of horse sweat and unwashed bodies. The soldiers had placed the large form in the center of the bed and clustered around it.

Their backs were to her, but in the dim, wavering light, she saw a mismatched ensemble of uniform pants, jackets, and homespun shirts. She glimpsed only part of the body that occupied the great berth, but the marauder wore Union blue trousers. The yellow cord sewed into the side seam of his pants leg indicated cavalry. The fact that these men knew their way around her home was puzzling.

Regardless, she wanted no part of them.

Emaline's heart rammed against her ribcage, yet she took a fortifying breath and stepped into the lamplight. The Adams pointed straight at the intruders, though their features remained lost in the haze.

"Move away from the bed." Her finger curled around the trigger when they swung to face her. "I'll kill the first one who as much as twitches."

"She's gonna shoot us," one soldier shouted, lunging sideways.

The other two dropped beside the bed out of sight.

Her gaze cut to the lean, shaggy-haired ruffian left standing near the side table. A thick, scruffy beard covered his face. Something about him made her finger ease off the trigger. Recognition swept through her just as his stoic face brightened into a beloved grin.

Her knees went weak.

Her jaw dropped open.

The hair on the nape of her neck tingled. "Oh my God," she whispered. The Adams fell to her side at the end of her limp arm. "Brennen?"

"Yes. And dammit, Em, don't shoot me."

Emaline laid the revolver on the highboy and surged into the room toward him. She flung herself into his outstretched arms, the impact causing his slouch hat to tumble from his head and hang by its leather lanyard around his neck.

Brennen hugged her. "You scared me witless waving that gun around."

"Well, you scared me half to death sneaking around in here like this. Why didn't you just holler?"

"Good God, deserters from both sides have been ransacking plantations all along the Rappahannock. We couldn't just barge in here screaming. We didn't know what the hell we'd find inside."

She buried her head against his chest, her hands splaying across his gray, unadorned shell jacket. Relief that he was alive engulfed her in joyful waves.

She pushed back and stared at him. "I'm so glad you're here." She looked at his soldiers.

No one smiled back.

She cast her eyes down to the bloody figure on the bed and let out a sharp gasp. Her pulse quickened so fast she could scarcely find her next breath. Everything else around her faded into oblivion.

Reece.

A sense of urgency engulfed her, overriding all other cascading emotions. She pushed from her brother's embrace, nearly toppling him backward.

Brennen sidestepped to give her more room. "We'd been fightin' over near the Wilderness and stumbled across him, Em. I think he's still alive."

Emaline assessed the wicked gash across the forehead, then the deeper, more critical wound in his chest. With her concentration solely on Reece, she raised her left hand and grasped the grubby coat sleeve of the closest soldier. She pulled him to her, her voice cracking under the oppressive weight that pressed down upon her heart. "I'll need water, and lots of rags. And, I'll need a fire laid." She met the stranger's solemn expression. "Also, downstairs in the kitchen, you'll find some pots. Bring me the biggest one you can find, filled with water, and suspend it over a fire in here. Go now!"

The stranger shifted his eyes to her brother for approval. He must have nodded. The soldier pulled from her grasp and left.

"Since the colonel helped me escape last year and all, I couldn't just leave him out there in that mess," Brennen said. "He'd have died for sure."

The truth of his words cut her like a knife. "You did right to bring him to me, Brennen. Please hurry. Down in the pantry you'll find my medical pouch. There's still medicine left from the supplies he sent me." She swallowed. In a shallow breath, she added, "And fetch Euley. She's out back with Israel. The last cabin on the right."

"I'll get her but we can't stay. We've slipped away only long enough to bring him here." Brennen motioned for the other two soldiers to leave the room. "We'll gather some wood and get a fire going up here, but then we've got to go."

"But...you just got here." Her eyes widened.

"I know," he muttered, cupping her face. "But we've got to go back." Worry starched the creases that etched his gaunt features. "I'm sorry to dump him on you like this, but I figured you'd want to try to save him, if you could. It's the best I can do. I'll go get Euley now." His hands dropped and he headed out the door.

Emaline turned back to Reece.

Only the sporadic rise and fall of his chest told her he lived. The beard stubble, dark and smeared with blood, was the only color on his face. She leaned over, intent on unbuttoning his blood-soaked shirt. At least she'd remove the uniform before Euley arrived. Sounds echoed through the house downstairs as her shaky fingers worked the pewter buttons. Heart-pounding memories of time spent with this man rushed through Emaline.

Tears filled her eyes and then spilled down her cheek in a chilly passage.

She swiped away the moisture with a hasty brush of her shoulder and refocused on her task.

Chapter Twenty-Two

Impatience wrenched at Emaline's emotions.

Minutes before, Euley had pushed her from the bedroom, urging her to give Brennen a proper farewell. Torn between telling him good-bye and wanting to dash back upstairs to Reece, she paced the weathered boards of the front veranda in frantic steps. Blood smeared in red splotches across her blouse and the material stuck to her skin. Her arms wrapped around her waist and she hugged herself against the chill in the air. A brisk wind swept around the corner of the mansion, bringing the promise of rain ever closer.

She stopped in front of her brother again.

"This war can't last much longer, Em. I just have a gut feeling about it." He glanced over his shoulder; his men had already galloped out of sight.

"Don't go, Bren. Please. Just stay here."

He frowned, pulling her into a quick embrace. His words brushed warm across the curve of her ear. "Let's not start this again, all right?"

She sighed and folded against her brother, pulling him closer. "Thank you for bringing Reece here."

Brennen encircled his arms around her waist, squeezed her tightly and then released her, stepping back. "I've put his saber and revolver in the kitchen along with his leathers." He tromped down the stairs, the warped boards squeaking under the pressure. He shoved his foot into the stirrup and then pulled up into the saddle. Lamplight spilled over him from the open front door. "His buckskin suffered a bad wound on its flank but Tacker said he'd clean it up." Brennen patted the saddlebags. "And tell Euley thanks for packing up the grub."

Emaline nodded, fresh tears welling. He raked back his long hair and then reached over his shoulder and pulled the sweat-stained hat into place. Stiff with dirt and age, the lanyard slid down the front of his jacket. His Morgan sidestepped and Brennen pulled back on the bit.

"Please be careful," she whispered.

"I'm always careful, Em." He smiled down at her. "You keep remembering that, and just keep on lovin' your colonel."

A nudge to the flank sent the horse into a strong canter.

Less than an hour after arriving to turn Emaline's world upside down, her brother disappeared into the darkness, the drumming of his horse's hooves fading into silence. Another loud crack of thunder resonated overhead. A chilling mist blew over her flushed face and she swerved on her heel and dashed back inside. The door slammed shut behind her just as the clouds ripped apart and released the promised deluge.

She hiked her work dress to her knees and took the stairs two at a time.

Another thunderclap rattled the windows as she reentered the master suite. Heavy raindrops pelted the glass panes like pebbles and lightning once again illuminated the room. "They're gone," she announced, heading straight to Reece. "How is he?"

Euley pulled thread from the boiling water with silver tongs, then fished out several sewing needles. "No change. Let's get started."

Emaline nodded, leaning over Reece. His erratic breathing fused with the oppressive panic that scaled the ramparts of her emotions. Reaching into a nearby bucket, she squeezed out water from a scrap of cloth, then swabbed the lingering grit and dried blood from his face. Seeing her brother alive and well brought joy to her heart, but Reece gave it the reason to beat. Indeed, this powerful man, who once wrapped her within his glorious embrace on a soft pine bower and kissed her with a passion she'd never known…this man could not possibly be lying like this before her.

"You ready, Miz Emaline?"

"Yes." She swallowed, hard, and returned the cloth to the bucket before reaching for the needle and thread her servant offered. A quick glance to the side table revealed a bowl holding debris that Euley had already removed from Reece. Emaline resettled her gaze on the jagged wound zigzagging across his chest.

She inhaled to steady herself then leaned closer. Her hands rested on a defined row of ribs that underscored his loss of several pounds over the past year. Her thoughts settled on the much-repeated task of bringing together the torn, ragged flesh across Reece's chest. The needle pierced the bloodied skin. The thread slipped through. Every stitch counted. Every stitch different. Every one bringing her closer and closer to another rush of tears.

She tamped them down and continued.

Dawn's light slipped through the break in the curtain to spill in a wash of pinks and yellows across the room. Emaline straightened from the bed and finally laid aside the sewing needle. On the floor beside her lay a pile of rags, bloody testament to a long and harrowing night.

Bolstered by Euley's encouraging words, she had finally completed her task.

"War is cruel," she whispered, her voice cracking. "Wickedly cruel. And pain-filled. May God forgive those who've started this nightmare for they surely didn't foresee such madness."

From across the room, Euley looked up from the bed sheets she was ripping into bandages. "Men don't look dat far ahead." She dropped the cotton strips into the boiling pot of water suspended over the low flames. "It's always been like dat, I'm afraid." The servant straightened from her task and padded to the bed to stand beside Emaline.

"There's nothing honorable in this tragedy." Emaline ran a hand through her disheveled hair and pushed a dark strand back over her shoulder. "Do you think he's suffering?"

"He don't feel da pain yet. But he will soon."

A half-empty morphine bottle stood on the side table waiting for the time when—*when*, not *if*—Reece would need it. Her thoughts tumbled backward into last night's macabre scene. After extracting more slivers of iron, she eased his torn flesh together and sewed closed the wounds. At her elbow, Euley prepared the topical that would cover the score of neat, precise stitches. When Emaline began to place the lint on top of her handiwork, her servant stopped her, a gnarled finger pointing to the boiled water in a nearby bucket.

"Dip it first, Miz Emaline," she whispered. "We don't want no pustulence."

A dozen times or more, Doctor Evans had told her laudable pus was acceptable, but she didn't argue against the woman's sage advice. Emaline did exactly as Euley instructed. She plunged the lint into the purified water and then applied the dripping aseptic poultice directly to the track of stitches below Reece's left breast. She then sprinkled additional chloride over the compress, added another dry, medicated poultice and several more clean muslin strips.

All night long, Euley whispered in her ear, reminding her repeatedly that the colonel was strong, he would survive. All night long, Emaline clung to those words. When her back muscles spasmed from leaning in one position, when tears filled her eyes to break her concentration, when she impatiently swiped them away and refocused on her task, she held fast to that belief. Reece Cutteridge was indeed the strongest man she had ever known, but there was no denying his now-precarious hold on life.

They had done all they could. His survival solely rested in God's hands. Her gaze swept his form. The bottom half of his naked body lay hidden, but the thin coverlet seemed out of place across such brawny magnificence.

Never had Emaline seen a more beautifully formed human.

She stared past the material that draped his hips, to the place where the hair grew dense and dark and traveled downward under the cloth to his groin. Her eyes shifted away and she swallowed, fighting hard to control the frenetic trip of her heart. She gathered a cloth in her hand.

Exhaustion eked through her and she nearly swayed.

Her right hand sought anchor around the bedpost, her left gripped tighter the cloth she held. She stared at his wide shoulders and again contemplated the impact his presence had brought back to her life. Behind her, Euley shuffled around the room, clearing away the bloodied implements she had wielded in the battle against death.

Only time would tell if Reece would be the victor.

"I's carrying dese things downstairs," Euley mumbled. "Be right back." The woman disappeared into the hallway.

Emaline stared at Reece. His pallor worried her. Bandages covered the gashes across his forehead. His hair, unkempt and long, lay in tousled hanks against the pillow. The neatly trimmed beard of her memory was gone, replaced by a full, shaggy growth that spread over the lower half of his face. Dark, sunken shadows hugged the skin beneath his closed eyes, and gaunt indentations shaped the area beneath chiseled cheekbones. A whisper of silver dusted his hair.

Only his mustache remained the same—a dark chevron that rode the curve of his mouth.

For just a moment, she allowed the memories, surrendering to the taste and feel of him, the tickling texture that brushed against her skin. Her eyes slipped closed. Her hand tightened on the bedpost. Prickles danced along the column of her throat where his mustache had brushed, his teeth nipping, his tongue savoring, salving the delicate skin near her ear.

Emaline swallowed and pressed the damp cloth against her heated cheeks. The coolness did little for the burning ache that bloomed inside her, radiating across her breasts, descending in an undeniable rush to nestle in the most intimate place between her legs. She buried her hand in his hair, her head lowering to the pillow beside him.

Her eyes slipped closed.

"Please, God," she begged, pleading into the cradling softness of the goose-down pillow. "Please don't let him die." From across the room, the embers of a dying fire popped as charred logs settled into the grate.

Three days later, Emaline stretched on tiptoes and placed the just-washed bed sheet across the clothesline. Sun beat down upon her and she swiped away the sweat trickling down her cheek. The back door slammed shut and seconds later Euley appeared, carrying more soiled clothing to the waiting cauldron over the fire.

Emaline turned toward her. "Don't you think we should at least try to give him another sip of water?"

"He ain't takin' it. I done tried." Euley tossed the clothes into the bubbling water.

"But his fever broke last night! We should see some kind of response by now." Emaline headed for the back veranda, throwing the words over her shoulder. "I'm going upstairs to check on him again."

Several minutes later, she leaned over the bed, pushing aside the wicker basket that contained a pile of clean cotton strips. Carefully, Emaline peeled away the blood-spotted bandages across Reece's forehead and plopped them into the bucket beside the chamber pot. The black stitches pulled tight in a snaking track of angry flesh but the faded purple edges of the wounds showed indications of healing.

Her hope rose, buoyed by the sign.

She placed the new dressing, then settled the basket of bandages on the side table. A guttural groan filled the space.

Startled, Emaline reared back from his chest.

"Reece?" she queried, not at all sure she'd actually heard him moan. She stared down at him, waiting for another sign, anything at all, to indicate he'd responded to her presence.

Then, he moaned again. The lament drawn out and full of pain.

That was more than enough for Emaline.

In a flash, she bounded from the bed and dashed to the window. She nearly ripped the fabric as she brushed aside the curtains.

"Euley, come quick," she bellowed into the clearing below. Standing by a row of turnips in the garden near the summer kitchen, the servant raised her head and shaded her eyes with her hand. "He's waking up! Euley, can you hear me?"

The old woman waved back. "Yes, yes, I hear you and so do all da folks in Richmond too. Hold on, I'm comin'." She trudged toward the veranda and

Emaline impatiently watched as she disappeared under the eaves of the house.

Reece tried to swallow, but a fiery sensation burnt through him and stopped any further attempt. Undulating pain crashed over him and he moaned again, struggling to eradicate the horrific sensation. The effort proved futile. He felt more than heard the groan tearing upward from deep inside his throat. Claws dug into muscles and tendons. He struggled to repulse the fiery demons that bored their way into his chest. Another keening wail fell from his parched lips. Seconds later, he felt something cool slip beneath his neck. His head rose and soothing tones, angelic and pure, cascaded over him, gliding in between the heaving waves of hell.

He must be dead, and this angel of mercy now begged for his soul.

Cooing words wedged aside his fear.

Something pressed against his lips.

Reece swallowed and a cloying sweetness trickled down his throat, bathing the fires of Lucifer in a wondrous rush of relief—until he coughed and the fleeting respite dissolved. Unbearable pressure returned to crush his chest. He fell backward upon the softness beneath his head. He tried not to scream, but the wail only ripped from his throat in another guttural moan. He raised his arms in an attempt to remove the wicked weight, but the gentle pressure stopped his efforts.

His angel spoke again, her dulcet words beckoning.

"No, you mustn't move." Her churring demand floated over Reece and he resigned himself to her counsel. "The morphine will ease your suffering. You must give it time." He struggled to acknowledge her command, but his awareness of her dulled under the onerous hook that cleaved his ribs.

The compelling force returned to his lips. Once more, he swallowed.

Comfort oozed his raw throat and the honeyed words purled again, pulling him past his torment, transporting him farther and farther away from the suffering.

"Don't fight so hard. Let go..."

He surrendered, curling up next to his angel. The comforting haven of her affirmations, her sweet presence, at last brought him escape. His mouth opened. He tried to speak, to tell her how much he needed her, but the words remained locked behind a rasping whimper. Then, the ebony curtain floated back over him and returned him to the convivial abyss.

Reece opened his eyes. Shadows danced before him. A flickering golden glow, blurry images, all twisted and leaped together across the hazy field of vision. He slowly blinked. Once. Twice. Attempting to identify the cloudy reflections.

His eyes drifted closed.

Coolness radiated through his hands. His fingers flattened, then peaked. He accepted the presence of something wonderful…the plane beneath his fingertips, soft and smooth. Then the sensation spread, penetrating into the skin beneath his arms, the underside of his legs, the aching muscles that stretched across his back.

A bed.

His eyes opened again. And this time the images materialized and entwined across a sea of pale green leaves. He blinked and forced his vision to stabilize. A wash of firelight flickered across wallpaper and highlighted the images of hunting dogs; pheasants drooped in death between the animals' clenched jaws. The distinct crackling of logs in a fireplace underscored the aroma of burning pine.

He tried to roll his head toward the light but searing pain pierced him again and he squeezed his eyes tight to contain it.

The explosion.

He remembered the moment now. Why wasn't he lying on a battlefield somewhere? The soft mattress beneath him, the warmth in the room, the wallpaper all said he wasn't in an army hospital tent. No hospital on earth smelled like this room—fresh and clean, an elusive fragrance of lavender.

The wondrous scent of my angel.

He'd memorized her soothing voice, pleading and praying, begging him to return to the living, begging him to return to her.

Then he heard a sound.

A snip?

His foggy mind scrambled to identify the source. He scanned the hazy-lit area above him. His gaze trailed down the mahogany posters of a huge bed. The whole thing swathed him in sheer curtains.

Again he heard snipping and peered sideways.

The bent form of a woman sat beside the bed, her hand dipping down and then pulling away from an object cradled in her lap.

Sewing?

Reece struggled to adjust his eyes. Firelight caressed her delicate features, the flickering glow framing her beautiful profile. Murkiness lingered inside his brain and testified that he'd been sedated, but he didn't think he'd also lost his mind.

He closed his eyes and slowly reopened them. The precious apparition shimmered back into focus. This vision seemed so real, so different from the thousands of others he'd had of her in the past. The myriad of other dreams had tormented his soul every night since he'd left her at that cramped hotel room in Falmouth nearly a year and a half ago, all swirled in a blur of regret.

Reece stared, mesmerized by the way her hand rose and fell with each stitch. Several strands of hair cascaded over her far shoulder from a loose chignon resting at the nape of her neck. He dug his fingers into the bed sheet. An aching need to touch her raged through him. His eyes burned with a need to blink, but he refused to do so, afraid she would disappear just as she had in all those other dreams.

So he opened his mouth and uttered her precious name. "Emmy?"

The garbled name grated outward from the covers and Emaline stopped sewing. She swiveled toward the bed. "Reece?" A flash of elation tinted her voice. "Y-yes? I'm here, Reece." For fifteen long days, he'd incoherently mumbled—words about the war, the horrible carnage he'd witnessed, everything ran together in a disjointed hodge-podge of mangled torment.

All pain-filled.

All drug-induced.

But not now. This time, her name left his lips in a clear whisper. Her gaze met his and her throat tightened. She surged to her feet, her sewing and the scissors tumbling to the floor. Leaning, she placed her ear next to his lips.

"Emmy?" His shallow query was barely perceptible, yet a giddy wave of disbelief fluttered over her.

She cupped his face. "Yes. Yes, it's me, Reece."

"Are you...real?"

"Yes. Yes. I'm real," she whispered, tears rushing into her eyes. She blinked faster. "I'm very real." After a long pause, his eyes drifted closed again. "Reece?" She reached for his bare shoulder and squeezed his warm skin. Her breath held while seconds ticked past.

Then, he reopened his eyes and peered up into hers.

"How...long?" he groaned.

She brushed his hair from his face. "Over two weeks. You've been badly wounded." He nodded, and the obvious pain of moving his head brought forth another groan. "My brother found you and brought you here."

"How?"

"On a scouting mission. He stumbled across your group of men. You were the only one left alive." She'd removed his stitches several days ago and there'd been no seepage to his wounds. Soon, he'd be up and moving to avoid atrophy to his strong muscles. "I'm going to remove the dressing on your chest now."

His eyes opened wider. "You're my angel," he whispered.

Emaline smiled at him, smoothing her hand over his head. "I'm glad I'm your angel."

The whole time she administered to his wounds, he watched her. Even when she poured medicine down his throat, he continued to stare up at her, even when the pain flowed over him and he moaned aloud; when the tears slipped from the corners of his dark eyes, he still refused to close them.

Chapter Twenty-Three

Euley had finished shaving Reece when Emaline eased open the bedroom door, carrying a tray laden with breakfast.

"He's in a foul mood dis mornin', Miz Emaline," the woman mumbled, moving past her and on into the hallway. Emaline anchored a smile. She wasn't sure she wanted another set-to with Mr. Cantankerous.

"Good morning, Reece." Her cheery voice matched the lively yellow-and-green plaid of her day dress.

"Morning," he mumbled, struggling to sit up in the bed.

She placed the tray across his lap. "I've brought you a nice bowl of fish chowder."

"Again?" He stared down at the opaque liquid in the bowl. Chunks of cooked vegetables bobbed in the broth like buoys. His gaze tracked back to hers. "We've had this same talk every morning for the past three weeks. Can't anyone rustle me up a slab of meat and some eggs?"

She fluttered the cloth napkin into the air and then settled it across his chest. Benjamin's cotton nightshirt engulfed him in soft white billows. "And I've told you the same thing every morning too, remember? Euley says you're not ready for anything more substantial quite yet." Dour-faced, Reece had been especially long-suffering these past few days. Emaline sympathized with him, though. To coop up this man for so long proved daunting, especially since he didn't crave the depending-upon-others role he now faced. Emaline refused to let him see her empathy and instead changed the subject. "Tacker informed me this morning your stallion has greatly improved. The wound on the flank is nearly healed."

"Lucky horse."

She stifled a sigh. "You're getting stronger every day, Reece. This takes time."

"Yes, but I've got things I need to do."

"What is so pressing for you?"

"The war, to name one." His eyes locked with hers and silence filled the room before he gruffly added, "I don't even know what's going on or where the hell my men are now."

Don't scream.

"Ah yes, the war again," she said, surprised her voice remained calm. "It appears to me you've already paid your dues." She gestured to the wounds. Even though they were mending at an incredible rate, Reece was still miles from being saddle-ready. Emaline pursed her lips. Each day, the argument of war and the important role it played in his life, swelled higher.

He shifted higher against the headboard. "I've got an obligation to nine hundred men."

"Yes, well let me relieve some of your concerns. Tacker heard from a passerby this morning that the Yankees are somewhere down around Petersburg."

She debated the advisability of giving him the news, foolishly thinking that by keeping him in the dark about the war's progression, he might forget his urgency to leave. As she saw the light of interest brighten in his eyes, along with a smile that popped up across his smooth-shaven face, Emaline realized the sheer impossibility of that dream.

Her heart sank further as his grin widened. "Petersburg? Good. That's only twenty miles south of Richmond. If Grant can get the railroads blocked, that'll cut off Lee's supplies and then we'll definitely have the bastards cornered. That's excellent news."

"For you perhaps, but certainly not for the southern soldiers."

He sighed. "It's only a matter of time. You know this. The sooner we get this damn thing over with, the sooner our country can heal."

"I'm tired of war," she whispered, turning away from his inscrutable gaze to straighten the few medical supplies still left on the side table. "This has all been an exhausting waste of precious lives and resources."

He nodded, picking up his spoon. "You'll get no argument from me on that one."

Her chin rose. "It appears you're ready to eat on your own today?"

He brought the broth-filled spoon to his lips and then offered a broad smile before sipping off the liquid with a tad more fervor than she expected. "Delicious," he said, plunging the spoon back into the bowl for a refill.

Emaline laughed, crossing to the fireplace. She stooped to tend to the ashes from the night before. Sweeping them up with the hearth broom, she placed them in the bucket, and laid a new fire for the evening light.

Appetite assuaged, Reece pushed aside the empty tray and leaned back against the mound of pillows. His arms nestled behind his head. "Emmy?" he said, his eyes drifting closed.

She stood, dusted off her hands, and then turned back toward him. "Yes?"

"Thank you for saving my life."

"You saved yourself."

"Not true, Angel, 'twas you that brought me back."

Emaline traversed the room and removed the breakfast tray, placing it on the table next to the supplies. *Angel*, his new pet name for her. The connotation behind the word disturbed her. Did he just appreciate her simply for her nursing skills? Like the admiration that so many wounded men gave to their caregivers or sanitation commission workers. Or was she truly important to him?

"Why do you call me that?" she asked.

His eyes opened, his smile returning. He lowered his arms to the quilt. "Because you are."

"I'm no angel, Reece. Believe me." She tossed his napkin on top of the empty bowl. "Sometimes I'm wickedly mean." She turned back. He appeared so much better today. His color had improved. Good health was returning, and though he would bear multiple scars from his injury, he should suffer no other ill effects.

And when he left this time, she would miss him dreadfully.

Their relationship had shifted into a strong friendship and she felt comfortable with the easy camaraderie of the past week. Aside from his frustrations about the war, which seemed to escalate at a steady pace, they had spent many an enjoyable afternoon talking about his ranch out west, and his sister, Callie.

Emaline cherished every moment spent with him.

She lowered to the edge of the bed and scooted back onto the mattress. "But sometimes, I'm nice too," she said, a chuckle in her voice.

"Yes, sometimes, I think you're very nice." His teasing words tangled up inside her heart. A long silence stretched between them and forced her gaze back to his. "And then sometimes I think you're a little wicked." He winked at her and sent a flush burning hot across her cheeks.

She remembered exactly how *wicked* she'd been while wrapped in his arms.

His eyes narrowed and the tone of his voice shifted. "You know you're an integral part of me now, don't you?" She glanced away. His words wrought havoc with her heart. Gone was the comfortable banter of moments before. His penetrating words continued. "Lying here, day after day, I've done a lot of thinking. I haven't always been honest with you."

Emaline closed her eyes. How much did she dare believe this time? The rich timbre of his voice rippled through her frustrations.

"I should never have said those unkind words to you after I discovered your brother that night. You don't know how often I wished I'd done things differently." He reached for her hand, his fingers closing around hers. The warmth and weight of them forced her eyes closed. With a will of their own, her fingers opened and then interlocked with his in a strong clasp. "I'd come back to talk to you, but then I discovered Brennen and everything went to hell after that. I'm so sorry I hurt you."

Chirping birds beyond the window promised another beautiful morning and the bustling sounds of Euley beyond the open bedroom door declared work that needed doing.

But they all faded into the background. As long as Emaline lived, she would remember the pain of that night.

Her emotions threatened to overwhelm her.

She knew it was only a matter of time before Reece climbed back upon his horse.

Caring for this man had consumed every waking hour this past month. As much as she longed to believe him, she knew she would never be able to endure another heartbreak of such magnitude.

Living without this man would be hell on earth.

So Emaline did the only thing she could do. She buried her desires deep within and denied herself her happily ever after.

"I appreciate your kind words, Reece. And you surely know how important you are to me too. I have always admired your strength and how you helped my brother escape." Tears welled in her eyes as she turned her head away from his steady appraisal. "But it's important you rest now." Her words tumbled over each other as her feet hit the floor. She shoved off the bed, pulling her hand from his to break their clasp. "I've many things to do this morning, so I must go now."

"Emaline, wait."

She gave him no opportunity to reply. Gathering up the tray, she fled the room, her heart pounding under the enormous weight of her decision.

Reece watched her leave, his outstretched hand dropping to the bedcovers. "Dammit," he snarled. The mood had shifted so abruptly. One minute she was smiling and laughing, and the next he was spilling his guts. From the tears she tried to hide, it was apparent his words had upset her all over again. Frustration filled him as he attempted to sort out confused emotions. He simply wanted to thank her again for saving his life, and off he went instead, like some rambling asinine idiot, pouring out his feelings for her.

Reece balled his hand into a fist and slammed it upon the coverlet. Damn this helpless sensation of need, this emotional dependence. He was tired of lying on his back in bed. He needed to get back to what he knew best. Soldiering was something he did well.

And he was sorely out of practice in all the subtleties required to woo a woman.

Chapter Twenty-Four

Reece waited in stony silence while Euley entered the room and placed his dinner tray beside him. He narrowed his eyes at her, his arms crossing in front of him. Three days had passed since he'd last spoken to Emaline.

Irritation clawed a hole through his patience. "Where the hell is she?" he growled.

"She's busy," the woman retorted.

"She's not that busy." He ground out the words, harsh and low, and threw them toward Euley. "Tell me where she is right now."

"I was told to bring up da food an' if'n you eat everythin', den I's to get you up to walk dis evenin'."

"I don't want to eat or walk. I want to see her."

"Yes, Colonel, I know what you's wantin', only I don't know what else to say." She shifted the tray closer and reached behind his head to plump his pillows. "I was told to bring up da supper an' dat's all I'm doin'. Now if'n you don't want to eat, then I'll just be taking it back down stairs wif me." Euley leveled her head and stared into his eyes. Hers narrowed into determined slits. "You get to make da choice, Colonel. Now pick."

"I haven't seen her for three days. Is she ill?" The disturbing thought banished his selfish disappointment.

"No, she's just busy." A smile revealed a row of crooked white teeth.

Reece simmered under the woman's smirk. This crafty old bat had him nailed against the wall and there would be no intimidating her. A grudging respect settled through him and he reached for the dinner tray, pulling it to his chest. All the while, his eyes remained locked with hers.

Euley nodded each time he brought the spoon to his lips and smiled each time he swallowed. Evidently she planned to remain right where she'd planted herself until he finished every damn drop.

Reece ate quickly.

He was tired of being waited on hand and foot, and tired of waiting for Emaline to reappear, whenever that might be. His words softened. "You know, I didn't properly thank you for helping save my life."

"Don't thank me. Miz Emaline did most of the saving. I jus' tore up yo' bandages. She on the other hand, hovered over you, day an' night. No one else could even get close."

"Except now," he snapped, shoving away the empty dishes. They rattled on the tray, underscoring his frustration. "Now she doesn't even come around. Why is that?"

"You'll have to be askin' her dose questions."

Euley placed the tray on the side table and turned to pull the cover off him in an exaggerated swish of color. "Come on, Colonel. It's time you started walkin'."

He didn't argue. The sooner he could ambulate, the sooner he could find Emaline.

Euley steadied him as he swung his legs over the edge of the bed. After several attempts, he finally stood, Benjamin's nightshirt ballooning around him. The wound in his chest unmercifully throbbed and he leaned upon the old woman for support.

His foot shuffled forward and he completed his first step.

"Dat's good, Colonel. First one foot, den da other. You's doin' fine. Yes, sir. Keep this up, you'll be back on dat horse in no time." Euley pointed to the chair beside the fire. "Let's work our way over dere and you can sit a spell while I change da linens." Several hellish steps later, Reece eased onto the chair and watched as Euley went about her chores, stripping and remaking the bed and straightening-up the room.

All the while, his frustrations percolated. His glare alternated between the open door in hopes of catching a glimpse of Emaline and watching the servant tidy his room. Twice, he nearly slipped from the chair while craning his neck to peer into the hallway.

An hour later, Reece returned to bed even more annoyed than he'd been before.

A week later, Emaline sat in the chair beside the open window.

The sweet smells of a mid-summer night wafted in on the breeze and washed the fragrance of bluebells, blue-eyed violets, and trilliums around her.

A discouraged sigh left her lips. When the door to the upstairs library squeaked open, she stiffened. "Well?"

She continued to stare out into the darkness.

Euley padded across the room. "He won't tolerate being caged much longer."

"Did he walk on his own again?" She tossed the words over her shoulder.

"Yes. An' he's done real good too. I had him up for nearly an hour, but he ain't quite ready to take on the stairs just yet."

"The sooner he heals, the sooner he'll be gone." The pain inside her chest swelled. "Thank you for helping with him."

"He cares for you a great deal, Miz Emaline. You sure you want to keep avoidin' him like dis?"

"I'm sure," she replied.

"Well, he's sleepin' now." Euley crossed to the door and opened it. "If'n you don't need me any longer, I'll be leavin'."

"I'll see you again in the morning. We'll work in the garden early while it's still cool."

The woman nodded and then disappeared from view.

Several minutes later, Emaline eased off the chair, smoothed the front of her dress, and drifted down the darkened corridor and across the upstairs landing to the master suite. Pushing open the door, she peered inside.

Amber firelight bathed the room in a subdued glow.

Reece slept soundly, his breath issuing in and out in a soft, steady rhythm. Emaline checked the corner of the room. His uniform, revolver and saber waited for him. Last night, she'd retrieved them from the kitchen cabinet and Euley brought them upstairs. The tools of his trade defined Reece; he would need them when he left.

Emaline slipped into the room, the pad of her leather house shoes muffled in the lush Aubusson carpet beneath her feet.

She came to a stop beside the bed.

Deep in the throes of a healing sleep, his mouth slightly open, peace claimed Reece. With the beard gone, she could see the healthy return of color to his skin. Earlier this evening, Euley had washed his hair, and the long strands lay in a thick and silky wave across the pillow. A few streaks of gray marked the passing of time since they'd first met. The sight undermined Emaline's resolve for distance. Her hands curled at her sides, the need to slide her fingers through the dark locks unraveling the enormous ache inside her heart. There was no use denying, she cared deeply for this man.

She lowered her mouth, stopping just short of touching his.

"I love you," she whispered.

From where he stood at the upstairs window, Reece watched Emaline move among the rows of corn. Laid out near the summer kitchen, the garden held a bounty of crops and would yield an abundant harvest this year.

He sighed. More than a week had passed since they'd last spoken, and he could move fairly well around the upstairs bedroom. Despite their rocky beginning, he and Euley also had developed an unexpected friendship. Reece found he enjoyed hearing the woman's views about many things.

His thoughts shifted backward to his shave this morning where he learned how much the old woman admired Emaline.

"After Master Benjamin died, she told us we could leave if'n we wanted to, even gave us official papers drawn up at the county court house to prove it, though most white folks disapproved of her doin' so." Euley chuckled, holding the mirror in place while Reece angled his jaw for the blade. "Miz Emaline been good to me an' Israel. So we stayed." She placed the mirror on the side table and handed him a towel, her chatter continuing. "Our daughter lives at Wildwood plantation over near da Rapidan River. Wildwood's owners refugeed to Richmond last year and just left dere people behind to fend for themselves. We's leavin' tonight to go visit Bertie for a few days. Gonna spend time rockin' my new grandbaby." Euley removed the basin of dirty water, and Reece nodded.

"You both take care on the ride over," he said. "There was heavy fighting on the Rapidan near Morton's Ford earlier this year and deserters from both sides could still be roaming the area."

"I appreciate yo' concern, Colonel. We'll keep our eyes wide open."

A smile tugged at Reece's lips as he watched Emaline gingerly step across the rows of carrots, their emerald tops ruffling where her skirt's hem brushed. A building excitement wound through him like a whirlwind.

She would serve his evening meal tonight since Euley would be gone. And a quick glance at the clock told him just how many hours remained.

He looked back. A hot June afternoon beat down upon Emaline, but she couldn't hide from him beneath the wide-brimmed hat. Her face, now a golden tan, bore small creases near her eyes. She worked hard, tirelessly turning the soil, pulling away the weeds, and watering her precious food supply. With each passing day at this window, his feelings for her grew right along with her bountiful stand of vegetables. He longed for her touch and envied the plants she tended with such caring, devoted hands. They received so much of her and he now nothing at all. He starved for her touch, her smile, her breath against his skin.

It had been an eternity since he'd kissed her.

Reece pushed away from the window, his feet slamming against the patterned rug with muffled force.

Tonight.

She would not be able to avoid him tonight.

Emaline finished lugging the bucketfuls of warm water upstairs.

Even though she'd used the servant's stairway, being quiet during the many trips up and down had been the hardest part. She repeatedly poured in water, but on this final trip, she misjudged the distance between the bucket and the side of her slipper tub.

Metal clanked against metal.

Her lips compressed and she glanced to the door, but the promise of a much-needed bath shoved aside all lingering caution. Working in the garden had drained her, physically and mentally, and she closed her bedroom door, then stripped from her soiled garments.

The breeze from the open window wafted across her nakedness. The faint, familiar trace of pine, the piquant aromas of horses and mules from the stable, Rappahannock's brackish hint, all mingled with the lavender oil skimming the surface of her bath water. Tired arms wrapped her body and her eyes drifted closed. Though Reece slept down the hall, her mind brought him to her.

For a moment, the raw, renewed strength of the man enveloped her.

Emaline opened her eyes, and settled her gaze on the portrait above the fireplace. The muted oil, an Edmund Blair Leighton original, had been another one of her husband's long-ago gifts. A single candle burned low on the mantel and plunged the angst-filled features of *Tristan and Isolde* into shadows. Isolde clutched a gilded harp, and Tristan a dragon's head—lost lovers bound by the dictates of their day; they smothered their mutual passion and pretended indifference.

Another sigh filled the room. Wavy candlelight washed across the dark, distressed mantel, highlighting the sleek stallion carving in the center of the oak. Powerful and magnificent.

Like Reece.

It would be so simple to open the door and go to him. And yet, regardless of what she said or did, he would still leave. That fact would never change. Emaline stepped over the edge of the metal and slid into the bath, willing the water to wash away all her desires for the man.

Reece clasped his hands behind his head, staring at the dark ceiling. He listened intently, trying to place the far-away sound.

Clanking metal?

He swung his legs over the edge of the bed and sat up. A moment later, he paced across the room to the door. Tomorrow he would take on the challenge of descending the main staircase. The resolution came directly on the heels of discovering his dinner sitting on the floor outside his bedroom, three hours earlier. One small knock upon the closed door announced its arrival. The retreating footfalls only fueled his determination to be up and moving. He was finished with lying in bed.

Emaline had avoided him for the last time.

Reece steadied himself at the door, then eased it open and peered into the hallway. Darkness prevailed, except for the wafer-thin slice of light coming from beneath the door at the end of the corridor. She was in there. Alone. Reece traversed the hall and stood just outside the closed door. Faint, muffled humming, angel-sweet and low, mingled with splashing water. He wiped his palm on his pants leg, then turned the brass knob.

The door swung open on silent hinges.

Light from a single candle illuminated the room in muted shadows. A small bank of orange coals in the fireplace bounced off a copper tub on the hearth, setting the metal aflame. The ethereal image of Emaline bathing ignited a fire that blazed straight to his groin.

His breath locked up somewhere inside his chest, his heart stopping in mid-beat.

With a will of its own, his erection pulsed into life. Hard and heavy, pressing against the buttoned fly of his pants. A rush of desire, urgent and unremitting, engulfed Reece. Locked in a fervent trance, he could only stare at the breathtaking woman in the center of the tub.

She sat angled away from him, the small swell of her breast visible just above the edge of copper.

Water glistened in shimmering droplets across ivory shoulders. She was a goddess sculpted in marble. As Emaline lifted her right arm, his gaze followed her hand. Inch by luxurious inch, she smoothed lather across the slender length. Small, slick, lavender-infused bubbles glistened in the candlelight and then broke a twinkling moment later. She cupped her hand and sluiced water over her shoulder.

Tiny rivulets caught the candle's glow.

Iridescent beads sparkled over her collarbone, then spilled in a provocative sweep down her spine to nestle at the wondrous curve of her back. Unbound hair, a glorious mass over her far shoulder, darkened into the color of a raven's wing, the subdued light reflecting through damp, luxurious strands—all around her, steam radiated upward; caressing, embracing her polished and perfect curves.

Reece swayed. His hand slammed against the doorframe to keep him upright. In a strangling effort, he brought a rush of air back into his lungs as a blinding ache for her burned through him, begging for release.

He would deny the beast no longer.

His groan reached Emaline's ears from across the room.

Her gaze lanced over her shoulder, her eyes widening as they locked with his. She gasped his name, the word tumbling from her lips in a raw whisper. For a long, stretched-out moment, he held her gaze; his lungs heaving in another quart of air while his passion for her strengthened. "You've avoided me for days." His voice scraped across the room. "Now I want to know why."

A maelstrom of emotions swirled through Emaline. In the time she'd known this man, she'd confronted so many chaotic sensations. No other male on earth had seen her bathe. None had seen her naked. With Benjamin, she'd been swathed in darkness, encased in cotton. She'd always closed her eyes.

With this strong and stalwart man, such thoughts seemed ludicrous.

Emaline fought for control, surprised she could find logic, or her voice, amid the quaking awareness rippling through her. "I thought it best."

"For whom?" he rasped, his hand still bracing against the wood.

She skimmed his magnificence. Barefoot, tight-fitting cavalry pants, no shirt. Across the smattering of dark chest hair, a fading bruise encircled the eight-inch scar, a malevolent serpent carved on his skin to forevermore remind him of the price he'd paid in war.

"Don't do this, Reece," she whispered, drawing her legs up to shield herself. "We both know you'll be leaving soon." Her tone sounded much too rational—the words presented with a weeklong rush of practice. "I thought it best that—"

"You should've asked what I thought." Amber light fell across the hard planes of his face. The searing heat, the intensity in his eyes bewitched her. "I've been driven mad waiting for even a glimpse of you." He was a powerful beast and his burning gaze ordered her to surrender, his low words flowing over her in a ragged whisper to push aside her foolish fears. "I would never knowingly hurt you, Emaline. Surely to God, you know this by now."

She knew. Deep inside, the pleading of the forgotten woman begged her to respond to this provocative man. Yield to him. Welcome him with all the wild abandon she saw reflected in his eyes. As futile as she knew it to be, however, she tried one last time to deny the inevitable. "Your upcoming departure is hurt enough."

With a muffled curse, Reece pushed from the wood and stepped over the threshold. He slammed the door behind him as he headed straight toward her. "I'm here now, Angel. That's all that matters tonight."

Chapter Twenty-Five

Reece came to a stop beside the tub, then dropped to his knee. Leaning forward, he captured a wet tendril of hair that draped her shoulder.

"I've missed you," he said, his eyes narrowing.

"Please don't…" Her words trailed off into a strained whisper. His gaze shifted lower and he brushed the end of the curl over the lush swell of her breasts.

Her nipples instantly hardened under his strokes.

"Your lips say one thing, Angel, but your body tells me another." One more sweep and her eyes slipped closed. Reece knew he could no more leave this room than he could stop the Rappahannock's relentless flow to the sea. His hand turned over, coiling the wet tendril around his fingers. He pulled and drew her forward.

Her eyes opened.

And a moment later, she surged upward until her mouth covered his.

Her succulence enveloped Reece, the sweet taste of her lips, a homecoming.

His mouth slid over hers, claiming more. Frantic. Forceful. Possessive. His arms wrapped her body, his hands gliding over her flawlessness. Water slipped down his forearms. Moving from her lips, he trailed kisses to her earlobe, nibbled his way to her throat, and then back to her lips. "Every minute of every day, I've wanted you," he whispered, low and husky. And then his mouth captured hers again and he kissed her, forcing her back against the cool edge of the tub. She was everything a man could want, and he wanted to give her everything. His lips caressed her face, tracing kisses across the bridge of her nose, sweeping over her cheeks. His heartbeat slammed against his chest, want for this woman thundering through his veins.

His voice slid out on a rough-edged plea. "Make me yours, sweet Angel," he murmured into the curve of her mouth. Her dead husband had turned her into an old woman long before her time. With his kiss, Reece would breathe life back into her. With him, she would know the vast difference.

Ragged moans fell from her lips as he burned a fire trail down her neck with his kisses. And then, a moment later, he covered her breast with his mouth, and felt the moisture-glistened peak puckering beneath his tongue's warm laving. A heady sense of power engulfed Reece.

He shifted sideways and slid his hands under the full curve of her hips, immersing his arms deeper in the water. He wrapped her body and drew her closer...and closer still. With his next inrushing breath, Reece tightened his hold and then lifted her up and out of the tub.

Water ran in rivulets down his arms, coursed through the hairs of his chest, soaked the waistband of his pants. Lavender-scented moisture sluiced over him to disappear into the woolen rug beneath them. In the next breath, Reece settled them onto a nearby chair.

Pulling Emaline across his lap, he shoved aside the throbbing reminder of the wound that had shattered his chest. Instead, he gazed into her eyes. His hands caressed her everywhere—from waist to hip, down each slender leg still slick with warmth and wetness. He palmed her breasts, as pure and silky as the moonlight that spilled into the room to mate with the candle's glow.

Enchanted beyond words, he became lost in her gaze—sultry, sensual, her need for him emanating from the depths of her shimmering eyes.

She wanted more of him.

And he soared.

Her cheeks aflame with desire, she whispered, "You control me so easily."

"I'm glad," he said, a perceptive smile lifting his lips. Masculine pride in his prowess and a blinding need to possess her inflamed him. His hand moved lower and explored the lushness between her legs. She granted him access; her courage to shove aside the last vestige of shame and offer to him this precious gift thrilled him beyond words. He cupped her womanhood, groaned aloud at the musky softness he found there. When his finger slipped inside her warmth, Emaline shuddered so fiercely in his embrace, she swayed.

With his first silken stroke, Reece freed the remainder of her inhibitions. He found her pulsing nub and melded his finger to it, sending Emaline careening into quivering madness. The faster he stroked, the tighter she coiled, garbled, gasping moans ripping outward, climbing higher while she panted toward release. And then, finally, Reece unwrapped for her the gift she so desperately sought.

Her back arched.

A keening wail ripped from her lips.

She repeatedly gasped his name and collapsed against him to buck in helpless response.

Several moments passed before she whispered, "I've never known...I was so afraid you'd die...afraid I would never get to..." Her words tumbled out, individual phrases choppy and sporadic.

As a whole, they told the story.

"Never get to what?" Reece coaxed. "Tell me, Angel fire. What do you want to do?"

She gazed at him and her hands slipped past his ribcage, down the planes of his stomach. Reece issued a strangled groan, the swelling surge against his pants reminding him that the beast beneath blue wool still begged for freedom.

Her hand settled atop his hardness and Reece caught his breath.

Emaline's chin dipped.

A slight smile touched her lips.

She pressed again.

His hands banded her arms and Reece squeezed, the animal inside him panting for deliverance. "I live for you," he ground out between clenched teeth.

She pushed from his clasp and stood, her nakedness glistened. Candlelight laved each curve. Her breasts, small, softly drooping could nourish him for an eternity, the rosy-hued areola surrounding each taut nipple, lush and dusky and a perfect size for suckling.

Her tousled mane shimmered over one shoulder like a mahogany curtain. Reece swept back the strands to send them into a damp tangle down her back, wanting nothing to mar the exquisite vision standing before him.

"What is it you want…exactly?" she teased, gazing deep into his eyes.

"You." He leaned his head back. "I want you."

"Then you shall have me." She reached down. As each pewter button on his pants slipped free, Reece pulsed beneath her fingers to remind her of his impatience. He lifted his hips and with an easy tug, she removed his pants.

His erection swelled before her like some wild and savage beast.

Her breath caught and she peered at him.

He shifted his lips into a lop-sided grin.

The uniform pants landed at his feet with a heavy thud. Emaline leaned over, smoothing her hands up his legs.

Reece issued a low moan, his impatience growing.

She moved forward and with surprising ease, she straddled him. "Is this how it's done?" she whispered, enveloping the demanding length within her slick sheath.

Amid the silver and amber of night, his deep groan answered.

With frantic fingers, Reece clutched her hips and drove in and out of her, a man mad with need. He wanted nothing held in abeyance—every piece of her mattered.

"Oh God," he ground out, the words ripping from his throat.

As his body rose, she lowered, matching him rhythm and speed. When she leaned forward, he rewarded her fully, and when she curved back, Reece sank deeper and died a little bit more in her arms. Their breaths fused together, their gasps a symphony of one.

They rose on the currents and floated on air. He demanded, and with a wild possession, she obeyed. When Reece speared the mark inside her, she cried out in passionate moans. Her hair swept forward in a damp curtain, skimming against his chest and enveloping him in the essence of lavender. He had never wanted a woman more. She was a provocative creature born from years of denial—a siren that could suck away his strength and soul.

When she at last reached the pinnacle, her fervent sobs poured into the night. Yet Reece waited...and waited some more...stroking her still deeper, leading her onward into paradise.

And then, with his next deep stroke, he felt the incredible quickening. It built, tormenting in its scale, overwhelming in its power to possess him. He cried out in surrender, his guttural voice, raw and panting as he released eons of need. He crested over into heaven-sent bliss, fully pumping into her. When he had nowhere else to go, Reece finally relinquished and released his seed deep inside his angel.

Chapter Twenty-Six

Jackson lowered the crumpled letter. "Unbelievable," he murmured, glancing up at Lieutenant Glave. The envelope fell to the desk. He angled the missive toward the aid-de-camp. "Where did you get this?"

"A Reb cavalry captain under a flag of truce brought it in to one of our picket posts this morning."

"Did they give you a name?"

"Yes, sir. Captain Brennen Benedict. He told the picket to make certain only you got the sealed envelope."

Benedict. The prison breakout.

Jackson scanned the contents again, a broad smile flooding his face. "He says the colonel's still alive."

"Alive? But…he was killed at the Wilderness."

"We never found his body, did we?" Jackson reminded. "Hell's fire, I searched for two days myself and couldn't find a single trace."

"But, Major, we never found lots of missing soldiers in that mess."

Jackson snapped the paper. "This is from the widow McDaniels's brother. He scouts for Stuart's cavalry. If he says he found the colonel wounded on the battlefield and took him back to the plantation, I believe him."

Confusion flooded the young aide's face. "But why would he do that?"

"It's a long story, Lucas, and one I'm not at liberty to share, but the fact is, Reece is alive and we're going to get him. Find Sergeant Conners and have him report to me. We'll leave in an hour."

"Yes, sir." He saluted with excitement, then rushed from the tent.

Jackson smiled and leaned against the chair, the letter falling to the desktop. Since Reece's disappearance, the war had shifted to a different type of fighting, consisting mostly of digging trench lines and earthworks. With the Rebs bottled up in Richmond and Petersburg, the Federal army now worked on putting a stranglehold on Lee's besieged troops. Siege lines tightened around the capital, and the regiment had moved several times over the course of the past two months. No wonder it took Captain Benedict so long to get the news to him.

Jackson uncorked a bottle of whiskey, sloshed a generous serving into his tin mug, and brought the metal to his lips. "Thank God," he muttered around the rim. His friend was alive. Soon Reece would be back where he belonged. The liquor burned a path to his stomach.

This rescue mission was one command Jackson would enjoy leading.

Mid-July arrived hot and humid. The afternoon sun beat down upon Emaline. She poured a bucket of water around her plants. Tacker hollered a greeting and she straightened, waving at him. The old man shuffled into the stable and Emaline sighed. Any minute, she expected Euley and Israel to return home from their visit to their daughter.

They were family now, and she missed them.

Emaline stole a glance toward the mansion and a smile broke across her face.

So was Reece. He, the most important member of her clan. The rutting beast had kept her up half the night. Emaline giggled, a flush heating her cheeks. She recalled his prowess and power. After their first frantic coupling near the tub, he'd taken her to the bed and possessed her in slower, mind-numbing ecstasy, showing her all the ways a man could love a woman.

Multiple times, in fact.

Reece slept soundly, his healing body demanding rest. She laughed again as she swung the empty bucket in a circle around her. A hum spilled from her lips. All afternoon, her outlook had been light and cheerful as the hope inside her grew.

Distant hoof beats of galloping horses interrupted her thoughts.

Emaline swung to locate the source. She raised her hand above her eyes to shade them from the sun. A shimmering haze radiated across the open fields and she saw the wavering approach of several riders. Was it three? Or four?

Could it be Brennen?

"Tacker! We've got riders," she hollered, pushing the straw hat off her head. It hung down her back by a soiled ribbon tie.

Yes, definitely three riders, she could see them.

They crossed to the edge of the field and angled toward the house. As they drew closer, Emaline determined two of the riders wore Confederate gray. A third wore Union blue. And not one of the three was Brennen. Disappointment gripped her, followed by an ominous unease. The empty bucket rattled when it hit the ground.

Deserters.

She turned and raced toward the stable.

"Tacker!" she screamed. "Hide!" She made it to the north side of the garden when the soldiers rode into the service yard. Emaline spun to face them. They reined their horses to a stop before her.

One of the men in tattered gray spoke first. "Afternoon, ma'am."

Black, waist-length hair lay in a greasy strand down his back. The sleeve of his jacket bore sergeant strips. Gaunt hollows carved out the area below each cheekbone and violet shading stained the crepe-like skin beneath his rheumy eyes. He appeared diseased.

Emaline swallowed. She corralled her spiraling fear and pointed to the well. "There's the water. Help yourself, and then keep riding."

"That's right neighborly of you," he said, stifling a cough.

"There's nothing left to steal," she added. "Your kind have been here before."

"And what kind is that?" a red-haired man with a shaggy beard, the other one dressed in gray, quipped. He reined his horse in a tight circle on her left.

The black-haired sergeant spat a stream of tobacco juice onto Emaline's tidy row of turnips. "Probably not the kind she'll dig up her silver and china for, you dumb jackass."

Emaline's heart hammered against her ribs, her fear escalating. The third man raised a long leg and nudged her on the shoulder with a dust-covered boot. She swiveled to glare at him.

"Where's your menfolk, Missy? Or your darkies?" He scanned the area before settling his gaze on her again. "Or are you all alone here in this great big house?"

Reece slept soundly upstairs but her fear for his safety mounted by the moment.

"There's no one else here." Her chin lifted. "And I'm not afraid of you."

"Did you hear that, boys? She's not afraid of me."

Red's laughter joined his. "Hell, if it was me, I'd be afraid."

Emaline gauged the distance to the closest place of refuge and made a wild dash between the two horses toward the open stable door.

"What the hell—" Blue reined his horse around and drove spurs into the flanks of the beast. The animal bolted, closing the distance. She heard him approaching. He leaned low, ripping away her hat before his fingers snaked into her hair. Carved-bone hairpins scattered, sending her chignon down her back in a heavy tumble. Except for the strands entwined within the man's filthy grasp. He jerked her up short, banging her into the side of his horse. The hot stench of the unkempt animal assaulted her nose, sweat from his hide soaking the front of her blouse. Tears coursed from Emaline's eyes. The pain tightened across her scalp.

"You ain't going nowhere, Missy, cept'n where we're takin' you." Blue slipped his boot from the stirrup and entwined a lean leg around her just as the others rode up to box her in.

"Turn her loose," the diseased man snapped and Blue released his hold, shoving her away from him. Blackie leaned over and smoothed his hand over her tangled curls. "I ain't had me a woman in weeks," he whispered. "Leastways, not a clean one like you."

Tears spilled out and ran unchecked down Emaline's face. No one saw Tacker emerge from the stable except her. The late afternoon sun glinted off a pitchfork clutched in his gnarled hands. Inch by inch, the old man closed the distance, the deadly tines aimed straight at the closest intruder.

"We aim to take you so you might as well give up," the diseased sergeant said, threading his fingers through her hair. "Holy shit, this feels just like corn silk."

"Please. No," she mumbled, attempting to move from his touch.

"She wants nothin' to do with you," Blue jibed, poking the barrel of his Henry rifle into her back to prevent her from moving. "We'll have none of this foolishness, Missy."

Emaline opened her mouth to scream, hoping her cries might somehow carry to Reece, but she never got the chance. Blackie grabbed her around the waist, a dirty hand snaking out to cover her mouth. Her shriek only muffled against the sergeant's calloused palm as she tasted salty grime.

Tacker rushed forward but his labored breathing announced his presence long before the deadly tines could reach their mark.

Red jerked around and shrieked, "Lookout!"

Blue deflected the strike with his boot, but the tines managed to scrape against his thigh. "Sonofabitch!" he bellowed before slamming his rifle butt on top of Tacker's head. The farrier crumpled beneath the crushing blow, the pitchfork rattling to the ground beside him.

"Damn nigger!" the deserter muttered, tucking the Henry under his arm to examine his wound.

Emaline struggled against Blackie's hold, her fingernails digging into the backs of his sweaty hands. Red spurred off toward the stable to search its interior as her frantic gaze dropped to Tacker. A deep zigzagging gash laid open his skull.

"Ain't nobody else in there," Red yelled, emerging from the stable. He rode up beside his partner who still inspected the small puncture wound.

"He nicked me is all," Blue proclaimed, then pointed to the prone body. "There's one nigger who ain't gonna enjoy freedom." They both laughed.

Blackie released his hold on Emaline and dismounted. "One more sound, woman, and I'll blow your damned head off," he hissed. She nodded, dropping to the ground beside Tacker. Before she could determine if the farrier still lived, the sergeant jerked her back to her feet, then scanned the area before his eyes once more burned into hers. "Who else you got livin' here?" His breath moved the wisps of hair caught in the perspiration across her forehead.

She nearly retched at the stench yet she forced herself to swallow her revulsion. Despite Reece's growing strength, how could he hold his own against these three monsters? "Th—there's no one else," she mumbled.

Red kicked at Tacker's prostrate form. "You think he's dead?"

Blue pressed the barrel against the old man's head. "I'll put a bullet in him, just to be sure."

Emaline gasped.

"Put that damn thing away," Blackie snapped. "We've got better things to do than kill some worthless old coot." He headed toward the stable, tugging Emaline behind him. She balked with every step, fighting to free herself from his grip.

"Take care of the horses," he tossed over his shoulder.

Blue sulked. "Hey, I'm wounded here, I should get her first. Remember what happened the last time? No one had a chance after you got done with the damn wench."

"Just don't use a knife on this one," Red pleaded.

The sergeant cast a threatening scowl in their direction as he shoved Emaline through the doorway.

"He always goes first," Red grumbled, looping the reins of the horses over a post.

Blue pushed past him. "Not anymore."

Chapter Twenty-Seven

The cool interior enveloped Emaline the moment she stumbled inside the stable. The soldier shoved her toward the closest stall.

"That's far enough," he ordered.

She spun around, and scanned the hazy room to search for some kind of weapon. Her skim came up empty; Tacker kept everything in its proper place.

"It's time to see what you've got hidden under all this," Blackie said, lust brightening his watery blue eyes. Both hands seized the front of her blouse and he gathered up the material. With a hard jerk, he ripped away the ivory buttons.

They scattered into the hay beneath Emaline's feet. Her heart beat so fast, she nearly fainted. Swaying, she caught herself and shuffled her feet wider apart.

Blackie's hands dropped to the scuffed buckle of his worn belt. A sarcastic chuckle reached out from across the dim interior to halt his actions.

Blue stood inside the opening of the stable. The sun penetrated the paper-thin spaces between the planked walls, illuminating the challenge scrawled across his features. "This time I'll take the woman first. Kindly step aside."

Emaline pulled the ragged edges of her blouse closed and melded back into the shadows.

Blackie pivoted to face his comrade. "You know, you're startin' to annoy me."

"Well, that's too damn bad. I'm tired of you givin' the orders around here. If I wanted that shit, I'd have stayed in the army."

"If it wasn't for me, you'd have been dead long ago. I got us past them pickets, didn't I?"

"I don't need you to get me past any guards." His wicked grin widened. "In fact, I don't need you for a goddamn thing."

Blue lowered the repeater and fired, sending lead into the center of Blackie's chest. The jacket washed crimson with the final beat of the man's heart.

The deserter collapsed to the ground inches from Emaline. Her ears rang from the rifle's report. Her gaze slowly shifted from the dead man back to Blue. He showed no mercy, his calm demeanor that of a man who had murdered before and knew nothing of remorse.

He was quite insane, the act a cutting blow of hatred.

Emaline's breath quickened, the flash of panic inside her expanding. The horrific picture bruised every corridor in her mind. She stepped back. He followed. She bumped into the plank boards of the empty stall, her body shaking in abject terror, yet she met his scowl with a determined glare.

Her chin lifted.

Red rushed into the stable to encounter the bloody scene. His voice penetrated the haze of gunpowder. "What the hell...?"

The maniac turned, and offered a grin. "We had a disagreement over who would be first and I won. You got a problem with that?"

Red's hands splayed wide. "I don't mind at all. I never much cared for the sickly sonofabitch anyway." He inched his foot out to nudge the body. "You take all the time you want with her, my friend. I'm more than willin' to wait my turn."

Emaline fought back another wave of nausea, then gasped, her eyes widening further when Blue pressed the warm steel barrel against her throat.

"Nooooo!" she screamed, kicking at the barbarian.

He backhanded her across the mouth, rocking her head to the side. Emaline recoiled to glare at him, the taste of blood filling her mouth.

The murderer loomed closer. Grasping her arms, he pinned them behind her back, wrenching her shoulder blades together. She tried to tear herself away from him, but the attempt sent a wracking jolt of pain down her spine.

"If you do exactly as I say," he whispered into her ear, "we won't have to bury anyone else today. You got that?"

Emaline nodded frantically.

"Now stand still while I undo this pretty little thing." He released her and she immediately shuffled sideways and grasped the edges of her torn blouse. She tugged the material together but he knocked aside her trembling hands, and ripped the material off her body.

Emaline squeezed her eyes shut against the raw, visceral shock coursing through her. In Reece's arms last night, she'd found exquisite paradise. She now floundered in a cavernous pit of hell.

In her mind, she willed herself to float away from the ordeal. Tears gathered, skimmed down her cheeks. If she fought this vicious violator, he would simply kill her. But if she complied, perhaps he might let her live. In the deep recesses of her mind, her surrender resembled nothing so much as a victory.

Another hard tug from the monster's hand and Emaline felt the delicate stitches tear. The peach-colored ribbon snaked through the tiny casing to scour her skin. The batiste camisole drifted from her body like a broken wing.

Her breath caught in her throat when he shoved her backward into the wooden planks of the stall. The smell of the mules mingled with the stink of the man.

Her wildly pounding pulse echoed in her ears.

"I don't believe you need this either," Blue mumbled. With a greedy roughness fueled by his growing lust, he wrenched her chemise downward. Her head snapped back from the force, sending a spike of pain down her spine. The stitches yielded and the organdy also fluttered to the ground. Her bare breasts met the sultry air. A low growl rushed up from deep in his throat and she heard the rifle drop. Calloused hands cupped her fullness, his fingers squeezing her already sensitive flesh.

Nausea rolled upward and Emaline feared she might vomit.

Reece jerked awake.

He hadn't slept so deeply in ages, but too many times over the past three years, he'd been awakened by the same sharp sound. The seasoned soldier inside him identified the unmistakable report of a rifle.

He surged from the rumpled bed sheets. Pulling on his pants, he scanned the room.

Emaline was gone.

He shoved his arms into a white cotton shirt and stumbled into the hallway. Pushing open several doors, he peered inside the upstairs chambers. All were empty.

I damn well know I heard a shot.

Four strides took him to the bedroom window that overlooked the service yard. He scanned the area near the summer kitchen, skimmed past the outbuildings and chicken coops, the water well and the smokehouse. His gaze finally settled on the garden.

Reece leaned forward. His fingers gripped the window sash as his eyes narrowed on the prone body.

Tacker?

A pitchfork lay at a cockeyed angle near his legs. Even from this distance, Reece saw the smattering of dark blood coagulating in the tight coils across the top of the old man's snow-colored head. Reece glanced around wildly until he spotted Emaline's sun hat flattened on the ground near the stable's entrance. To the left, three horses hobbled together, their reins looped over the plank railing in front of the building. They'd been ridden hard, their coats unkempt and matted with sweat.

A movement caught his attention and his gaze lanced to the open door.

Someone's inside.

Emaline?

Panic nearly suffocated him.

He reached for his holstered Remington and in one smooth move brought the belt around his hips. He buckled it as he headed down the hallway. This was not the way he envisioned taking the stairs for the first time, but he'd get down the damn things one way or another.

Reece reined in hard on his emotions, and descended. He shoved aside the throbbing ache in his chest and as he reached the last step, he slid the revolver from its holster and checked the blue-chambered cylinders.

Dammit, only two rounds...

...and three horses.

There was no time to reload; he had no choice but to push on. He slipped from the house and stumbled down the back steps. Crouching as low as he could, he headed for the dubious protection of the garden and Tacker. Working his way down a row of corn, Reece reached the body lying prone at the other end. His fingers pressed against the old man's throat to check a pulse.

He found the strong heartbeat.

"Tacker?" he hissed into the farrier's ear. "Wake up!" He shook the frail shoulder until a low moan fell from the thin, pale lips. Anxiously, Reece repeated, "Come on—wake up."

"C—Colonel?" Tacker stammered, trying to shift to his side. "Are dey gone?"

"Who? Damnit, man, tell me what's happened."

"Th—three of 'em...dey's got Miz Emaline. Dey be violatin' her." He paused, unable to complete the rest without a ragged breath. "I-I tried to stop 'em, to help her, but..."

A raging, raw anger breathed to life inside Reece and he heard no more. A nauseating feeling of dread enveloped him.

Dear God, not again. First his wife...and now Emaline!

With a mighty heave, he rose from the ground and crossed the thirty feet to the stable, then flattened against the wall near the open door.

Chapter Twenty-Eight

"Get over here and drag him out of the way," Blue ordered, never taking his glower off Emaline. "I'm gonna need more room to satisfy this one."

Red shrugged and followed orders, grabbing one of the dead man's boots. Unceremoniously, he pulled the body through the dirt and dumped him a short distance away.

Blue pointed to a mound of straw near the back of the stable. "Now you just lie down and do exactly what I say. And if you're good, I just might let you live after I'm finished."

"You sure as hell ain't gonna kill her before I get a piece," Red scoffed. He pulled a stool over and sat down to watch.

A hard shove sent Emaline to the ground. Her gasp zipped through the stable.

"You stupid wench. You'll move when I say so." Eager fingers fumbled at the buttons on his pants. "You're gonna like this 'cause you ain't never had a real man—"

A cocking revolver resonated through the hazy stable. Blue sliced his gaze toward the entrance. Sunlight poured around a tall form silhouetted in the doorway. "As a matter of fact, she has. Me."

Reece would only need to kill two now, having spotted a third body sprawled nearby. Streaks of blood across the straw-strewn ground told the story.

Regardless, the odds had narrowed.

A red-haired, pot-bellied mongrel closest to him, surged to his feet, knocking over a stool in the process. His hands rose slowly. "Take it easy, mister. We didn't know she was your woman."

Reece dismissed him, glaring instead at the man straddling Emaline's nearly naked form. Her sobs wrenched an agonizing hole in Reece's heart. The blood in his veins, already a hard boil, bubbled over into a blistering roll. He carved out words from deep inside his throat and threw them toward her tormentor. "If you so much as breathe in her direction again, you're a dead man."

Focusing on the horrid sight, Reece sorely misjudged the danger posed by the man on his right. The pistol had already cleared its leather holster before Reece reacted. Pivoting, he squeezed off his first round. The bullet blew a gaping hole in the bastard's chest that drove him backward into a rack of saddles. Blood spread in a scarlet bloom as the Colt slid from a lifeless hand and hit the ground with a thud.

A warning scream from Emaline and Reece swung back. The last deserter clutched a sixteen-shot Henry. Reece emptied his second and final round, but with unexpected agility, the man lunged sideways and the shot burrowed instead into the wall.

Reece dropped to the ground just as the Henry levered, then fired. Again and again, sharp reports rang through the stable. Reece rolled, and bullets chased him across the hard-packed earth, inches from his thigh, his shoulder, his head. Chaff and dust rose into the hazy air.

Pungent gunpowder fused with the smell of fresh hay.

The shooter readjusted but aimed too high, his next shots thumping into the wood, shattering glass, embedding into a bag of grain behind Reece. A spilling hiss joined the clicking dissonance of the Henry and shell casings dropped to the ground in chinking pings.

The bray of the mules coupled with the high-pitched shriek of horses.

Reece slammed up against the stool and his hand swept across the ground near the dead man's boots, fingers scraping the dirt in a wild search. They closed around the wooden grip of the Colt.

An eyeblink later, Reece angled up onto one hip, sighted in the bastard, and fired before the Henry could lever again. The pistol ball struck the man between the eyes, snapping his head backward.

He crumpled into a lifeless heap.

"I said you'd be a dead man," Reece hissed. His slitted gaze stayed in constant motion and a split-second later, he saw Emaline climb to her feet, tears streaming down her face. She scrambled toward him in a stumble, her breasts jostling with each frantic step she took. Pieces of straw clung to the tangles in her hair. She tripped over her skirt, then righted herself.

Reece surged to his feet and met her halfway, sweeping her into his arms. He pushed the dull throbbing in his chest to the back of his mind. She melted against him and his mouth found hers in a frantic kiss, his fingers plowing through her tangled mane. He swept his lips over her face, his breath warm gasps that still carried his fear. He kissed her cheeks, the side of her head, inhaling deeply in an effort to control his pounding heart. Heavenly lavender fused with the stench of gunpowder.

"Did they…are you hurt?" he asked, his voice a rush of concern and frustration. He smoothed his hands over her bare shoulders, brushed away the dust and debris that clung to the curve of her back.

"No, no, I'm fine. You got here in time." She muffled her words against his chest, her hands sweeping up and over his shoulders. She climbed higher in his embrace. His hold tightened around her. "You saved me, Reece."

The emotional impact of her words swelled inside him. All the years of heartbreak, everything that defined him to this moment, Jenny's death, the fears, the scars he carried deep. With his next inhalation, Reece buried them forever.

His gaze swept the stable, spotting a faded work shirt hanging from a nail near the entrance. He guided Emaline toward it, his hands folding around the faded cotton. He eased her into the butter-soft folds.

"They k-killed Tacker," she sobbed, her fingers trembling. She tried to push the garment's small wooden discs through the buttonholes, but she struggled. "He was t-trying to save me and they killed him."

"No, love, no," Reece reassured her, sweeping her fingers aside to finish the task. His lips pressed against her damp forehead, slid over the tear-streaked curve of her cheek. He nipped her lips. "He's alive—just took a nasty blow to the head."

She stared at him. "W-What?"

"I spoke to him. Come on, I'll show you." Reece ushered her from the stable and across the service yard toward the old man. Tacker still sat on the ground next to Emaline's vegetable garden, the pitchfork once again clutched in his hand. She dropped to her knees beside the farrier. Ignoring his protests, she inspected the wicked gash on his head. The rattle of an approaching wagon caused them to look up. From around the side of the mansion, Euley and Israel came into view, a mixture of curiosity and concern highlighting their ebony faces.

Chapter Twenty-Nine

Unmarked graves left no tales.

Reece dusted his hands against his pants, then leaned on the shovel to catch his breath. His chest throbbed from the unexpected exertion of the afternoon.

"You shouldn't have lifted him, Colonel," Israel said. "You ain't done healin' yet."

Reece glanced at the black man beneath the arm he wiped across his sweaty brow. "You did most of the work."

Sweat ran in shimmering beads down the field hand's weathered face. His features momentarily disappeared behind the folds of a blue-checked handkerchief before the ragged cloth crumpled into a pocket. "What you done to put 'em here was a heap more important than me diggin' dese here graves."

Reece nodded, then gestured toward the line of shanties in the distance. "Let's go check on Tacker. He took a bad hit."

"Oh, he's a tough ol' coot, Colonel. He be just fine." Israel heaved both shovels upward, settling the implements across his brawny shoulders. Long arms draped over the durable ash handles.

The men crossed the field, heading in stony silence toward the last cabin in an orderly line of twelve. Inside, the women cared for Tacker's wound.

Cotton strips encased the top-half of the farrier's head. He squirmed on the rickety chair as Euley secured the dressing.

"Sit still," she barked.

Tacker groused. "You's pullin' my hair, woman."

Emaline stepped back. After the ordeal, she'd donned a clean work dress while Reece explained to the new arrivals what had happened with the deserters. When the men guided Tacker to the cabin, Emaline returned and trailed behind them, expounding on the heroism displayed by both men.

"Well, if'n you quit your fidgetin', I won't." Euley's words to the old farrier brought Emaline back to the moment. She gathered up the scattering of medical supplies and slipped them into the pouch, smiling at the other two in the cabin. Euley stepped back to admire her handiwork. "Dem stitches should hold as long as you don't go out and dance a jig."

"Don't have to worry 'bout dat none," Tacker said. "I'm done wif being a hero."

Emaline sidled up next to Euley, and slipped a hand over the old man's bony shoulder and squeezed. "Thank you for helping to save me from those horrible men."

"Ain't me dat saved you, Miz Emaline. Yo' colonel be da hero."

"Yes." She nodded, love for Reece filling every chamber of her heart. "But you were equally brave and I shall always be grateful." From across the room, Euley's voice filtered through her thoughts.

"You spoilin' dat ol' man again. He'll get used to being praised an' glorified an' Lord knows I ain't got time to be fussin' over him like you do." She accentuated each word by waving a tallow candle toward them both before jabbing it into an empty pewter holder.

The cabin door swung open and Reece bent his tall frame to step inside. His head nearly brushed the rough-hewed ceiling. The room seemed to collapse around him. "They're buried," he said, stepping sideways. His comrade entered behind him.

"Dat's right," Israel confirmed. "Dey's buried in the garbage pit where dey belong."

Euley handed Reece a ladle of water. Nodding his thanks, he passed the still-full metal dipper on to Israel. "Here, my friend, you did most of the work. You drink first."

Israel hesitated for a moment and glanced at Euley, then accepted the proffered gesture, downing the liquid in several gulps. "Thanks, Colonel." He handed the ladle back to Euley. "I was mighty parched, at that."

The woman re-dipped, then offered Reece a serving. The water disappeared in three swallows. His gaze met Emaline's over the wide metal bowl, and he winked.

She smiled, a flush brightening her cheeks.

Several moments later, hooves drumming against hard-packed earth pulled Reece to the window. Emaline joined him as he shoved aside the muslin curtain. The silhouettes of a half-dozen mounted soldiers filled the clearing, and the glint of well-tended brass tack and leather accoutrements testified to an organized squad of men. When one soldier dismounted and headed toward the mansion's back veranda, a smile lifted Reece's lips. He crossed the small shanty, and pulled open the door.

Cupping his hands to his mouth, he shouted, "Jackson! Over here!"

Emaline sat in the rocking chair and stared across Shapinsay's front lawn. Reece stood beside her, his foot propped on the bottom rail that ran the length of the second-floor veranda. She refused to talk to him despite his many efforts.

His frustration grew as he stared into the darkness. "This just makes things easier," he said, trying once again to get her to respond. Beneath his frock coat, his heart pounded against sore muscles. His healing wound throbbed and he shifted his saber into a different position alongside his thigh, then leaned on his upraised knee. The air resonated with the familiarities of summer, the sweetness of evening wafting across him to belie the anguish that coursed through his veins. He felt incredibly small, perched on the unseen shoulders of the ticking bastard called time.

And Emaline's silence proved damning.

Reece dropped his foot from the banister and turned around, leaning against the railing. His arms interlocked across his chest, his fingers brushed the place where she'd mended the jacket the night he'd returned from the dead.

A dull ache lingered, but his heart hurt worse.

With this woman, he'd been reborn and though the seasoned soldier had once again returned on the outside, the accoutrements of war anchored into their proper place, inside Reece stood naked before his lover. The reason for returning to war had dramatically shifted, and he no longer needed the escape battle had once provided. Only the responsibility of command drew him now. *She must understand this.*

From somewhere inside the mansion the muted clamor of milling soldiers reached out to him, their voices floating up the stairs and onto the veranda with a reminder of his enormous obligation. The clock continued to tick as his men waited to depart. The truth pressed in on him from all sides.

Reece no longer desired to ride away from the only thing that mattered in life.

But how could he turn his back on his men, tell them to leave him alone with his newfound happiness? He couldn't. He wouldn't. And still...more precious moments ticked away.

He must make her understand.

"At least refugee to Richmond, for God sakes. Deserters are roaming everywhere now, and I don't want a repeat of what just happened. You'll be safer around people until this thing ends."

Her gaze shifted. And locked with his. "This is my home and I'm staying."

She was lost in torment and he agonized with her. Since stepping from the shadows of the cabin earlier this evening to reunite with his men, Reece hadn't had a single moment alone with her...until now.

"So, you're leaving tonight then?" she asked glancing back into the darkness beyond the veranda.

He nodded. "Yes, it's a long ride to Petersburg."

"Well, you'd better get started then," she quipped. "The sooner, the better."

"I'm so sorry about...all this."

Her gaze snapped back to his. "About what? You've done nothing I haven't allowed you to do."

A heavy sigh spoke his distress. "Neither of us has done anything wrong. We've only followed our feelings—"

"Our feelings?" Her words slid out in a heavy rush. "Is that what we'll use to describe what you brought to my life?"

The lump in his throat refused to move, his heartbreak so potent, he could almost taste it. He saw her grip tighten on the arms of the rocker, her pale knuckles straining against the chipped white wood.

"I stopped believing in miracles a long time ago, Colonel."

Colonel?

An intrusive voice beckoned him from the bottom of the main stairs. "We're ready to ride, sir, whenever you are."

"Just a damn minute," he hollered. The anxiety building inside made him more a snarling creature from hell than a mighty leader of men. They had so little time left. Reece leaned over and folded his fingers around the braid that draped Emaline's shoulder.

Lamplight fell across her from the open bedroom door.

"I want you to know my life has changed forever because of you," he said.

"Don't," she begged, the single word, a sickening sob that erupted from her trembling lips. He stared down at the silken plait as soft as brown satin in the palm of his hand. He tugged on it, trying to draw her upward but she refused to budge.

He tugged again and this time she rose, the seat of the rocker bumping against her legs. A heartbeat later, she surged toward him and Reece met her halfway. He would not repeat the mistake of riding away without telling her how he felt this time. His breath brushed her face and sent the tendrils dancing.

Tears slipped from Emaline's eyes and chilled her cheeks. His arms folded around her like a steel vise and he pulled her against him. "You've given me a reason to live again, to love again...and I do love you, Emmy. I'm begging you to give me a reason to return."

On her half-sob, his mouth found her lips, capturing them in a kiss fierce with love.

Her bitter disappointment dissolved under the pressure of his questing mouth. His embrace, strongly possessive, stole her breath. His passion consumed all of her and rendered her helpless. Her arms rose over his shoulders and she clung to him as the sorrow of his leaving inundated her in wave after heartbreaking wave.

When he broke apart their kiss, her words tumbled out in a frantic series of broken whispers against his mouth. "I...l-love you too...without measure...f-forevermore..." He nipped her mouth in fierce little bites. She sobbed the words again, trailing his lips down her throat, then back to her lips. She arched against him in a desperate attempt to pull him closer, to crawl inside his skin. "Y-Yes, please. Oh Reece, I beg you...p-please come back to me."

The love in his eyes poured over her. "You're my world now." He shook her to drive home his words. "Never forget this, Emmy. When the war's over, I'll come back to you. I promise this with my life." And then he shifted sideways. He pulled her arms away. They separated, and an agonizing emptiness enveloped Emaline. She sobbed, the floor beneath her feet shifting sand. Her knees threatened to buckle, forcing her to grope outward for the railing. Shaking fingers wrapped the wood as her eyes clenched shut. Her shoulders drew forward and she closed in on herself, her breath laboring under a rapid exchange of air.

She heard his long strides carrying him to the doorway.

The bedroom rug muffled his crossing, his steady footfalls echoing back. He descended the main staircase. And moments later, Emaline heard the faint resonance of a slamming door.

And then, the galloping horses.

She crumpled to the veranda, falling prone across the wood. Only the sultry summer wind and the fireflies flickering over Shapinsay heard the prayers she sobbed as she pleaded with her heavenly father to bring her lover safely back to her.

Chapter Thirty

The Federal infantry at Petersburg prepared for another major move. All around, the crackle of small-arms fire penetrated the rumble of thunder. The Union had strengthened its lines over the winter and now encircled the city.

The death hold on the Confederacy had begun in earnest.

Capturing the Southside railroad, the Northern forces cut off supplies to the starving Southern troops. The Rebels were barely hanging on, their numbers dwindling over the winter as desertion ran rampant. Under General Philip Sheridan's leadership, the Union cavalry prepared to move westward into Dinwiddie County, their destination now the strategic crossroads of Five Forks. Torrential rain fell upon the Union encampment, drenching it under another afternoon of storms.

Rivers of mud flowed down each Company street. Men prepared to move.

Reece stepped into the tent just as Jackson looked up from the regimental ledger. "Got a minute?" Droplets of water fell from the wide brim of his slouch in a steady drip.

His friend's face brightened. "Where the hell've you been? I haven't seen you in over a week."

"Been busy. But wanted to drop by for a minute and see how you're doing. Besides, I've a proposition for you, if you're interested."

"That all depends on what you've got in mind." Jackson leaned back in his chair. "If you want me to take the regiment out into this sloppy mess again, then my answer's going to be I'm busy. Go away."

Reece chuckled. "What I'm offering's got nothing to do with the war."

Jackson shoved out the other chair with his boot. "Well, in that case, have a seat. I've got all afternoon."

The rubber-backed rain slicker Reece wore crackled as he settled into place. "You still toying with the idea of going west after all this?"

"Absolutely. I'm riding where it's warm and dry."

"Oh, it's dry out west. And hotter than hell most days," Reece laughed. "But, I'm not talking about the weather right now. You remember our discussions about my spread near Tucson?"

"Dos Caballos? Yes, I remember well your fifty-thousand-acre horse ranch. God's gift to the world, I believe you said. And one of my stopovers will be at your place, to rest and recoup and visit a few lovely *señoritas.*" He winked.

Reece removed his hat and tunneled his hand through his damp hair before resettling the slouch. "You interested in buying me out?"

Surprise creased Jackson's face, and he stared for a moment before frowning. "What the hell you talkin' about?"

"It's simple. I'm looking to sell my portion, and I want you to make me a reasonable offer. That is, if you're interested."

Jackson retreated into quiet thought, his gaze rambling around the room, before he spoke again. "Why are you selling?"

"I'm only selling my half…I'm going back to Emaline instead."

"Well, hell I figured that much, but…how can you forget everything—"

Reece raised his hand to stop the flow of Jackson's words. "I'm happiest when I'm with her, so save your breath. There's nothing left out west for me."

A derisive snort filled the space between them. "There's your sister, for one. She might have a thing or two to say about your quick decision."

Low rolls of thunder punctuated his words as Reece slid to the edge of the seat and leaned forward. "You, of all people, know my decision was neither quick nor easy. Callie's a grown woman. She'll understand." Above them, rain thrummed upon the tent roof like a herd of stampeding horses. "I want to sell to someone who'll take care of...my half, and I can't think of another living soul better suited to the monumental task. You're the only man I know who'll be able to handle my sister's...sweet disposition, and still do a fine job of managing the spread." His voice dropped into a smooth whisper. "And did I mention she's so beautiful in the moonlight, she'll take your breath away?"

Jackson's brow arched. "Your sister?"

"No, you jackal. My ranch. Look, all I'm asking is for you to think about this. You can let me know later if you're interested. Make me a fair offer and she's yours."

Jackson leaned back on two chair legs, his arms crossing his chest. Reece stared at him. His friend had changed. Hell, they'd all changed. After spending the past four years wallowing in mud and blood and killing more than their share, Reece had no doubt Jackson would never return to Philadelphia and sit behind the family desk at the Neale Savings and Loan Bank.

An uneven smile ambled across Jackson's lips. "I'll give it some thought."

"Good." Reece climbed to his feet. "Now see to it you stay alive so you can give me the answer I want to hear." He headed toward the canvas flap that fluttered with the breeze. Water pooled on the ground around the center post, and the canvas flooring beneath his boots squished. Slipping his hand beneath the leather slicker, Reece pulled a daguerreotype from his vest pocket. "Oh, by the way," he said, tossing the image of his little sister onto the desktop in front of his best friend. "You can make your own call about Callie." He swept aside the flap and stepped into the rain-soaked afternoon.

The Cincinnati Enquirer
Major battle fought at Five Forks, Virginia
April 2nd, 1865
Twelve-thousand Federal cavalry under General Phillip Sheridan take critical crossroad near the Southside Railroad outside Petersburg, Virginia. Rebels fought with wild abandon but were unable to staunch the tide of Union blue. Reports state Confederate General George Picket was routed by a savage Federal charge and

General Meade verifies the United States Army has dealt the Confederates a mortal blow, but at a huge cost to the Union. All reports indicate heavy casualties among the Ohio Regiments participating in the assault, and several commanders, including the colonel of the 6th Ohio Cavalry, were listed among the officers killed. More information forthcoming as soon as details become available.

Brennen pulled up into the saddle and shoved the crumpled newsprint into his saddlebag. The colonel had been dead for almost three weeks and he had to find out from some damn Yankee newspaper?

Sonofabitch.

He swallowed, then wiped his shirtsleeve across his face. In the past four years, he'd seen good men splatter their guts all over the battlegrounds of hell, but this made him purely sick. He'd faced things no man should face, but what he knew he must do now would be tougher still. He gripped the leather reins so hard, his knuckles cracked.

I have to tell Emaline.

His breath tripped as a shudder lanced through him. He sighed, then settled deeper into the saddle. The war was over. The monumental task of putting back together shattered lives could finally begin.

Except for Em.

Brennen's throat went dry. He swallowed his anger and remade plans. He'd been stripped of all personal possessions except his revolver and horse, and the Yanks let him keep those only because he wore captain's bars. And thanks to the bastards who'd burned his manor house in Richmond, he had no place to call home. He would stay in Virginia no longer. Out west, he could begin again. There were rumors of railroad expansion. They'd surely need help. But he'd postpone his travels for a few more days.

Several men who'd been under his command stepped from the tavern and shouted at him. Drunk, defeated, unsure of what they would do now, they issued a shaky salute in his direction.

Brennen nodded and raised a couple of fingers to his hat brim in response.

His lips pulled into something he hoped resembled an amiable reply, but inside he felt like hell. The bottle of whiskey he'd consumed with them roiled in his gut.

His smile faded with the light of day.

Smells from the rail yard reached his nostrils. A multitude of rotting horse and mule carcasses waited to be burned and their stench fused into putrid accord with the tangy breeze off the ocean. His skin crawled with perspiration. Unexpected heat bubbled up from somewhere inside. The colonel had been the only goddamn Yank he'd ever admired.

The only one.

He remembered the man's grin when he unlocked the handcuffs that night, the way his sister and the colonel looked at one another—even then their feelings deep, Emaline's frantic efforts when the man lay wounded in her house. All the recollections tumbled together and sent waves of sorrow over Brennen.

After all, she loved the big Yank.

Tears threatened, and he compressed his mouth into a hard line to staunch an unforeseen sob. Chin lowered, he withdrew into the shadow cast by his hat brim. The glow of the setting sun burned over him.

He'd had a bellyful of death.

He jerked his reins to the right and the war-weary horse obeyed. Setting spurs, Brennen headed north before he changed his mind. Fifty miles separated him from Shapinsay, but even the two days it would take to reach his sister would not be enough to figure out what the hell he would say to her.

Chapter Thirty-One

Emaline removed the stopper from the decanter, poured the whiskey into a tumbler, and then handed Brennen the glass. His hand tightened around it. He'd been here a full day, and still couldn't bring himself to break the news.

I don't want to break her heart.

The whiskey disappeared in two swallows.

Last night, she'd told him all about the Yank's recovery and return to war, and skimmed the details about deserters, a near rape, and Reece's heroic rescue. She left off the part about the colonel bedding her, but a blind man could read between the lines from the brightness in her eyes and the glow she emitted.

He placed the empty glass on the side table, and leaned forward, clasping and unclasping his hands between his bent knees. He couldn't put off the gut-wrenching duty any longer.

Just tell her.

"Sit down, Em," he said, his words much too abrupt.

His sister obeyed, easing into the nearby chair. Her voluminous skirt settled around her in a rustle of satin. Emaline had grown into a woman of true courage over the past four years. She would need all her fortitude to withstand what he was now about to share. Brennen offered a small smile, but he feared his eyes gave away the truth.

"There's something I need to tell you," he said. The whispered words barely registered in his own ears. Had she even heard him?

"I don't want to hear any more of your plans to travel west. You've talked of little else since you arrived. You can live here. There's plenty of room."

Brennen glanced at Euley, busy clearing away the empty dessert plates. He slid a hand over his face, brushing against several days' growth of beard. His gaze skimmed back to his sister. The lamp in the room cast a soft, butter-yellow glow over her. He swallowed. Everything around Brennen reminded him of happier times, but now the furnishings, the carpet, his sister's polished pretense, even his own skin pressed in on him.

His heart rammed in merciless thumps against his ribcage. "No. I'm still going west."

"Well then, what? Are you leaving sooner? Is that it?"

"Yes, soon. I'm headin' out soon, but…for Christ's sake, Em, will you let me finish what I need to say!"

Her eyes widened and she leaned back, staring at him. Across the parlor, a fat stub of tallow burning on the mantel pushed ominous shadows up the wall. Bloody hell, this was going to be much harder than he'd expected. "I don't know how much you've heard about the battles fought around Petersburg."

Emaline's brows drew together, her forehead creased. "Not much, only from a few passersby. Why?"

He paused to clear his throat and then straightened himself in the chair. His sister clenched her teeth and Brennen fought the bile rising in his throat. "Well…the fighting was especially hard on the Yankee cavalry over near Five Forks, Em. One regiment in particular."

She leaned forward, her eyes boring into his. "What are you trying to tell me?"

"What I'm trying to say is…the regiment who took the most casualties in that campaign was the 6th Ohio." He paused when he heard her sharp intake of breath. Brennen hesitated, knowing his sister's world was about to fall apart. "And one of the officers killed was—" *God, how can I say this to her?* He softened his voice even more. "Em, I'm so sorry but…your colonel's dead."

She stared at him, unblinking. One second. Two. "W-what?" she finally mumbled, her hand surging to her throat as stomach-turning horror darkened her eyes.

He dug into his pocket and retrieved the folded newsprint. "I had this confirmed by one of General Pickett's aides. He was there when it happened."

Her shaking fingers reached for the wrinkled paper. Denial blazed bright in Emaline's eyes. "M-Maybe they're mistaken. Maybe it wasn't Reece." Panic flooded her voice and her face flushed.

She bent her head to read.

Nausea welled inside Brennen when tears gathered behind her dark lashes. Several slipped down her cheeks, dropped onto the newsprint. His pain deepened. He leaned forward, resting his hand on the arm of her chair. "I'm so sorry, Em," he whispered.

Silence hung in the air between them, oppressive and heavy. The article slipped from her fingers, drifting to the floor. Euley moved behind her and laid a hand across her shoulder.

A grimace creased her black face. "You sure 'bout this, Masta Brennen?"

He nodded.

Emaline's shoulders hunched forward and tears flowed unchecked down her flushed cheeks, dropping into dark splotches on the bodice of her burgundy dinner dress. Her head moved back and forth, her anguish building. Overwhelming. Unbearable.

She stared at him through a veil of tears. "N-no, Bren," she sobbed. "You're so wrong. H-he said he'd come back to me."

Brennen swallowed hard and slid forward to the edge of his chair. She was so pale now, so stricken he feared she might shatter into a million pieces. "I know," he whispered, ready to catch her if she did. "And I'm so sorry, Em. He was a damn fine man. Decent and honorable."

She slipped forward, crumpling off the chair to collapse into a satin puddle on the carpet before him. "Noooooooo," she cried. "No, noo, noooo."

Brennen dropped to his knee and slipped his arms around her. He bent his head, his words pleading. "This damn war's destroyed everything else, don't let it destroy you too, Em…"

But a deep, dark chasm split Emaline's soul in two.

She tried to pull from his embrace, but he held firm. Crushing pain warred with a bottomless disbelief as she stared up at her brother. Her words slid out on a wail of grief. "H-he promised me." Horror writhed up from inside. Her brother's sympathetic face distorted behind a blur of tears.

Brennen's arms tightened, but she struggled again and pushed free. *No... No...No...this cannot be true. Reece...Reece...* Slipping sideways, Emaline crawled across the carpet only to tangle in the bands of her crinoline. She bumped against the side table. The glass toppled, then fell to the floor and shattered. Tremors reverberated down her spine and darkness threatened to drown her.

She slumped to the floor, entangled in her dress. Her fingers dug into the carpet beside the glass slivers. And great wracking sobs poured from the bottom of her heart.

"Don't do this," Brennen begged, his whispered words slipping around her wretched grief. "Euley, get the hell over here and help me lift her back into the chair. Be mindful of the glass."

Emaline stiffened when strong hands slid under her arms. "H—he can't be gone, Bren. H—he can't be." She fought to free herself, but they managed to raise her to her knees. "Euley," she stared into the sympathetic eyes of her dearest friend. "H—he can't be gone." Heart-wrenching sobs erupted again along with her wet, hiccupping words. "I...l-love him s-so much. He promised..."

Her brother leaned over her, his head shaking. "I know, honey. But, come on, let's just get off the floor now." Her legs were too shaky to bear weight. She heard the harsh rattle of her breath, felt the chair beneath her, then seized up when another wave of anguish crushed her chest.

Her need and fear escalated.

She drifted in mind-numbing darkness. With each stuttering breath, with each tear that coursed down her face, with each ragged sob, Emaline felt her sanity slipping farther and farther away.

Chapter Thirty-Two

The front door opened with a soft whoosh, bringing the redolence of baked bread onto the veranda. The flame inside the lamp Euley clutched in her hand flickered. She settled the container onto a table beside the rocker where Emaline huddled.

"You can't keep sittin' out here like dis, honey. You've hardly moved since your brother left. Let's go back inside now and get something to eat."

"Leave me alone," Emaline mumbled, staring into the darkness beyond the veranda. The lamplight tossed shadows up the railing and across the weathered wood. Tear-swollen eyes squinted against the harsh brightness. Her hair lay in a tangled mess over one shoulder, hadn't met a brush in nearly a week, and she didn't even care.

Euley drew a second rocker close, the curved bands that defined the chair scraping across the creaking planks. The noise speared through Emaline's misery. A low groan slipped from the old woman as she eased onto the worn pine.

"Now it's been nearly a week since you heard bout the colonel, Miz Emaline, and I ain't said nothin' out of respect, but now we's all gettin' worried." She clasped her hands in front of her, the thin fingers working around each other. "Dis ain't like you to give up. I mean, sitting out here, day after day… you's scarin' us."

Emaline pushed aside the caring words. "Please go away." Somewhere in the darkness, the forlorn hoot of an owl floated back on a passing breeze to mingle with the soft sobs that fell from her lips. Clouds parted. A quarter-moon spilled ivory light from its slivered end across the rutted ground that spread out before Emaline. "Th—there's no reason to care anymore."

A heavy sigh met her ears.

"Dat's the sadness talkin'," Euley whispered. "You's got lots o' reasons. We need you. And yo' home needs you. Da colonel wouldn't want you to forget dat, honey." The woman reached over and smoothed a calloused fingertip over Emaline's cheek, pushing back a tangled curl. Cold air met the tear-stained path and tingled. "'Member when Masta Benjamin died? You didn't let the sadness stop ya then. You got up and began again. Dat's what you gotta do now."

Soft sobs coalesced into sharp sputters. Emaline buried her face in the palms of her hands. "But I—d-didn't…care for Benjamin the way I did Reece." The serpent of loss slithered through her, coiling and strangling all her happily-ever-after plans. "We'd b-become so…close, Euley. So…very close." She muffled the inference of their intimacy behind shaking fingers as the roots of her despair dug deeper. The hollowness inside her burgeoned. Another keening cry spilled out and wave after wave of grief rolled into the sultry night.

"I know, honey. Dat's how flames burn, hot an' full o' passion. But if loving the colonel proved anythin', it proved you's got da strength to face dis grief. He's still part of you, the golden threads dat hold together yo' fabric of life."

Euley patted her shaking shoulders but Emaline's words grated toward the woman in a bitter whisper, "But I don't want to live without him. Don't you all understand this?" The lamplight rippled again, pirouetting through the darkness as a cloying, rain-swollen wind tossed her unbound hair. Reece was in her every thought, in every passing breeze. Her hands gripped the arms of the rocker, seeking any way to anchor the man's memory, to somehow make him flesh and blood and bones again. She sobbed, knowing each long night without him brought her one more day closer to madness.

Euley's sigh embraced her, her words barely heard. "I understand yo' sorrow, Miz Emaline 'cause I've lost people too." Her voice lowered, woven around a pain-filled whisper. "My oldest boy ripped from my arms while still young and sold away while I begged Masta Benjamin to let him stay. My arms still ache even now. And remember my baby boy Jimmy? One minute so full of life, the next he lay dead in my arms from da fever. I…I thought I'd never get through those times, like God hisself reached inside me and pulled out my heart. But 'member what you told me back then?" The servant smoothed tangled strands over Emaline's shoulder with a gnarled hand. "You came to my upstairs room an' drew me into yo' arms an' said, 'we'll take each day real slow', dat's what you said to me. A day at a time. Nothing more."

Emaline pressed her head against the back of the rocker and rolled it from side to side, her crying soft and steady. "I'm s-so sorry Benjamin took your firstborn from you and Israel. I begged him not to, Euley. I pleaded with him for days on end…but he wouldn't listen."

"I know'd it wasn't you, and I long ago made my peace wif God." Euley's comforting, caramel-colored hand slipped over Emaline's fingers and squeezed. "Now you listen to me. Da colonel admired yo' strength an' courage. He told me you was da bravest woman he'd ever met. Yet here you sit growin' weaker an' weaker every day. How does any of dis honor the love he had for you?"

Emaline stared out at the shadows. Five-thousand acres of land waited beyond—and a broken down woman, half-crazed from grief sat weeping at its helm.

Minutes passed.

They sat in silence, their hands gripped together.

Emaline allowed Euley's strength to flow into her. Slowly, the sobbing trailed off into ragged sniffles as Emaline turned toward her loyal friend. Age lines edged kindly ebony eyes. This incredible woman could staunch the flow of blood one moment, can turnips and green beans the next, roast a pig for the multitudes, and yet still managed to coax a brokenhearted lunatic back from the precipice of hell.

Shame seeped past her pain. "I—I'm so sorry to frighten you all," she whispered, wiping her other hand against the tears. "I hadn't realized how selfish I'd become." Just beyond the veranda, the winds swirled off the Rappahannock and sent a tide of strength as old as the Commonwealth surging through Emaline's veins. At the river's edge, the towering pines seemed to welcome her back with rustling, balsam-scented whispers.

"You ain't selfish, honey." Euley smiled and slipped her hand free from Emaline's grasp to pat her shoulder. "You's just prostrate wif grief right now. Dis pain may take years to go away, but getting weaker an' weaker won't bring da colonel back. It'll only take you away from us too."

Emaline clenched the folds of her work dress, twisting the black and cream plaid through her fingers. "The very thought of living without him is... unbearable." Recollections of strong, warm hands skimming her bare skin, the rich warmth of his voice, the words *I live for you* rasped against her throat—all careened together to underscore her agonizing loss. Reece washed sunshine over the empty void that had been her life.

Emaline shuddered, unable to voice her fear but it was there hovering between each strangled breath. Would the strength of his memories fade over time as Benjamin's had? Would she be all alone again in the mundane routines that defined her?

"You ain't without him," the old woman whispered as if reading her worried mind. They stared at each other, then Euley leaned forward and pressed a finger to the middle of Emaline's chest. "He'll live forever right dere. Ain't no one gonna take dat away from you. No one. Now, come back inside. Just like we did before, we'll start all over again."

Emaline slowly inhaled, nodding, then slid to the front of the rocker. She paused and reached for Euley's hand, once more interlocking their fingers. She wouldn't have to live without love. She was surrounded by it in a million different ways. In the wise and caring form of this proud, battered woman and the two old men, huddled in the hazy light of the entryway, waiting for her return. In the work-worn routines of the plantation, the place which again embodied her purpose in life. How had she not seen this before?

With each stuttering breath, Emaline's panic and fear receded. She'd always been surrounded with love, but hadn't realized the magnitude until one man rode into her life and forced her to feel again. Until she'd loved Reece, she hadn't known the depth of her own soul. Until she'd loved Reece, she could never have found the truth. Until she'd loved Reece, she had no inkling of the power of her own heart. She stared beyond the veranda at the multitude of flickering fireflies. In silent perseverance, each tiny beacon emitted a steadfast hope for survival.

Once more the aroma of baking bread reached out to embrace her, warm and yeasty—reminding her of the people who still remained. A faint stirring of hunger nudged aside the oppressive weight inside her chest, nipping at the edges of her sorrow. "I'll try, Euley," she whispered. "That's all I can promise." Seconds stretched into minutes. Her healing slowly began. She turned toward her dear friend, the fragile smile returning. "For all of you, I shall surely try."

Euley nodded, then stood and drew Emaline to her feet. "Dat's good enough for now, child. Dat's good enough for now." The front door eased open and a heartbeat later, Tacker and Israel stepped out to welcome her home.

Chapter Thirty-Three

Moonlight draped the man as he reined his horse to a stop beside the brick entrance posts. His breath slid out in a low sigh and he straightened in the saddle. He was dog-tired, but at least his responsibilities to everyone else had finally ended.

He wanted peace…and he knew he would find it here.

Slowly, he turned the horse up the winding lane. Almost a year had passed since his last visit, yet he remembered everything in precise detail. His gaze settled upon the four-columned mansion at the far end of the lane. Under the silvery wash of moonlight, the house beckoned with open arms. He reined to a stop before the wide steps and dismounted, looping the animal's reins over the railing.

He turned and rested his hands over the saddle, scanning the grounds. Dappled streaks of light shimmered through the trees and highlighted the area where he'd laid out his regimental streets.

So swift does the plowshare of peace cover up, and the emerald mantle of nature conceal, the wrath and destruction of war.

The poignant words of some unknown Washington reporter seemed quite fitting now. What had the past four years actually proved? Other than instilling a seething rage in people that would last a lifetime, they proved not a damn thing.

The front steps creaked as he climbed. Four strides later, he stopped at the front door. He leaned sideways and peered through the glass panes that graced the barrier. Faint light radiated from the back of the house.

Should he knock? Or just go in?

Will she still want me?

His hands fisted then relaxed. It had been so long since he'd held her. He swallowed, then exhaled, slipping his hand around the doorknob. The brass felt cool against his palm and a muscle tightened in his jaw.

It didn't matter whether she still wanted him or not...he wanted her. And he'd lived every agonizing minute of the past year in anticipation of just this moment. A smile quirked his lips. Oh yes, before this night moved into a new dawning for them both, he would make his Angel want him all over again.

And she would know exactly how much he loved her.

Reece turned the knob and entered the house.

Emaline lifted the container of tallow candles from the table, then paused to listen. Muffled footsteps echoed from beyond the kitchen door. She inhaled, then exhaled in a thin rush of air. A veil of frustration passed over her. They must stop this incessant checking up on her every minute of the day and night.

I'm fine, Euley, now go back home.

No...don't be angry with them.

They just care.

Behind her, the kitchen door swung open just as she slipped the sandalwood box onto the pantry shelf. Emaline drew her hands through her hair to shove aside the ever-present wisps that clung to her damp forehead.

Worn loose, she let her hair hang in a tangled mess down her back.

Without turning around she quipped, "I said we'd finish tomorrow. Please go give Israel his supper." She reached over to the rows of canned foods. Only the routines of her day kept her sane.

How many times have I told them? The green beans go on the left, the tomatoes on the right.

Glass jars scraped across the wood as Emaline jerked them back into their correct positions. *Order—the brittle thread that holds me together.* "I'm perfectly fine, I'll see you again in the morning."

Silence filled the room.

Emaline turned. A single candle illuminated the winter kitchen. Her gaze settled upon a large figure leaning against the doorframe, his arms folded across his chest.

Her eyes widened. A strangled gasp lodged deep in her throat. She stiffened in shocked surprise. Her left hand rose to encircle her throat as every fiber within her tightened at the inconceivable sight.

Emaline didn't dare breathe.

She refused to blink for fear the image would disappear into the disparaging loneliness that her every waking hour had become. Six unbearable weeks had passed since she'd heard the news of his death.

And now, in her grief-stricken state, she realized she'd at last lost her mind.

Then a familiar grin tipped the corner of his mouth upward. The richness of his voice crashed over her, filling every crevice of Emaline's parched and lonely soul. "I promised you I'd come back."

A split-second later, amid a whoosh of brocade, she crumpled to the floor in a dead faint.

Reece surged into the room.

"Emaline!" he bellowed, reaching down to sweep her from the floor. He cradled her in the crook of his arm. Several steps backward brought them to a kitchen chair. He lowered onto the smooth oak, his arm wrapping more securely around her. "Come on, Emmy, wake up." His fingers traced the curve of her cheek, patting softly. "Please, love...open your eyes."

She began to stir, a soft moan reaching his ears. He waited, his heart thundering inside his chest.

Her eyelids fluttered and then opened.

Their gazes locked.

"Welcome back," he whispered, his lips quirking again into a smile. "Are you all right?"

She nodded, then raised a trembling hand to his face, touching his lips. Reece gently nipped her fingertips, his smile widening behind them.

"I-Is it really you?" Her words were low, filled with hope.

"Yes, my Angel. It's really me." He chuckled at the expression brightening her features.

"But, I thought you were…dead." She pushed against his chest and sat up, still cradled across his lap. "Brennen said you'd been killed at Five Forks."

His eyebrows slanted inward. "Five Forks?"

"Yes. He showed me newsprint that said the 6th Ohio's commanding officer had been killed."

Reece hesitated, then slowly understood. "Oh, I know why he might've thought that. And he was right, my regimental commander did die that day."

"But I thought you were in charge?"

His arm tightened and he lifted her into a better position. "A week before the battle, I was promoted to Brigade commander. I took Jackson and a few others of my immediate staff with me. Colonel Brady died that day." Reece leaned his head against the back of the chair. "I've spent the past six weeks discharging men and finishing paperwork. And then, I had personal business to tend to. I should've known the letters explaining my delay wouldn't have reached you?"

"N—no, I received nothing."

"Doesn't surprise me. The postal service is still in shambles."

A tear slipped down her cheek in a silver streak. "Oh, Reece," she said, burying her head against his chest. Her fingers splayed across his shoulders. "I'm so happy you're finally here."

"Look at me," he said, his expression softening as his hand slipped under her chin. He lifted her head and emerald eyes met his. He framed her face with his hands, brushing back the soft curls. "For the remainder of my life, I will always be right here."

Under the swell of her tears, love shimmered back at him.

Moisture welled in his eyes too.

"I've waited far too long to do this." Reece leaned forward and claimed her lips in a fierce kiss. She ran her palms up his arms and across his shoulders, embracing him tightly. He nipped down the smooth contour of her neck, whispering against her silky flesh. "I've thought of little else except loving you."

She moaned and tugged at him in a frantic pull until he met her lips again.

Her breasts flattened against his chest. She issued a tremulous whimper when his tongue swirled into the softness of her mouth. The kiss heated him to a fever pitch, his arousal, a pulsing commander of will now. "Forever and always you're mine," he said.

"Yes…only yours," she moaned against his lips. "Forever and always."

Hot pressure welled in his groin. She trailed sweet kisses over his face, her hand slipping between them and traveling down his frockcoat, scraping over tarnished buttons and the hard plane of his stomach, sliding past his belt buckle until she at last found the swell that proclaimed his burgeoning need.

She pressed.

And Reece hissed, dragging his breath inward in a rush of air. Her touch, raw. Wonderfully bold. His blood rolled through his veins. He lolled his head back against the chair, and groaned between clenched teeth, "Careful, Angel, it's been a while."

A pleasing shade of pink flushed Emaline's cheeks and highlighted the faint freckles that swept across her nose. She giggled and leaned into him. "For me too."

A slow smile curled his lips. With his next gulp of breath, Reece looped his arms tighter around her, and then stood. Dear God, she was a banquet set before him…and he, a mere mortal, fresh from war and famished for her delicious offerings.

"I'm finished with our greetings, how about you?" She nodded and dipped her head against his chest. Cradling her in his arms, Reece surged from the kitchen, her voluminous skirt sweeping in a black curtain across him. He crossed through the parlor and headed toward the stairs. All thoughts fled his mind but one—undressing her with a need honed by months of denial. She commanded him—her whispered promises of love would nourish him a lifetime.

Emaline tilted her head back and laughed, the sound honey-rich and rewarding. Her hair fell in a dark curtain over his arm and Reece nipped along the curve of her throat, pleased to feel her skin flushing warm beneath his mouth. Her moans were a heady invitation that drove him onward at a determined pace. She curled into him and nestled her head into the curve of his neck. A feeling of true completeness settled over him. "I'm home, Angel. That's all that matters now."

Reece ascended the stairs in a dozen strong strides, then headed down the darkened hallway. He crossed the threshold into the bedroom and Emaline reached over his shoulder, pushing the door closed behind them.

They spent the remainder of the night in paradise.

Chapter Thirty-Four

Waking came slowly to Emaline.

A glow of contentment simmered through her. She wiggled her toes and sighed. The tingling in her lips reminded her all over again of the exquisite night they'd spent in lovemaking, passionate most times, a tender rejoining, others.

She reached out only to find the bed empty.

My God…did I dream the whole thing?

Panic seized her. She glanced sideways. The rumpled place where Reece had slept was empty, but he'd been here. His scent, their scent, still lingered on the sheets to embrace her. The panic slowly ebbed.

He's alive and he's home forever!

I must tell the others.

The drumming beat of galloping horses brought her bolt upright. Emaline tossed back the covers, scrambled from the bed and raced to the window to peer outside.

Sunlight radiated down upon an astonishing scene.

Her heart slammed in her chest and she dashed for her robe and slipped the fine lawn fabric onto her sensitive skin. Jamming her feet into leather slippers, she hurried from the room. She hiked the robe up around her knees and descended the main staircase two steps at a time, then dashed out the front door and across the veranda. Dust swirled around her as she came to stop on the top step.

The wooden planks beneath her slippers vibrated as dozens upon dozens of horses galloped past her, their hooves pounding against the hard-packed earth.

The sun's midday glare nearly blinded her. Emaline shaded her eyes, staring in disbelief at the blurring haze of riders and sleek-coated beasts.

And then she spotted Reece riding alongside the magnificent column.

He guided his buckskin toward her, reining Saguaro to a stop beside the front steps. "Is this the Shapinsay Plantation, ma'am?" he asked, his eyes shadowed beneath the brim of his slouch hat.

An odd flutter raced through Emaline's chest. "Oh you. Where did you…?" she stammered, searching for words, but her voice stuck in the back of her throat.

A devilish gleam lit his eyes. "What, my love? No rifle this time?"

Love for him surged into every chamber of her heart and she could not contain her laughter. From the corner of her eye, she caught sight of Tacker and Israel waving their arms in wild attempts to redirect the milling beasts toward the corrals. And though she couldn't see Euley, Emaline heard the old woman bellowing orders to keep the critters out of the garden.

Reece narrowed his eyes, then leaned from the saddle toward her. "I've decided to return the horses I confiscated from you. You remember that day, don't you?" He rubbed an imaginary spot on his cheek where she'd slapped him that long-ago morning.

Emaline blushed. "Oh yes, Colonel Cutteridge. I remember that day very well. In fact, you thought to kiss me in broad daylight in my own study, much to my chagrin."

Tears flooded her eyes. Couldn't he see she needed to touch him, needed to tell him in a million different ways how much she loved him?

He straightened, instead. "Yes, that I did, and don't regret doing so for one moment." He pushed his hat back a bit farther on his head and dark hair fell in waves over broad, dust-covered shoulders. "And while these aren't exactly the same horses, I'm sorry to say, they're still a good start."

"A start?" she asked, laughter bubbling outward. "There are hundreds of horses here, Reece."

"Yes, two hundred and twenty, to be exact. Callie shipped them to me from *Dos Caballos*. Appaloosas, mustangs, paints and palominos, all bred for speed and agility, and all possess the strength to survive any elements. Since Jackson bought my half of the ranch, I've nowhere to go with them. So I'm completely at your mercy. You must say yes to my plans."

Her arms wrapped her waist. Oh, how she ached to kiss him. Between sobs of delight, Emaline gasped, "What plans?"

"Our future, my love." He gestured toward the horses. "The war has critically depleted the horse population in the east. There'll be a true need for stock again, and it's my intention to have everyone in Virginia buy them from us. No more tobacco farming for you." He stared off across the fields. "This will make excellent pastureland for the horses." He turned back and inhaled. Happiness mingled with the expression across his face. He then peered down at her. "So…can I stay?"

She gripped his pants leg. "Oh my God, Reece, I'm so glad I didn't shoot you back then." Laughing so hard now her cheeks hurt, she said, "Yes. Yes, you may stay here forever."

The corner of his mouth quirked up. "Come here," he ordered in a wickedly delicious tone. He bent down and with an ease born of solid strength, Reece swept her off her feet.

Her breath caught and for one magnificent moment, Reece cradled her in midair in the crook of his arm before settling her sideways across the saddle in front of him. Blood pumped through Emaline's veins as dust swirled around her carrying deep inside the aromas of horses and ancient pines and the spicy hint of her lover.

Yearning reflected from the depths of his eyes and his hand sank into the tangled waves at the nape of her neck. He cupped the back of her head and pulled her toward him. "Shall we seal the deal?"

Before she could offer a reply, his mouth came down on hers. Hard. Searching. Demanding. Emaline readily surrendered, opening for the sensual sweep of his tongue. Desire for this man zipped clear to her toes and set her soul aflame. When his lips lifted from hers, she groaned aloud, limp with longing for more. She arched her neck and he nipped a path down her throat, sending quivering shudders careening through her again.

"Marry me," he whispered, his words burning against her skin.

Emaline opened her eyes, and stared up at the turquoise sky. "Wh-what?" she stammered, blinking several times. She straightened, her chin dropping as she stared at him.

His powerful features shimmered into focus. "Marry me," he repeated.

Emaline splayed her hands across his chest, then leaned forward, skimming them over his broad shoulders as she nestled into the incredible strength of this man.

Tear-filled eyes rose to his and ever so slowly she lifted her lips into a smile. "Yes, I will marry you." The simple words, brushed against his lips in a warm rush, carried all the love she felt for him. He tightened his hold around her trembling body, and from that moment forward, she knew he would never let her go.

Epilogue

April, 1866

Shapinsay Plantation

"Here's another letter from your sister." Emaline handed Reece the envelope just delivered by courier.

"Again?" He looked up from the ledger, a grimace crossing his face as he ripped open the vellum envelope. "Good God, poor Jackson. I've sent him into the viper's pit."

Emaline laughed and crossed the room to the wingback chair. Settling onto the soft cushion, she tucked her feet beneath her. Things were going well for them now, and the plantation's profits stemmed directly from Reece's hard work.

She was happy. Beyond happy. And she could hardly contain her own news.

His chuckle broke through her musings. "Looks like Jackson is insisting Callie stop swearing. He wants her to start wearing dresses and start acting like a lady." Another quick laugh followed. "She's praying for the day he drops dead."

"Well, if anyone can cajole your sister into satin, it'll be that smooth-talking man." Emaline well remembered the major's implacable charm.

"You know, don't you, this was my intention all along when I sold him the deed." He tapped the letter on the desk and offered a bright smile. "Callie needs someone like Jackson, though she'll never admit it. Someone who's strong enough to stand up to her. And Jackson, well, he needs to be more flexible. In fact, they both need to learn that two heads can be better than one. Their narrow views about how the world should work need adjustments and it'll be fun to see which one will get the upper hand. Yep, I'd say things are off to a rollicking good start for them."

"Do you regret it?" she asked. "Selling the ranch, I mean?"

Reece smiled at her, his gaze lingering a moment longer than needed.

A delicious sizzle zipped straight through her.

"Not one single day. You, this place, are my life now. I'm quite content." He winked at her, then placed the letter into the drawer, his attention returning to his books. A lock of dark hair drifted over his forehead and the sight sent Emaline's heart into a thrumming beat.

She wanted to run her fingers through the thick strands again.

She knew if she but arched a brow, he would oblige. Here in the study, on the kitchen table, nestled in a mound of soft hay in the stable, it didn't matter where to Reece. His appetite for her had no end, and neither did hers for him.

The sensations he'd created as they headed downstairs for coffee this morning, floated over her again to reel her thoughts. Total conviction gleamed in his dark eyes as he swept her into his arms, pressing her against the wall. With his robe opened to reveal his magnificence, Reece offered her a grin, then eased her down onto him. A raspy hiss of pleasure filled the hallway as he buried himself deep inside her. And for several delicious minutes her diaphanous nightgown curtained them away from the world.

Emaline giggled and snuggled deeper into the chair.

To busy her hands, she lifted her tatting from the side table. The sweet little secret that nestled inside her begged for revelation, but this was too important to simply blurt out while her husband tallied their books.

No, she would wait until later to share the glorious news Euley had confirmed for her this afternoon. After verifying her suspicions, the old woman beamed from ear to ear. And with a loud whoop, she proudly proclaimed that all Emaline needed was the right man after all. A miracle, that's what Emaline called the baby growing inside her. And come winter, that precious little miracle would be suckling at her breast.

Her breath slid out in a contented sigh.

Another lingering glance in her husband's direction washed a current of love so strong over Emaline, she nearly sobbed. Theirs was a union born of strength and passion, created during a time that had tested both. They had surmounted all adversities and risen from the ashes of war into a magnificent Phoenix ready to embrace a new dawn.

Indeed, there could be no greater glory than that.

About the Author

Say hello to USA Today Recommended Read Historical Romance writer, CINDY NORD...who hopes you enjoyed reading NO GREATER GLORY, book one in her bestselling 'The Cutteridge Series', as well as the #1 Civil War Romance at Amazon for over one full year. Each book of this popular series 'stands-alone', but you won't want to miss the ongoing excitement of the great west in WITH OPEN ARMS, book two of her beloved series, as well as a #1 bestselling western historical romance. The recent debut of book three, AN UNLIKELY HERO, also surged onto the coveted 'Top 100 Romances at

Amazon' list thxs to her devoted readers. Book four, BY ANY MEANS, debuts the spring of 2018. Cindy is a member of numerous writers groups, and her work has finaled or won countless times in writing competitions—including the prestigious Romance Writers of America National Golden Heart Contest. A luscious blend of history and romance, her stories meld both genres around fast-paced action and emotionally driven characters. Indeed, true love awaits you in the writings of Cindy Nord. Please join her on Facebook at her popular Monday-thru-Friday morning "Coffee Klatch", as well as on Twitter at @cnord2. And keep up with her appearances, booksignings, and her love of sharing historical tidbits at her webpage: www.cindynord.com -- Long live historical romance! ♥

Website: www.cindynord.com
Facebook: Cindy Nord - www.facebook.com/cindy.nord.9
Twitter: www.twitter.com/cnord2

With Open Arms

A war-weary ex-soldier. An untamable woman. Love doesn't stand a chance in hell...

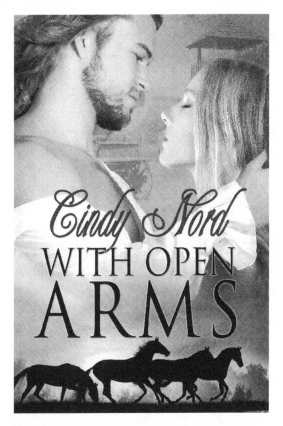

The Cutteridge Series, Book Two

Hardened in childhood by the death of her parents, then left to run the family's southwestern territory ranch when her brother rode off to fight for the Union years before, Callie Cutteridge hides her heartbreak behind a mask of self-sufficiency. Breaking horses for the army proves she's neither delicate nor helpless. When a former cavalry officer shows up claiming to own her brother's half of the Arizona ranch, she steels herself to resist the handsome stranger's intention to govern even one single aspect of her life. After all, loving means losing…to her it always has.

For months, Jackson Neale has looked forward to putting the bloodstained battlefields back east behind him. Callie isn't the agreeable angel her brother led him to believe, but he's damned well not the useless rake this foul-mouthed hellion thinks he is, either. His quest for calm stability contradicts sharply with her need for control, yet still their heartstrings tangle. But how can these mistrusting partners transform their fiery passion into happily-ever-after when all Callie knows how to do is fight… and all Jackson wants is peace?

Enjoy the following excerpt for With Open Arms:

The warmth of day vanished with remarkable speed, shrouding the desert under a bone-chilling twilight. Murky shadows crept across the Rincons' rocky ridgeline as Jackson Neale slipped into the concealing darkness. Seasoned by four years of war, his body tensed with a caution that defined survival. His fingers folded around the worn, wooden grip of a well-oiled Colt. He could count on one hand the people he'd befriended on the trek westward from Virginia, and knew with absolute certainty the person riding into camp tonight wasn't one of them. Only a fool would enter without hailing first, yet this stranger displayed a boldness that amazed him.

In stony silence, the uninvited guest guided a horse toward the saddlebags by the fire. Small, flickering flames inside the ring of fieldstones washed a glow across the bay's ruddy flank.

His gaze moved upward.

Mexican spurs strapped around the heels of silver-tipped boots caught the fire's glint. Leather batwing chaps encased long legs. And despite the chill, a jacket hung open to reveal a .44-caliber Remington strapped around denim-covered hips. A flat-brimmed hat, its crown encircled with a *concha* band of hammered silver, hid the face of the evening caller.

The visitor dropped to the ground, the rowels on the spurs chinking when they hit the sand. He glanced around, then crouched on a knee beside the saddlebags.

Jackson tightened his lips as all caution evaporated. He knew full well how to deal with bandits, having met a few already on his ride westward. He bolted from the shadows and slammed full-force into the unsuspecting thief. Momentum drove them both to the ground. In an instant, he pinned the fool against the sand. His right hand rose in a tight fist, his left shifting across the cotton plaid shirtfront to seek a firmer grip. In an instant, all the fight, all the pent-up energy, everything inside him dissolved. He'd never be too cold or too tired to forget the lushness of a female breast.

His eyes widened as his arm dropped to his side.

On a sharp breath, he rasped, "You're...you're a woman. I thought you were—"

"Get off me, you stupid son of a..."

The profanity spilled from her mouth with such ease that Jackson swallowed a lungful of air. Indigo eyes blazed up at him like shards of broken glass, and wild wisps of sun-stained hair danced against the curve of her cheek. Swathed beneath layers of trail dust, the hellion's hard edge and tone of voice contrasted sharply with what his eyes told him about the rest of her. His heart responded with an engaging hitch, but he blamed the rush of heat that flushed his face on the nearby campfire, not the comical fact that this frosty little tart had taken him by complete surprise.

He gained control of his emotions. "Why are you riflin' through my gear?"

Leather-gloved hands rose to thump against his chest. "I said get off me. I...can't breathe."

He shifted sideways, pushing against the ground to stand. With a muffled oath, Jackson staggered back another step as she bolted to her feet. She bent to retrieve her hat and slapped it against her thigh. As she did, his gaze raked down the noteworthy curves of her body. Her masculine outfit provided a disguise, yet closer inspection did little to hide her figure. The fringe on her leather chaps rode both shapely legs, and the sight reminded him of the pleasures a woman could offer—sultry, sexy and full of endless possibilities. In this particular woman, however, all softness appeared to end with the supple leather.

Anger sealed her mouth, and the scowl that creased her features indicated not a shred of sweetness filled her body, either.

An involuntary clench seized his jaw. "Good God, woman, I could've killed you."

She issued an impatient huff. "I live with danger every day, so your words barely register." With a quick flick of her wrist, she twisted her hair into a knot atop her head, then jammed her hat back over the tarnished curls.

Jackson had never expected to see such a raw woman, and the enmity in her bright eyes held all the subtlety of baying hounds. She cursed cruder than a camp-following whore, but she'd die young if she needed to steal from a passerby to survive. He peered into the darkness but heard no other threatening sounds. She obviously rode alone.

His attention drifted back. "Since you're so nicely groomed now, start explaining what you're doing in my camp."

"Your camp?" Her razor-sharp laugh bit straight through him. "You might think this is your camp, but you're standing on Cutteridge land and I own every damn acre." The heat in her eyes branded him where he stood. "And, I sure don't recall giving you permission to trespass here or anywhere else."

Her statement brought Jackson up short. He'd ridden more than twenty-five miles today, but hadn't figured on reaching Cutteridge property until sometime tomorrow morning. The image on a faded daguerreotype, tucked beside the worn map in his saddlebag, flashed across his mind. The woman's likeness, given to him months ago by his colonel, had been branded into memory. There was barely a whisper of resemblance between the serene beauty reflected in his picture and the foul-mouthed hellion who stood before him now. Somehow, Jackson kept the blistering bile of disappointment from reaching his voice. "Cutteridge land, is it?"

"You heard me clear enough." Her expression hardened as she pressed closer. She brought her point closer still. "All Cutteridge. And all mine."

From somewhere beyond the campfire's light, the forlorn howl of a coyote underscored her words. Smoke curled upward in lazy tendrils. Jackson's nerves constricted as the woman's words slipped around him like a noose. And tightened. He tipped back his head and stared at the wide expanse of stars inundating the ebony canvas above him. "Oh God," he mumbled, the lump in his throat refusing to move. "Please don't let this shrew be Colleen Cutteridge."

A bolt of raw adrenaline shot through Callie when the sound of her given name spilled from the tall, hard-angled man. Her pulse hammered in her chest. She squared her shoulders, her chin jutting higher as his gaze reconnected with hers.

"We've never met," she snapped. "I'd have remembered you." Obviously, he wasn't some cowpoke looking to encroach on her land. Not this one. A red flag rippled inside her, and she pointed to the campfire in an attempt to hide her unease. "I spotted this a half mile away. A fire this bright's a blatant invitation for Apache lookin' to lift a scalp."

Stupid oaf.

A smug smile lifted the man's lips and a slash of white appeared. "I appreciate the warning."

From his chiseled jaw carved straight from granite, to his cool, collected calmness, the man possessed an ease of manner that unnerved Callie, and she didn't appreciate the feeling one damn bit. A stubborn spirit, her companion and strength these past five years, spiked through her. She rubbed her midriff where his thighs had bruised her ribs. And for one disturbing moment, she couldn't help but admire his impressive strength. Granted, he'd bruised her ego more than her body, but—

Callie caught her thoughts and jerked them back into control, exactly where she liked things best. She took a full step backward, the rowel on her boot heel chinking across the tension. "Look, mister, I don't give a squat if the Apache scalp you this night or the next. I just don't want the bloody deed done on my ranch." Her fingers curled around the grip of her revolver as her gaze scanned his belongings, then moved on to his horse waiting in the shadows. "I could shoot you myself for trespassing and spare the Apache the trouble of killin' you. Or…"

her gaze drifted back to lock with his, "…you can gather your gear, saddle that fine Morgan you've got line-tied over there, and get the hell off my land."

Seconds passed like hours before the dark-haired man bent to retrieve his hat.

He straightened slowly, pulling the brim of the sweat-stained Stetson low upon his head. Through dark, cold eyes, he stared at her.

With each thump of her heart, the stranger's unnerving quiet further frayed her nerves. A log from the campfire shifted deeper into the flames, sending a shower of sparks heavenward. The pungent aroma of burning mesquite filled her nostrils and fused with a raw, unspoken awareness that sizzled from the man.

He leaned forward, the brim of his hat bumping against hers. The thinnest hint of amusement lifted his lips. "It appears I won't be riding from your life quite so soon." His words were too soft, too controlling. "And this land isn't just *your land* any longer." Without removing his gaze, he reached into his frock coat. With the speed of a striking rattlesnake, an envelope appeared in his leather-gloved hand, then rose between them until level with her eyes. "The name's Jackson Neale and this makes me your new partner."